THE CAJUN

Joe Barfield

Moran Publishing, L.L.C.

Moran Publishing, L.L.C.

THE CAJUN

Copyright 1994 by Joe Barfield
All rights reserved. For information
address Moran Publishing, L.L. Co.
Houston, Texas

This novel is a work of fiction. Characters resembling actual persons living or dead are purely coincidental. This work is a product of the author's imagination and creativity.

ISBN: 1-884797-01-6

Book Concept and Design by Joe Barfield

Cover illustration by Kyler Sharp
@
Carrousel Productions
Houston, Texas 77099

Printed and bound in the United States of America
by
Gilliland Printing, Inc.
215 North Summit
Arkansas City, KS 67005

Special Thanks For the Help to:
Becky Moumouris
and
Henri Alonzo

Dedicated to Cajuns

People make comparisons to the Cajun dialect; French, Spanish, but it cannot be done because the dialect is unique. Only one word describes their dialect--**CAJUN**!

Cajuns have a zest for life and a passion for fun and food like none I have ever seen. Their story telling is next to none. I regret that I can't accurately show the Cajun dialect with the written word. To be truly enjoyed it must be heard.

THE CAJUN

TALE	PAGE
Prologue	
1. ATCHAFALAYA	1
2. Blue Dragon	11
3. SWAMP WITCH	22
4. Fever	31
5. Swamp Rats	39
6. Devil's Island	49
7. Jambalaya	56
8. Terrorist's Revenge	70
9. Snakebitten	80
10. Escape on Devil's Island	90
11. Labyrinth	100
12. HOSTAGES	113
13. TRAP	121
14. SPIDER MAN	128
15. The Hunted Becomes the HUNTER	138
16. Wyatt Earp	151
17. Cajun Justice	156
18. Return to Danger	174
19. Lost	181
20. Vengeance	189
21. CAJUN TERROR	198
22. Goodbye, Ballew Dragun	205

Prologue

The Atchafalaya

More is known about the deep seas and the jungles of the Amazon than the peoples of the Atchafalaya.

Animals found only in remote parts of the United States and Canada can still be found in the swamps of the Atchafalaya. Animals like the brown bear, cougar, bobcat, deer and raccoon can be found in the swamp along with swamp rabbits, nutria, eagles, hawks, owls and all kinds of geese and ducks. The nutria is a rat looking mammal that reaches almost five feet in length. The swamp rabbit is an excellent swimmer and will take to the water when in danger, with only its nose sticking above the water until it is safe. In extreme abundance throughout the swamps can be found alligators, timber rattlesnakes, water moccasin and the dreaded cottonmouth. The poisonous cottonmouth will not only strike but also chase its intruder. Related to the snapping turtle are loggerhead turtles with a head and neck the size of a mans leg and jaws powerful enough to snap a broomstick like it was a twig. The loggerhead can weigh as much as 140 pounds. Nighttime brings the bullfrogs and swarms of horseflies and mosquitos.

Filling the swamps are beautiful baldcypress with their knurled roots protruding above the swamp water and hanging gray-green Spanish moss. Also there can be found plants that are medicinal, edible and poisonous.

People can still be found living on what the Atchafalaya gives.

Hidden deep in the swamps of the Atchafalaya are a people untouched by modern civilization. Only through mans greed has he ventured into the swamps of Louisiana in his never ending search for oil. Even the Interstate 10 bridge, crossing more than 25 miles across the swamp, is suspended above the Atchafalaya as though it were an unwanted visitor.

Acadians fled to the swamps in search of peace, closely followed by Blacks, French and White.

For over a hundred years time stopped. In the swamp few knew of electricity, air conditioners or telephones.

Over time stories have filtered from the swamp of the Atchafalaya. Fierce romantic stories of the people known as the Cajuns.

Chapter 1

ATCHAFALAYA

In 20 years with the FBI, Richard Staley had protected many people, but never anyone as beautiful or stubborn as Kelli Parsons. Even in the midst of the dangerous terrorist situation, he found himself physically excited by her presence. He had protected people from hired assassins, Mafia hit men, even their own families--but this was his first time to protect someone from Islamic Fundamentalists. Thanks to an elaborate system set up by the FBI, he felt confident he and his charge would escape detection.

Contrary to the television versions of federal agents' fast-paced lives and dangerous missions, his life remained almost boring. None of his cases involved unusual incidents or even any gunfire, and he doubted this case would be any different.

A journalist, Kelli had written about the Muslim religion, provoking a similar reaction as that produced by Salmon Rushdie's tome, <u>Satanic Verses</u>. Her biting commentary into what she called "atrocious" religious domination and denial of women's rights in Arabic states had brought threats against her life and forced her into hiding.

"Sometimes I think writers don't have the sense God gave them to come in from the rain," said Richard Staley disgustedly. Smoke from the filtered Salem cigarette rolled from his mouth with each word. Staley twisted the burning stub in the ashtray of the armrest. Mechanically, he dug in his shirt pocket for his lighter and another cigarette. The woman Richard's orders demanded he protect sat beside him in the back seat of the navy blue government car.

"Nobody asked your opinion of writers," Kelli snapped. She quickly opened the passenger's side window in retaliation for the cigarette.

The interior of the car was as dark and cold as a coffin. From the comfort of the passenger seat, they argued about the present situation, while the driver sped hastily toward their destination in Houston. Wedged securely between two other identical cars, their vehicle headed west on Interstate 10. Baton Rouge lay behind with Lafayette just ahead.

They were traversing the 25-mile-long twin bridges stretching safely above Louisiana's Atchafalaya River swampland. The bridge cut through the swamp like an unwelcome foreigner, splitting to carry double lanes of traffic quickly in opposite directions and separated by a black void. Approaching headlights appeared to float in a vast darkness, the road sounds muted by the car's air conditioning. Other than the cars, there were no other signs of civilization.

A low-hanging fog crawled from the Atchafalaya swamp, weaving its way along both sides of the highway. No stars lit the hot, overcast, summer night. They were deep within an area of Louisiana with strange people and even stranger customs. Hidden in the Atchafalaya swamps were thousands of untold secrets. Secrets interwoven with danger and romance--mysterious secrets as haunting as the people living in the swamps. This was Cajun country.

"It's our right--no, it's our obligation--to expose the atrocities and suppression of civil rights committed in other countries," said Kelli strongly defending her beliefs.

"Sorry, Kelli," said Richard Staley, "I just don't buy it. Apparently you and other writers haven't learned from that Salmon Rushdie incident. You shouldn't have written what you did."

"Oh, you read my book?"

"I read your book--only to get familiar with your case. Not what I like to read."

"I suppose you prefer picture books like Playboy."

Richard shrugged his shoulders, "It wasn't so bad you wrote about their religious practices, but you should've kept it objective. When you inserted your opinion about the religion being--how did you put it? Barbaric and uncivilized? Oh, yeah, and their masochistic practices should be stopped by the world . . . a little heavy, don't you think?"

"It's true!"
"So is the fact they're chasing you."

He sucked long and deep, making the cigarette glow red, hoping to glimpse more of Kelli's lithe figure. He feasted his eyes on the full breasts, half protruding from the low V-cut shirt she wore, and the loose-fitting jeans did little to hide her fine figure. Smoke hung heavily in the car.

Kelli waved her hand in front of her face, turned her head, and frowned, "Those things are awful--you really should stop."

Staley gestured with his finger ineffectively in the dark and stuffed the partially used Salem into the ashtray, until the smoke ceased to rise. He touched the button on the door lowering his window only slightly.

"You're safe. The FBI has you in protective custody. Still, you should have left them alone." The smoke cleared, and he rolled the window back up.

Defiantly, she lifted her head. "I told the truth. Nothing more and nothing less."

"And now a foreign country has put a price on your head," he said, with a cold stare. Her silky blonde hair hung below her shoulders. Her presence excited him to a point he wanted to grab her.

"Is it too hard for the FBI to protect me?" she asked.

Richard's face showed anger, "You have nothing to worry about. As long as the Bureau is involved, those camel jockeys won't be able to find you. We'll be in Houston soon, and you'll be safe."

"Can't find me? They found us this morning. Ask yourself how! Your beloved Bureau has a leak!" she snapped, spitting out the words. Anger and fear echoed in her voice. "I've lived with those people. Don't underestimate their abilities. Remember, you couldn't prevent them from finding me this morning."

"We don't know if it was them. It looked suspicious, so we got you out of there," Richard explained. Although only mildly concerned, he wondered if Kelli was right. If so, then who revealed their location? Surrounded by his most trusted men, Richard was confident. He let his body relax in the comfort of the plush velour seats of the briskly moving automobile.

The green mile markers and blue call boxes flashed past the car. From each call box protruded a tall antenna, all equipped with a phone for stranded drivers to call for assistance.

The three-car caravan passed mile marker 131 and call box 1295.

Richard's four best agents accompanied them. Two long time friends, Del and Ralph, were in the lead car along with the driver, Jerry, a somewhat over zealous and agitating agent at times. Dependable and trustworthy, Ted and Ron brought up the rear.

For added protection, a young rookie FBI agent, Mike, rode in the front seat of the car along with the driver, Steve. Both excellent marksmen. A total of eight agents to protect one nutty writer.

On the last protective case, Richard harbored another woman so she could testify against Miami drug dealers. Not much of a looker, it took Richard only two days before he slept with her. Playing on their fears always enabled him to get close, and such escapades had cost him his marriage.

Now he sat next to a woman with a hot temper and the body of a topless dancer. He savored the anticipation. Richard would enjoy screwing Kelli. Soon he would convince Kelli she was safe-- but only if he was near. Then she would be his, like the others, he mused.

"If you plan on going to bed with me, forget it!" Kelli snapped.

Richard coughed self-consciously and fumbled nervously with a fresh cigarette, trying to hide his surprise and guilt. "I'm afraid you have me pegged wrong. My job is to protect you," he added defensively, wondering if she had read his thoughts.

"Yeah, sure, you bet. I've been around the world. I've met men from many places, and, let me tell you, men are the same everywhere. You won't get in my pants," she repeated, chiding Richard. "If I were you, I'd concentrate on keeping your zipper shut and your mind on business."

"Stop worrying, we'll be there soon," Richard said. The terrorists were of mild concern to him. Soon the morning incident would be forgotten.

Halfway across the Atchafalaya swamp, two automobiles approached rapidly from the rear. Both slowed as they pulled alongside. From within the lead FBI car, came two bright flashes. Instantly, Richard recognized them as gunshots from the driver's side. What had happened?

"Get down!" he yelled at the same time shoving Kelli's head down.

Suddenly the two charging automobiles started shooting at the trailing FBI car, killing Ted and the other agent. The car crashed viciously against the rail, lifted vertically, and pirouetted across the causeway ending with a violent somersault that catapulted it over the steel guardrail into the swamp below.

Unassisted, the lead FBI car slid sideways forcing Steve against the railing. The car bounced against the barrier grinding sparks from the steel rail before coming to an abrupt stop parallel to and less than six feet from the railing.

Richard forced the rear passenger's door open and pushed Kelli from the car as gunfire shattered the windshield. Fatally wounded, Steve slumped from the driver's door on to the highway. Mike escaped from the passenger door. Finding cover behind the right front fender, he responded quickly with his gun.

Richard crouched at the rear of the car, firing back at what he presumed to be those who pursued Kelli. For the first time, an agent on one of his assignments was killed in the line of duty. For the first time, Richard felt fear.

"This is fucking great! The FBI is going to let me die on some God forsaken bridge in the middle of a swamp," moaned Kelli. "Help! Help!" she screamed at the top of her lungs.

"Shut up!" snapped Richard as he shook her harshly.

"Don't worry, ma'am," said Mike, the young innocent-looking agent near the front of the car. When he turned to return fire, a bullet caught him in the face and he stood erect, screaming and clutching at the pain from his shattered jaw. A barrage of gunfire hit his defenseless body, hurling it over the railing to the watery abyss below.

"Oh, God!" gasped Kelli.

An eerie silence followed. Suddenly, a familiar voice broke the quiet, "Hey, Rich? Rich, can you hear me?"

The voice belonged to Jerry Hyatt, who had been driving the lead car. Jerry's relaxed voice and manner indicated he was not a victim of the assailants. Nor was it hard for Richard to figure that the flashes of gunfire had come from Hyatt's gun. Jerry had killed Del and Ralph.

"That motherfucker killed 'em," Richard mumbled. He wanted to kill Jerry, but he tried to make his voice sound nonchalant through his fear. "Jer, is that you?"

"You got it. These men want to make a deal. They're willing to give you $500,000 if you hand over Parsons." Jerry paused, "I hope she's not worth your life."

Both hands trembled while Richard ejected the clip from his .45 and replaced it with a new one, "Jer, what the hell is going on? When did you change sides? Why'd you murder Del and Ralph?"

"Listen, Rich, consider this a business deal. Del and Ralph wouldn't listen. Don't be as stupid as they were. This is a chance to leave the Bureau with more money than you could make in a lifetime--otherwise, you die with Parsons. These men can't be stopped, I promise you that."

The offer was tempting and for an instant he thought it over, but Kelli interrupted his thoughts.

"Well, Wyatt Earp, are you going to tell them to leave at sundown and defend your lady?" she prodded sarcastically when she noticed his hesitation.

Reality jerked him back, "Jer, the police will be here soon and your sellout will end."

"Sorry, Rich, but we stationed a half-dozen men down the road. They're dressed as FBI agents and are holding the local law enforcement at bay. If we have to kill you, the law will never know the difference."

A voice called out to Richard, a voice he had never heard before. He detected a heavy accent, but could not detect what nationality, although he suspected somewhere from the Mid-East. "Richard Staley! This is Kaja Aboujawdeh . . . we will give you one million dollars for Kelli Parsons! The woman **will** die, you don't have to die with her."

"Can't beat that, Rich," said Jerry enthusiastically.

This time, the numbers sank in, and the idea of turning this woman over became a real possibility. Why die? He could give her to them and live a life of leisure with a million dollars. Defend her and die, or surrender her and be a wealthy man. Wealthy sounded better than dead, he figured.

Carefully, Kelli watched his reaction. She had few alternatives and could do but one thing, "Hey, Wyatt, you and the boys can play O.K. Corral, but I really have to be going."

Confused by the statement and his own thoughts, Richard reacted slowly, "No . . . you can't."

"Really? Fuck you!" she snarled, giving the international one finger salute in front of her face. Before Richard could stop her, she took two quick steps, jumped to the top rail, and in a hail of gunfire, leaped to the black water 20 feet below.

Staley heard her hit the water. "Well, shit!" he responded angrily between clenched teeth. How would the terrorists react to her jumping from the bridge?

"Awww, Rich, you fucked up," said Jerry despondently. "We don't need you anymore."

An ear-piercing scream from the waters below finally penetrated the long silence.

"Jer, I was gonna give the bitch to you, but she got away," Richard whined. "Sounds like she's a goner anyway?"

"No deal!" said Kaja, "Kill him!" With a wave of his arm, the men opened fire.

Richard returned the fire until his clip ran out, then he replaced it with another. With only two clips left, his death seemed imminent and certain. There was only one way out. In a flash, he vaulted the steel rail and found himself hurling to the water below.

* * *

How far underwater Kelli had sunk, she could only guess, but her ankles were mired in some horrible muck. Trying to pull free, her tennis shoes were sucked from her feet. As she clawed her way to the surface, she brushed the body of the agent who died defending her. Gasping for air she burst from the water, and now she could feel the young man's body beneath her feet. Thoughts of snakes and alligators entered her mind. Where was land? Would this stinkhole be where she died?

Suddenly something large and slimy brushed against her hands. It felt cold and rubbery. Frightened at what she feared was surely an alligator, she started to scream with the hopeless thought the screams might scare off the intruder--she was wrong. Suddenly something slid under her arms and around her chest. Frantic, she screamed louder when she felt herself lifted effortlessly from the water. The new terror pulled her across the fearsome alligator-like clump. Another unseen menace took her from the waters of the swamps.

To her surprise, she found herself deposited safely within a boat. Turning catlike, she crouched, confronting her new antagonist. In the darkness, stood a giant of a man. She considered herself tall at five-feet-eight, but this powerfully muscled man stood at least a foot taller than she did. Without a word, he returned to a sitting position at the other end of the boat and watched her closely, saying nothing. She feared she had found a danger worse than the one she escaped on the bridge.

Death waited on the bridge, and while the swamps offered a slim chance of survival, the gentle giant offered her no harm. As her eyes adjusted to the darkness, she saw he wore a vest-type jacket and a shirt with half-sleeves to his elbows. A battered baseball cap laid atop his huge head of shoulder-length dark hair. Strapped under his left arm was a sheath, from which protruded the bone handle of a long knife. She reasoned the man was a Cajun living in the swamp.

"Help?" he asked as he pointed to her. The deep resonant voice carried a heavy accent.

"Yes, yes!" she cried gratefully, recognizing the strangely pronounced French word. "Help! Those men are trying to kill me. Can you help me?"

She cast apprehensive glances in the direction of the top of the bridge as the gunfire stopped.

The Cajun didn't answer. Instead, he turned and pulled on a small rope, lifting a cage full of what looked like shrimp and dropped it in the middle of the boat. Quietly, he watched as Kelli turned her head to the side and squeezed the water from her long hair, then shook her head.

"We've got to get out of here!" she cried.

Suddenly, gunfire erupted again. Both looked up in time to see Richard jump from the Interstate bridge, nearly landing in the boat with them.

Kelli's savior reached for the floundering man and grabbed Richard by the collar of his shirt. The Cajun held Richard in the air as the flat-bottom boat rocked from side to side. Only his years of experience and numerous fights with the deadly alligators of the Atchafalaya prevented the boat from tipping over.

Terrified, Richard tried to point his gun at the Cajun, a mistake Richard would not soon forget, as he stared full into the angry face of the giant Cajun. As easily as taking a toy from a child, the Cajun plucked the gun from Richard's hand, leaving him defenseless. He placed the gun in his belt, and holding Richard with his left hand, the Cajun reached for his knife and pulled it from his sheath.

"Oh, God, no! Don't!" whined Richard, trying to cover his face with his hands, while kicking viciously with his feet, but futilely.

"Stop!" yelled Kelli as she reached for the arm holding the

knife. Then she pointed at Richard, "He is with me. He is an FBI agent. Do you understand?"

The Cajun said nothing, but he threw poor Staley to the back of the boat where he cowered behind Kelli.

Above, on the bridge, four of Kaja's men shined bright flashlights onto the water below. Suddenly a light located the trio within the boat. Kaja barked a command and his men began firing on the boat.

"They're going to kill us," Richard moaned. "Make him do something," he begged of Kelli, pointing to the Cajun. "Tell him to give me my gun."

Before she could answer, the Cajun gathered his antiquated lever-action rifle and took careful aim at one of the lights above. A long burst from an Uzi chopped across the water, coming within inches of the boat.

The Cajun fired once, shattering a light, and penetrating the arm of the man holding it. The bullet traveled the length of his arm and exited out his back, instantly dropping the injured man to the pavement above. Three more times the rifle sounded in rapid succession. Darkness again covered the swamp. Guns continued to fire wildly into the swamp as the giant returned to the wooden seat and heaved mightily on the oars, forcing the boat through the water at incredible speed.

They had gone a short distance when he turned. The bridge disappeared, but the sounds of guns firing into the darkness of the bayou and men yelling continued. Soon, the sounds faded to nothing.

Kelli looked around the small boat. Tied to the side was a crocodile or an alligator. In the dark she could not distinguish which, but it looked dead and that made her feel better. She also realized she didn't know what lived in Louisiana swamps.

From the creature's head protruded a long slender wooden shaft with a thin strong rope tied to the end of the shaft. The neatly coiled rope lay beside a bow nearly as long as she was tall. Not a modern compound bow, but the older longbow that took a tremendous amount of strength to pull. After being lifted effortlessly from the water, Kelli was sure the shaggy giant was very capable of using the bow. The dead alligator was proof enough to dispel any doubts she might have.

One end of the wooden boat was flat to hold an engine. But the boat contained no engine, only two long oars attached in the center and much longer than most row boats.

In silence the Cajun rowed deeper into the swamp, farther from civilization and farther from those who pursued Kelli and Richard.

"This man is crazy. We gotta escape," Richard whispered.

"What's the matter, 'Richie Rich,' weren't they going to stick to the bargain? Don't be such a wuss, Richard. For the first time I don't think those people can find me. **Your** men told them where we were. **This** man did something yours couldn't. He saved us from those bastards--including your wonderful FBI killers."

"Tell him to give me my gun."

"You tell him," she snapped.

The Cajun stared at Kelli from head to toe, "Belle!"

Kelli recognized the French word for "beautiful." Yet, the word didn't quite sound French. The giant had a strange accent, surely Cajun. She regretted never learning the unusual dialect. In her home state of Kansas she never thought that one day she would use it. Cajuns were known for slurring their words and she was sure she would be able to understand more.

"He's probably some stupid hillbilly," Richard said.

"For your information, he is probably Cajun and I suggest you behave. He could kill you if he wanted to. So don't antagonize him," Kelli suggested.

The Cajun laughed and spoke in his native tongue. She could make out bits and pieces. Her quick mind formed the phrases.

"He's crazy, I tell you . . . and probably ignorant as hell," Richard repeated.

Kelli failed to hear Richard. Instead she concentrated on trying to translate bits and pieces of what the Cajun mumbled, almost undetected: "Crazy? Maybe stupid . . . It not me jump bridge . . . .take gun . . . If man gone, I have one less problem. Why lawman jump Atchafalaya? . . . men are dangerous . . . woman beautiful . . . woman trouble." She caught his eyes as he looked deeply into hers. He hesitated at the oars, ". . . maybe she understand me."

Kelli looked away and knew from his words he understood what they were saying. The Cajun smiled and resumed his steady rowing deeper into the darkness of the Atchafalaya.

Chapter 2
Blue Dragon

Local law enforcement officers organized the clean-up, and traffic moved slowly around the bad wreck on the bridge crossing the Atchafalaya River. Near one car, two men were talking.

"The locals have been told of the situation as you ordered, Kaja," Jerry Hyatt was saying.

"Good," snapped Kaja, "Keep the story straight. I want no one to follow. No FBI. No locals. The girl has been kidnaped. Understand?" Jerry nodded and Kaja continued, "I will take my men and find them. Also, I want to find out who this man with the rifle is. It will be my personal pleasure to kill him. Make sure there is no investigation around here so we can search for them unhindered. We don't want the FBI here."

"No problem," Jerry assured, "when I'm finished, they'll think the woman headed for California. Besides, I have a few friends in the Bureau who can cover things for me."

"Don't mess up, Mister Hyatt," ordered Kaja. "We have paid you too much money for you to do something foolish now."

* * *

Stiff and cold, Kelli awoke to discover she was lying against Richard. Awakened by his snoring, she swatted at the pesky mosquitos buzzing about her head, but without success. Three more replaced each one she killed. At the present rate, she was sure she would need a blood transfusion before dawn.

Tirelessly, the Cajun rowed without any sign of fatigue. The insects went unnoticed by the giant man. Mechanically, Kelli glanced at her wrist. Like her shoes, the watch was gone. She could only guess how much time had passed. No longer could she hear the sounds of cars or see their lights. How much time passed she had no way of knowing; maybe an hour or more, she thought. The Cajun continued his rowing and she marveled at his endurance.

For the first time she realized she knew nothing about the swamps of Louisiana. In school, she had studied all types of geography . . . the Amazon, the Congo . . . romantic and dangerous places. Less was known about the swamps of the Atchafalaya. Because the swamp was in the United States, did people give less attention to it than they did to other parts of the world?

She always thought that people in the swamps were backward and inbred, even incestuous. Yet the man sitting before her was not deformed by in-breeding. Neither did he have the signs denoting ignorance. His knowing smile suggested he sensed their situation and thought it amusing. If anything, the man was handsome and, physically, a fine specimen. He could've abandoned them to bullets or gators--but he hadn't.

She noticed he no longer wore his sleeveless jacket. Instead, he'd wrapped it around her.

"Thank you," she said as she pointed to the jacket. The Cajun just nodded.

When he saw her slapping at the mosquitoes, he handed her a small jar, "This stop biting."

Kelli unscrewed the cap but quickly pulled her head away from the vile-smelling contents. She refused to use the grease, closing it and placing it in the bottom of the boat. The Cajun smiled and shrugged his shoulders.

It only took a few more minutes of being hopelessly swarmed by countless mosquitoes before she relented and applied the unappealing grease. No sooner had she finished than the insects quit their attack. The Cajun smiled and nodded his head. For some reason, she felt secure and quickly fell asleep again.

Kelli awakened to the soft scraping of the boat sliding up onto the shore. Still dark, the starlit sky glistened across the waters of the swamp. The stars were clear and bright, not hidden by the lights and pollution of the large cities. With her eyes now accustomed to the dark, she saw, for the first time, that the monstrous object tied along side the small boat was indeed an alligator. Richard still snored.

The Cajun tied the boat to a log and started walking toward

a cabin less than 20 yards away. Kelli jumped from the boat, slipping the vest on, as she followed. The Cajun turned and pointed to her bare feet.

She shrugged her shoulders. "My shoes got stuck in the mud."

The Cajun nodded, turned and continued along a narrow path near the water's edge. Kelli stumbled and followed closely behind. Richard remained snoring in the stern of the boat.

Large cypress trees grew from the water and thick Spanish moss hung from the branches. In places the moss stretched down to, and in places even touched the water. They had come ashore on a small island, beautiful but primitive and deep within the swamp.

They had stepped back in time over 100 years. Nothing was different now than centuries before. The construction of the small house amazed Kelli. Surrounded with swamp reeds to the rear, land on the right and half of the front, and open water on the remaining sides, it stood 4 feet out of the water. On the island, she could see other small structures in the darkness.

Outside the door to the house, on the weathered wooden slat porch, the Cajun lifted the glass cover surrounding an old kerosene lantern. Next to the lantern he took a wooden match and, with the flick of his thumb nail, it crackled to life. The lantern flickered, then filled the rustic wooden porch with yellow light. The Cajun motioned for Kelli to follow. Inside, she found a well-kept attractive three-room cottage with a large living area, a small but adequate kitchen with an old wood-burning stove, and one bedroom. Through the open bedroom door she saw a large bed surrounded by mosquito netting. For added protection, the porch and windows were all screened. An expert craftsman had built the house.

In the yellow light, she could see the Cajun more clearly. He removed his cap and placed it by others on a hook next to the door. Carefully, he placed the rifle in a rack on the wall beside two others. He ran his hand through his thick black hair and lit another lantern. His jaw was square and firm and his smile filled with a set of perfect white teeth. The eyes were gray and intimidating. He wore handmade boots of alligator hide, and his belt and knife sheath were made from snake skin. His shirt, dark blue with gray half-sleeves, pictured a large cartoon of the Marvel Comic character, Spider Man, on the front. Around his neck hung a leather necklace from which dangled the rattles of a once formidable rattlesnake.

From the size, she doubted it could be real. She wondered if a rattlesnake could grow that large.

On one side of the room, near the bedroom, rested an easel and a partially completed oil painting of the swamps. Kelli noticed the walls covered with similar paintings depicting scenes of the swamp. The rustic framed canvas paintings looked as real as snapshots of the swamp. Who painted? Who had built such a fine house?

In another corner, a plastic chess set with an old playing board was perched on top of a small empty barrel. The corners of the old cardboard playing board were tattered with age and peeling.

Next to the chess set, leaning against the wall and beneath the window, was what could only be described as an aluminum washboard, but without the sturdy frame. Two aluminum bands, each forming two half circles, were attached at the top of the aluminum "thing" and on the floor beside it were four spoons. Close to this washboard was a well-used accordion.

The furniture filling the small house was old, but well maintained, and ornaments and oil paintings filled the four walls of the rectangular room.

On one wall hung the skin of an alligator, she estimated to be over 10 feet in length. Beneath this hung a variety of animal and snake skins. The colorful and deadly skins of the cottonmouth, rattler, and coral snake. For Kelli, it was a strange introduction to the creatures of the Atchafalaya Swamps.

Below the skins hung the shell of a large turtle. The shell reminded her of the snapping turtle she had found in a pond when she was a little girl. She remembered the vicious little thing and couldn't imagine a confrontation with a turtle the size of the one hanging on the wall.

The shell belonged to a Loggerhead turtle over 2 feet in length and a little more than one and a half feet wide. At one time, it had a neck the size of large man's calf and capable of snapping off a grown man's arm.

The Cajun motioned for Kelli to come to the kitchen where he had a large bowl filled with water. As she approached, he handed her a small clean towel and a bar of soap and pointed to the bowl. The water was sweet relief from Kelli's ordeal, and she quickly washed the dirt and grime from her face.

When she finished, the Cajun made her sit in a rocking chair and handed her a drink of water. God, it tastes good, she thought.

She smiled her gratitude.
 Beside the rocking chair was a stack of comic books, placed neatly in a wooden box. Casually, she fingered through them and saw that all were Marvel comic books of Spider Man.
 Abruptly, the man who showed only kindness took her left ankle in his hand, stretching the palm of his other hand alongside her small foot as though measuring it. Satisfied, he released her ankle, and handed her a large white T-shirt to wear. Then he stood her up and directed her to the door leading to his bedroom, where he pointed to the bed.
 "If you think I'm going to go to bed with you, you're crazy!" she snapped.
 With a frown and a disgusted shake of his head, he pointed to the bed. He pointed at her and said a single word. She understood the French word, "Sleep." The Cajun started to leave.
 "Who are you?" asked Kelli.
 The Cajun said something, neither English nor French, but with a unique accent she couldn't identify. However, she did understand the word, "Tomorrow." The Cajun then walked outside, leaving her alone.
 Kelli hesitated, but the sheets looked inviting. What of Richard? Exhausted, nothing seemed to matter. At first, she thought of sleeping in her cold wet clothes should the Cajun return, then she chuckled to herself, knowing he had the power to do as he wished. So she cast away her concern and fear as easily as she discarded her clothing. She slipped on the fresh clean T-shirt, then crawled beneath the inviting sheets.

* * *

 Long after midnight, two cars stopped in front of Happy Jak's, a small supply store and bar deep within the swamps of the Atchafalaya. Happy Jak's was the local gathering place where men could be found with information about the swamps. From what Jerry managed to learn from the locals, Happy Jak's was the place to secure airboats under the pretense of a fishing trip in the swamps.
 "Kaja, I don't think I should be with you," said Hyatt as he closed the door to the limousine.
 Two large mercury vapor lights illuminated the parking area. Four worn and rusting pickup trucks were parked in front of the old store. A hunting dog, chained to the bed of a truck, barked

as they neared the building.

In the shadows, a short pier extended from the rear of the building into the swamp where three airboats, a canoe, and a bass boat were moored. A stray dog with half its hair missing skittered away as they approached. If all went well, they would find information on the strange man they had seen rescue Kelli and Richard from the Atchafalaya. If they found him, they would find Kelli.

"You worry too much, Jerry," Kaja said, casually stopping before he climbed to the wide porch. "There would be no reason for the FBI to suspect you gathering information on the disappearance of the woman. Besides, I believe your price of half a million to be enough incentive to keep you near." He stepped to the porch of the old dilapidated building, half extending into the swamp. "You don't collect your money until she is dead."

"All right, all right, Kaja," Jerry said, waving his hands in the air as he relented to Kaja's demand.

"This is it?" asked Kaja.

"Yes," Hyatt confirmed. "This is the place to arrange for a fishing expedition into the swamps."

"Then let's find out," he said as he motioned his men to wait while he and Hyatt entered the old bar. "Jerry, don't call me Kaja. The name is too suspicious, call me Tom."

"Good idea," said Jerry.

So it was Tom and Jerry entered a strange world where neither belonged, a combination of Cajuns, Creoles, and mulattos. To patrons at Happy Jak's, Jerry, and Kaja were outsiders, men asking for a fishing guide in the swamps.

Two pool tables stood at one end of the smoke-filled bar. A dozen tables were scattered about the dusty wooden floors. The bar was separated by a locked door leading to the supply store, open only during the day. At the back of the bar were two wooden doors half filled with square glass panels. The doors led from the rear of Happy Jak's to a wooden deck and walkway over the water. Some patrons had their transportation tied to the pier.

The bar had a pungent smell of spice and pepper, mixed with a slight odor of old fish. The jukebox played, sounding nothing like music the strangers ever had heard before, heavy with whining violins and whirring accordions. The words were more of a slang and a slur. The unique dialect was nothing Jerry could identify. He felt uneasy.

But nothing bothered Kaja. The unusual surroundings had no effect on him. Deadly situations posed no problem for the terrorist, and there was nothing he and his men feared or could not handle. The stories he had heard about the people from this southern part of Louisiana had no effect whatsoever. If these Acadians posed any problem to him, he and his men would eliminate anyone in the way. The American people were weak and were of little concern to him. Americans were cowards when it came to the thought of death. Self-indulgent people who were not committed to the cause of Allah. Kaja had no reason to expect anything different from the backward people of Louisiana.

Two of the men playing pool stopped to stare at the intruders. A small, gray-haired man at the bar, bent over by time's unkindness, watched the pair, then said something unintelligible only the bartender understood. The stout bartender laughed and continued to clean glasses.

Together, Jerry and Kaja approached the bar and sat next to the small old man.

After wiping a glass clean and placing it on the shelf, the bartender approached the two men. "Can I help ya?" he asked in his heavy Cajun accent. Black hair hung over the bartender's ears. He was large and fat with thick bushy eyebrows, but he carried himself with the ease of a powerful man--a man with confidence he surely felt he could back up. With him behind the bar, a bouncer was not needed.

"Yes, we would like--" Kaja started to ask, but the bartender interrupted.

"Guides for a fishing trip into the swamps," said the bartender, smiling. He smiled when he noticed the anger in Kaja's face. "You do not look like fishermen."

Kaja, a slight man with a thick scar across his nose, the remnant of a ragged wound splitting his nose nearly in half, was anything but a fisherman.

"Who are you?" demanded Kaja angrily.

A small, paunchy man sitting next to Kaja listened intently. Across the room his friend stood playing pool, clutching his pool cue, watching, and listening.

The bartender spread his arms, placing both fists with the knuckles against the worn wooden bar top, "Here, **we** ask the questions. Strangers don't ask us questions." The bartender smiled confidently, while he glared at Kaja.

Kaja regained his composure, as all terrorists had learned to do when they had hostages within their grasp. "Pardon me, we have had a long day. We have everything we will require for the trip," said Kaja truthfully when he thought of the arsenal he and his men had brought. Again the vision of the large youthful man with the old gun danced in his mind. Kaja laughed, "We can catch anything with what we have."

With a shrug of his shoulders, the bartender responded, "You have came to the right place. There are guides here. Most of these men can take you anywhere you want."

"May I ask your name?" Kaja asked with extreme politeness.

With a thump of his huge chest the bartender responded, "I am Happy Jak Chamblee."

Kaja sized up the bartender much like a cat eyes a bird. Before he left the swamps, it would be Kaja's pleasure to personally kill this insolent American.

"Excuse me," said Jerry, trying to get Happy Jak's attention, "We were told we could find a man here. Saw him in the swamp yesterday." Jerry held his hand over his head to show the man's height, "He's about this big, wears a baseball cap, and sleeveless jacket."

The little old man beside Jerry answered with strange words, loud and clear, but barely understandable, spoken with a bit of awe: "Blue Dragon! You hunt the Blue Dragon." Then the old man turned to the patrons of the bar and yelled loudly in the Cajun dialect. Neither Kaja nor Jerry understood.

Jerry shook his head. "No, no. We're not looking for a dragon, we're hunting for a man."

Happy Jak's attitude changed abruptly. "I can no longer help you. If you not want to drink . . . " Happy Jak paused slightly, "then leave." The hint of humor had disappeared from his eyes.

The small, paunchy man jumped suddenly from his seat on the far side of the room and hurried to his companion near the pool table. Even across the room, his words could be heard as he spoke. "Delacroix, did you hear? They hunt Dragon!" he said excitedly.

"Shut up, Mamou!" snapped the large man, Delacroix, still holding onto the pool cue, more like a weapon than a tool of entertainment. With one free hand, he pushed Mamou aside. Still eyeing the strange men, he chugged the last of his drink.

With their business unexpectedly finished, Kaja and Jerry turned to leave Happy Jak's. When they reached the limousines, they were distracted by Delacroix who had followed them into the darkness. At his side came his short friend, Mamou.

Jerry nudged Kaja. "Maybe they have some information on the man we're looking for."

Delacroix and Mamou approached slowly.

"Can you help us find the man we look for?" asked Kaja.

Delacroix stared at the limousine and ran his hand along the finely polished paint. "You are no fishermen. You have money? Maybe you hunters . . . maybe I help you find the Dragon."

Kaja shook with anger. Were the people of Louisiana crazy to think he believed in dragons? "There are no dragons! Do you think I'm foolish enough to believe your story?"

"No, you don't understand me," said Delacroix with a touch of anger. "You hunt a man. You hunt Ballew Dragun."

Finally both men understood and Jerry asked, "Can you help us?"

A sinister smile Kaja understood flashed across Delacroix's face. "If you want to kill him, I will help you."

* * *

The summer fields of Kansas were green. Kelli walked through the fragrant grass and rainbow-colored flowers covering the hill for as far as the eye could see. Robins and Cardinals chorused the songs of summer. She was home on her father's farm.

Kelli stretched, opened her eyes to the cage of mosquito netting surrounding the Cajun's bed, and suddenly jerked back to reality.

She raised herself to both elbows and smiled. "Well, Dorothy this sure isn't OZ, and I don't think you'll be able to find the yellow brick road. Now is this Cajun the Tin Man, the Lion-- oh, hell, at least he isn't the Wicked Witch."

Slowly she sat up in bed and closed her eyes, then mumbled, "Oh, Toto, there's no place like home, there's no place like home." Kelli opened her right eye and smiled, "It was worth a try."

How she yearned for the safety of her father's farm. He was right when he had told her to marry and settle down. Now she was in a land, about which she knew virtually nothing . . . a land more foreign and more deadly than Iran and other Middle Eastern countries she knew well. But she wasn't in a foreign country; she was in America . . . in a small patch of swamp in the southern part of Louisiana.

Hell, I might as well be in the fucking Amazon, she thought, as she watched a spider on the wall.

Who was this strange man? Beside the bed lay an old worn pair of jeans and a shirt. The clothes had not been there when she went to sleep. She slid from the bed and held the jeans in front of her. The clothes were a little big but clean. She was thankful they were slightly larger, and she slid easily into the clean but worn clothes.

Cautiously she peered from her room, then she smelled strong coffee and something akin to biscuits or cornbread, sweet and appealing.

In the kitchen stood the Cajun with his back turned toward her. Next to him on the counter, standing on his hind legs, a small raccoon waited patiently for food. Kelli watched the Cajun fill a small dish with water, then hand the raccoon a morsel of food. Eagerly, the creature washed the tidbit in the water-filled dish and quickly devoured it. After each handout, the raccoon would again assume his beggar's stance and the cycle would be repeated.

Kelli stepped from the room holding her loose-fitting jeans with one hand. "Good morning," she said in as friendly a manner as she could.

The Cajun turned from the sink, but her voice startled the raccoon and it jumped backwards, bumping its head on the overhanging cabinet. The giant of a man moved effortlessly across the room toward his rocking chair, where he retrieved two boot-like moccasins made from alligator skin. She knew he must have just finished making them, along with a belt from some type of snake. He smiled and handed them to her.

"For me?" she asked.

The young, rugged man nodded his head and pointed to her feet and waist. She surmised him to be about her age, perhaps in his late twenties. The boots were surprisingly soft and fit well and all from only a crude measurement the night before. Now she understood why he had held his hand up to her foot. With one measurement, he managed to fabricate a boot fitting her perfectly.

"They're beautiful!" she exclaimed as she slid the snakeskin belt through the loops of her pants.

"Belle?" he asked, his face reddening a bit.

Kelli laughed, "Yes, belle!"

The Cajun seemed relieved. "Belle," he said pointing to the boots. Then he pointed at her and smiled, "Belle!" Just as quickly, he turned and mumbled something she could not understand, but his actions told her everything as he poured a cup of coffee.

"Thank you," she said, taking the pungent coffee.

The chicory coffee was strong, but she thought it tasted very good. In foreign countries, to dislike food or drink offered by another person was an insult. She was sure the swamps of Louisiana were no different. In fact, she rather enjoyed the unusual flavor of the chicory. Over the years, she had become bored with the watered down version of what Americans called coffee. She raised her mug and smiled. If someone wanted coffee, this was the only way to drink it.

"What is your name?" she asked casually and intentionally using English.

"Blue Dragon," he replied with the heavy accent.

"Blue Dragon?" she queried, not sure what he said. The fact he answered her question let her know he understood English, even if he apparently preferred not to speak it.

The Cajun shook his head negatively. "Ba--llew," he said slowly. "Dra--," then he pointed to Richard's gun, "gun."

"Ballew Dragun!" she said excitedly, trying to add the accent so it sounded proper. Her effort brought a smile from the Cajun, Ballew Dragun.

Chapter 3
SWAMP WITCH

Kelli sipped the dark strong coffee, all the while evaluating Ballew Dragun. From the kitchen she noticed the raccoon watching her much as she watched the Cajun.

Cautiously, Kelli approached the kitchen and the raccoon. Ballew stopped and handed her a piece of the biscuit he was feeding the raccoon.

"Give this to Rocky and he be your friend," said Ballew, also cautioning, "slowly."

Carefully, Kelli extended the piece of food toward Rocky. The raccoon looked to Ballew first and, after he received an affirmative nod, he readily accepted the proffered tidbit, which he quickly washed.

Kelli giggled like the little girl back in Kansas. The animals, the farm--another time far away.

"You called him Rocky?" asked Kelli, trying to draw the Cajun into more conversation.

Ballew smiled, "Yes. I find him when he was small. He look like he been in a fight, so I call him Rocky--after the fighter."

He spoke in clear but broken English, heavy with the Cajun accent, occasionally slipping into his Cajun tongue. Both were easy for Kelli to follow.

"Do you go to the movies?" she asked, thinking about the boxing movies of the same name.

"Movies? No, I go to movie many years ago when my mother, Belle Rose, takes me to Baton Rouge. I name him after the boxer, Rocky Marciano."

So he didn't go to movies. Kelli doubted he had ever even seen television. For now, there were more pressing matters--like hunger. Kelli was hungry.

"Eat?" Ballew asked. When she nodded affirmatively, he turned and placed two biscuits from the blackened cast iron frying pan onto a small plate. He sprinkled them with spices, put them on a larger plate and eagerly handed it to Kelli.

The biscuits were really rice fritters. Hunger overcame her wariness, and the spicy-sweet, hot, rice fritter covered with nutmeg, cinnamon ,and powdered sugar pleased her immensely. It was more like a rice doughnut, and she made sure her new Cajun friend noticed the delight in her eyes. She quickly finished both fritters, between sips of the steaming black brew.

Kelli was about to thank him when Richard burst into the house. Kelli had completely forgotten Richard being left in the boat. The Cajun showed no outward sign of surprise. Rocky skittered from the counter and out the screened door, pausing only long enough to push the door open with his paws.

Richard's face and arms were covered with red welts. He scratched furiously at the mosquito bites covering his body.

"I'm FBI," Richard said.

"And what is the FBI going to do?" Kelli asked.

"They will send men in to rescue you and take you to safety," Richard said confidently.

Kelli frowned, "FBI, what does that stand for? Famous But Incompetent? Fuck the FBI--I feel a hell of a lot safer here in the swamps. Besides, I hope your precious FBI doesn't have any more Jerry Hyatt's waiting for us."

The Cajun smiled.

Richard flashed his soaking wet leather encased badge at Ballew and ignored Kelli's words. "You must take us to a phone and get us to New Orleans and give me my gun."

The Cajun's transformation was evident and quick. No longer was he the gentle man who had served breakfast to Kelli. Instead, he became angry with Richard's demands--the man he saved from the swamps only hours earlier.

"Maybe I let gators eat you," he growled in Cajun.

Kelli understood most of what he said. "Richard, I suggest you shut up."

"No, Kelli, he has us prisoners. He has to free us. It's the law. Besides, it looks likes he's been poaching alligators," Richard added defensively.

"In case you don't remember, last night he saved our butts, you asshole!" she yelled.

Her comment again brought a slight smile to the lips of the Cajun. Both were surprised when he brought out Staley's gun. He removed the full clip and showed it to Richard. Then he slid the clip back into the gun and placed it on the table between them.

In broken English, he spoke as he backed away. "Go for gun . . . you win, it yours . . . you lose, well . . . " he said, with a shrug of his huge shoulders and a confident tone.

The unexpected action sent a cold chill up Richard's spine and his legs started to tremble and give beneath his weight.

"You can't do this!" said Kelli in shocked disbelief.

Ballew smiled at her. "He is coward. Don't worry--he won't go for gun," he said in the strange Cajun language that was becoming easier to understand with every spoken word.

"What did he say?" asked Richard nervously.

Kelli turned her head and covered her eyes, hoping the ruse would make Richard stop his foolish efforts. "I can't bear to watch."

Richard backed away. "Hey, guy, I'm not gonna have a shootout with you."

As though nothing had happened, the Cajun stepped to the table, retrieved the gun and placed it in his belt. He went to the kitchen where he poured coffee and found another fritter. These he offered to Richard, who quickly spit the coffee back in the mug.

"Jesus, this tastes like shit!" he snarled as he bit into the rice fritter, hoping to remove the taste of the coffee. He was not prepared for the sweet taste and promptly spit the fritter back onto the plate. "Look, I'm an FBI agent," he said, pulling the badge from his pocket. "You have to take me to the nearest town."

The Cajun's frown should have warned Richard into silence. But he didn't and Ballew Dragun jerked the badge from Richard's hand, walked to the door, and flung the badge as far as he could into the waters of the swamp.

"You can't do that," whined Richard.

"I'm afraid he already did," snickered Kelli.

"But I'm the law!" he insisted.

Ballew took one step, grabbed Richard by the front of the shirt and lifting him from the ground, said, "In the Atchafalaya, you be nothing--here, **I** am law!"

When the Cajun released his hold, Richard scrambled from the house, falling down the steps into the mud at the water's edge, and crying hysterically, "He's crazy!"

They watched as he crawled and stumbled his way back to the boat. Rocky returned to the porch, stretching his neck to see. Without the gun, Richard was helpless . . . naked . . . totally powerless.

From the porch they watched Richard rub the bumps covering his body.

"Shit, God, I'll die of malaria," he whined, as he scratched at the tiny mosquito bites he had received throughout the night while sleeping in the small boat. "Damn, they itch!"

Finally, Richard stumbled into the swamp, where he removed his shirt and splashed water on his back and arms. With the taste of bitter coffee still in his mouth, the cool water in which he stood looked satisfying. He bent over, cupped his hands, and scooped up a mouthful.

"No!" yelled Ballew when he saw what Richard intended to do. The yell startled both Kelli and Richard.

Richard was so unnerved by the yell, he reeled backwards and fell, half-submerging himself in the swamp water. Quickly, he stood erect in the knee-deep water. Defiantly, he faced the giant man on the porch. "Yeah, well fuck you, you backwoods sonofabitch! If I wanna drink water, I'll damn well do as I please." Then Richard bent over, putting his face in the water, and drank his fill.

The Cajun took one step and stopped. Even he realized the effort would be too late. A mighty fist pounded the frame of the house, shaking the whole structure as he shook his head in disgust.

"Ballew, what's the matter?" asked Kelli.

"No drink, water bad," he said, then pointed to Richard. "He get sick."

"What can we do?"

"Nothing, too late. Fever start tonight," he said. Gently he grabbed Kelli's shoulders and turned her so she faced him and spoke in his Cajun tongue: "Don't drink the water. I show you where be safe water."

The morning was bright and beautiful and the thick overgrowth shaded the sun. A pelican splashed in the nearby waters, quickly rising with a full gullet from which protruded a large fish tail.

She nodded her understanding and followed him from the porch. For the first time she could see the tiny island more clearly. She could see a large shed she guessed housed his tools and equipment. Outside the door to the structure were two wooden saw horses with planks stretched between the two. Next to the shed was a small building similar to the smokehouse her father had built on the farm in Kansas. Near the shed hung an alligator skin she surmised to be the one tied to the boat the night before. She wondered if the Cajun had slept at all during the night. What with skinning the alligator and making the shoes and belt she doubted it. Alongside the skinned alligator hung the pelts of various animals.

The thick grasses rustled and Rocky stuck his inquisitive head out. Soon he was following close behind.

Beyond the sheds and farther inland was a screened shed with a dozen chickens inside. After a momentary stop Ballew opened the pen so the chickens could forage for themselves. He continued, showing her the outhouse, then a wooden box containing an old mechanical pump attached to a deep water well.

Ballew stopped and hand-cranked the pump, putting his hand before the clear, cool liquid spilling into a wooden trough. This he drank, then gestured for Kelli to follow his example. She did so, then washed her face.

Next to the water pump was a wood stall 4 feet square and 5 feet high. Kelli stood before an ingeniously constructed shower. On one wall above the shower hung a tin pan painted black, holding, she guessed, ten gallons of water and covered with glass. Screwed to the bottom of the black water container was a shower head pointed inside the fenced area. A capped spout protruded from the top and rear of the tin box. Below the spout a pail hung from a wooden peg on the fence. Tightly laid bricks, packed with clean sand, covered the shower floor. She knew the black tin and glass would heat the water during the day and keep it warm during the evening.

The Cajun nodded for her to enter. This she did and pulled the chain hanging from the shower head. She jumped back to keep from getting wet and reached out and touched the still warm water. It felt good to run her arms through the water and wash the dirt from them. The water felt even better on her face. She pulled the cord and the water stopped. Oh, how she wished for soap and a real shower.

"Thank you for--" but she stopped short. The Cajun was

nowhere in sight. She looked toward the house and saw Ballew emerge, carrying something in his arms.

Ballew walked directly to Kelli, ignoring the sniveling man at the water's edge. Near the boat Richard sat dejectedly, picking up mud and throwing it back down.

"Wash," said Ballew, handing Kelli a large soft towel and a bar of soap.

Inside the shower stall Kelli reluctantly removed the clothes Ballew had given her and hung them over the fence. Slightly embarrassed, she removed her final garments. A quick glance showed the giant Cajun had turned his back and stood like a mighty sentinel.

Kelli felt helpless and safe at the same time. The desire to wash overwhelmed the instinct to be cautious. How could she trust a man she didn't even know? But all he did was offer help. Clearly the Cajun could do anything to anybody whenever he pleased and no one could stop him. She laughed, knowing she could do nothing, so she enjoyed the shower.

She scrubbed her skin until she thought it was raw, then she washed her hair until it squeaked. Her hair was still lathered when the water stopped abruptly. With one hand she wiped the soap from her face and opened her eyes. A pull on the cord indicated the tank was empty. She looked over the fence in Ballew's direction. His back was still toward her.

"Ballew," she said softly and when he turned to answer she pointed helplessly to the tank.

Kelli thought she noticed a slight redness in his face as he approached the stall and, looking away from her, reached blindly for the pail. He fumbled with the pail as he filled it. With a full load, he returned to fill the tank for the shower. Kelli tried to hide her nude, soap-covered body against the wooden wall.

Ballew poured the water accurately and not a drop missed the spout. Just before he finished Kelli reached over the wall and touched Ballew's arm.

"Thank you, Ballew," she said softly.

Ballew managed to get only half the remaining water in the tank. Kelli laughed as she watched Ballew return to his post.

She pulled the cord and was unable to restrain a scream of shock when the cold pellets of water cascaded against her body. She failed to notice the smile on her guard's face as she danced in the shower trying to remove the last traces of soap.

After the refreshing shower Kelli dressed herself quickly before stepping out of the stall. Ballew waited patiently. Together they walked back to the small house.

On the return trek, Ballew gathered a combination of strange-looking leaves from a bush and cut pieces off another aloe-type plant. He placed them in a small leather pouch at his side. They made a short stop at the smokehouse, then Ballew disappeared inside and returned quickly with a stack of fresh-cut steaks.

"Get him," Ballew said to Kelli, "He must eat now. Tonight he be sick."

Terrified as Richard was, Kelli convinced him to come into the cabin and eat, then she tried to help Ballew in the kitchen, but he was very proficient. Anyway, he cooks more than I do, she thought.

The old wood-burning, black, cast-iron stove had already heated. Water boiled in a small pot. In this, Ballew sprinkled some of the leaves he had gathered. Grease, placed in the skillet, sputtered and slid around the steaks. He sprinkled on more spices. The aroma of the sizzling steaks became mouth-watering.

"What are they?" asked Kelli pointing to the white steaks.

With a flip of the spatula, he turned one of the steaks. "Gator," he said calmly and added, "The one you saw last night."

Kelli fidgeted, but showed no outward signs of disgust. She had eaten stranger things, so she doubted alligator would not be any different. She was glad Richard had not heard the identity of the steaks.

In the corner, farthest from Ballew, sat Richard with his arms wrapped around his folded legs. What a pitiful sight, Kelli thought. The night before, he tried to defend her. Last night a civilized man, today nothing more than a lost, frightened creature. So complete was his transition, she no longer begrudged him wanting the money. Now he was like a sick cornered dog in surroundings foreign to his style of living.

Richard caught her eye. "Where's the telephone? I need to call the office."

"Sorry you're shit out of luck. No telephones here," she chortled.

"We have to leave," he snapped.

Kelli turned to Ballew, "When will you take us back?"

"Tomorrow," Ballew answered.

They ate in silence and when they finished, Ballew went

about his chores on the small island. Richard sat on the porch alone, while Kelli explored the house and all of its strange items. She thought the paintings were beautiful and wondered how he could afford such fine works of art. She did not understand the small wooden box filled only with comic books of Spider Man. Children's books, but no children to read them . . . only Ballew.

In the distance, they heard a small motor boat. She peered from the window to see a small, old woman nearing the island in a motor boat. As she watched, Richard entered the house and hid in one corner, behind a chair. Either the ordeal had become too much for him or the swamp water was taking effect. Maybe a combination of both, she thought.

Kelli walked to the porch to catch a better glimpse of the visitor. Ballew stood at the shore, waving his hand to the small woman. When the boat landed, he greeted her and helped her from the boat.

"Belle Rose!" exclaimed Ballew as he helped her along the shore.

Beautiful Rose, thought Kelli, as she walked toward the two. She was anything but a beautiful Rose. Her skin was dark brown from the sun and covered with moles, her face leathery and her lips wrinkled. When she took off her old sailor's cap, it revealed thinning hair turned white over the years. She even had a bald spot on the back of her head. Bare-footed and wearing a faded, cotton print dress, she looked ancient, but moved with a bounce and sparkle, excited at seeing people. Two dolls, one with a long needle through it, hung from a leather belt wrapped around her waist. Strange, thought Kelli, but they appeared almost like Voodoo dolls. The most appalling feature was when Kelli saw the tiny old woman spit and realized she chewed tobacco.

"Trouble's brewing, Ballew," she said in the heavy Cajun accent. "Men want you. Strange men, likes I never seen. Dey want you dead and--" She hesitated when she heard Kelli approach. Her eyes alert and full of life, Belle Rose spied Kelli, her wrinkled lips formed a smile, and she pointed a dry bent finger toward Kelli. "Dis beauty will be the dead of ya yet, son. Six men come. Dey come kill you and de woman."

"They can't find me," Ballew said flatly.

"You wrong. Delacroix and Mamou help dem search. Dese men got money and guns. Word says dey's not from our world." Then she tapped the dolls clinging to her waist and again her voice crackled, "But I done take care of dem for you."

"They are from other country?" Ballew asked.

"Muslims from Iran," interjected Kelli. "They are dangerous, just like she said. Maybe we should leave."

"No one make Ballew Dragun leave. I stay. They will leave," he assured her.

"You can't beat them. Our own government couldn't beat them," Kelli pleaded, pointing to Richard cowering on the porch of the house.

Belle Rose spit. "Duh girl be right. You know Delacroix like you dead. I don't want dem get my Spider Man."

"I'll be careful. Now you go, foolish woman," Ballew chided as he gave her a playful pat on the behind.

Ballew escorted Belle Rose back to her boat and after she cast off into the swamp, he returned to Kelli. "Why they want you dead?" he asked.

"They did bad things, and I told people by writing about it in a book," she said defiantly.

"Sometimes it is wiser to be quiet," he observed simply and returned to his work.

"Aren't you going to prepare for them?" she asked.

"I know when they come. Delacroix does not know where I am. It will take them time."

"Who is Spider Man?"

"It what Belle Rose calls me. I am Spider Man."

"What a strange name, Belle Rose. How'd she get such a pretty name?"

The reply was blunt: "You ask too many questions." After a moment of silence he sighed. "She my friend. I call her Belle Rose. In the Atchafalaya, she known as Swamp Witch."

Chapter 4

Fever

"Everything is ready," Jerry said to Kaja.

Nearby Delacroix and Mamou listened and waited with two airboats loaded and ready for their hunt into the Atchafalaya. Four of Kaja's men, two with Uzi's and two with shotguns, accompanied them.

A vicious smile covered Delacroix's face, "You must want the woman bad."

"It is none of your business," said Kaja coldly. "When I get the woman, you can do whatever you want with this Ballew Dragun."

"He is not easy to find or to catch," Delacroix said knowingly. "He killed my brother, and for that, I will kill him."

Kaja waved at his armed men, "He cannot escape. My men are professionals. We have brought *countries* to their knees."

"Where is Happy Jak?" asked Kaja as they loaded the airboats.

Mamou straightened up and stretched his back, "Happy Jak give us supplies, but he leave. Did you want something more?"

"No, it is not important," Kaja snapped.

He had plans for Happy Jak. A wicked death is what lay in store for him. Kaja expected to have the woman by the end of the day and Happy Jak dead by morning's light.

Jerry interrupted the men, "The boats are loaded, Kaja."

"Did you bring the money?" asked Kaja.

"Yes, but why will you give it to this Cajun?"

"You do not understand," said Kaja with a sly smile. "The

money is the bait. Any man can be bought. After he takes the money and turns the woman over to us . . . we kill him and take the money back."

"Now I understand," said Jerry, smiling at the plan. "What about Rich?"

Kaja shrugged his shoulders. "We kill him, too."

Delacroix made final preparations on the airboats as Kaja approached. Kaja pulled on the ropes holding the equipment and supplies giving them one final check. "All is in readiness?" Kaja asked Delacroix.

Delacroix glanced at Kaja and gave an affirmative nod.

A sinister grin covered Kaja's face, filling Delacroix with the foreboding of death he knew all too well.

"Take my men on a run so they can become accustomed to the craft. We will be ready to leave in the morning," said Kaja.

Again Delacroix nodded, his head filled with thoughts of Ballew Dragun's death.

* * *

"Someone's coming," said Kelli, anxiously peering from the window. "Who is it?"

Calmly, Ballew listened to the motors. A trace of a smile crossed his face as he grabbed his baseball cap and started to leave the house to greet his visitor, "It is Happy Jak."

Kelli recognized the name spoken earlier when Belle Rose had arrived. Happy Jak was Ballew's friend. Hurriedly, she followed his long graceful strides to where the drone of Happy Jak's airboat had stopped. The airboat scraped ashore, sending small waves splashing against the island.

"How you are, Ballew?" asked Happy Jak as he tied his boat to a log on shore.

"It goes, Happy Jak . . . it goes. What 'bout you?"

Happy Jak rolled his lower lip over his upper lip and tilted his hand from side to side. "Look what I find," he said as he joyfully tossed two shirts towards Ballew.

Both shirts were snatched from the air and Ballew held them up. One was gray and blue, the other had red half sleeves with a royal blue body, both with action pictures of Spider Man across the front. Next, Happy Jak tossed two rolled comic books in Ballew's direction.

Ballew's face lit up like a child who had received a new toy.

"I like . . . thanks!"

While Ballew admired the shirts, Happy Jak unloaded food and supplies. "Men come for you, Ballew."

"I know."

"Belle Rose?" asked Happy Jak. Ballew nodded. Only he and Ballew called her Belle Rose. Happy Jak rubbed his chin and spoke broken English in his Cajun accent, "I think the men want this woman. I bet she is one paper say died last night." With a box of supplies in his hands, he approached the woman and smiled devilishly as he extended his hand. "I am Happy Jak . . . I never met a dead woman before."

Kelli extended her hand. "Nice to meet you, but let me assure you, I'm not dead."

Happy Jak turned to Ballew, slapped him with his free hand, then spoke in the Cajun dialect, "Is the beautiful woman good in bed?"

Quickly, Ballew brought his finger to his lips, but too late.

"I can understand what you say," said Kelli in the same dialect, but with a different accent.

But Happy Jak laughed boisterously and slapped his hip, "Oh! And she be smart, too! Must be Cajun." Then he looked Kelli full in the face, "Please forgive me, but a man can only **dream** of finding someone as beautiful as you in a place like this. What I said was surely meant as praise of your beauty. If I could, I would take you for myself." Again he laughed loudly.

Suddenly he became serious as he put the supplies on the porch to the house.

"Ballew, you and the woman are in trouble. They are strange, these men. They walk with death. I saw weapons like I have only heard of. Short rifles, shoot many bullets. Many bullets, just like that," Happy Jak repeated, snapping his fingers together to get the point across. "More than you use in a year."

"Uzis!" cried Kelli when she understood what he meant. "Those men are Muslims."

Confused, Happy Jak asked, "I thought they live on other side of world?"

"They do."

"You must make someone plenty mad they come round the world to kill you."

"I wrote something about them and they want to kill me."

Happy Jak just shook his head, "It good you only write

something. I hate see how mad they get if you **do** something." Then he aimed his comments at Ballew. "Delacroix bring them to find you."

Ballew only nodded, seemingly unworried by the changing events.

"Aren't you going to do something?" asked Kelli.

"Yes. I forget your painting, Happy Jak. Wait I get them," said Ballew. He walked from the house toward the shed storing the paintings.

"Isn't he worried?" Kelli asked Happy Jak when Ballew disappeared into the shed.

Happy Jak gave a slight shrug of his shoulders, curled his lower lip, and rolled his big round eyes, "Ballew fear nothing. Do as he say, and you be fine. The men I see plenty bad."

"I've got to leave here."

"They have men waiting if you leave the swamps. The FBI think what you are dead, or plenty far away. They cannot help."

"Who wants the FBI? They told them where I was," Kelli said confused by her predicament. "Those men want me dead and the only ones I can trust have been paid off to turn me in."

"You can trust Ballew Dragun!"

"What can he do that the FBI can't?"

"I trust Ballew with my life . . . you trust him," said Happy Jak, as though it was a certainty. "He will help you. As far as your FBI help are concerned, remember this: In a chicken shed the chicken ladder are covered with chicken shit from top to bottom . . . you find bad even in high places where you trust."

"But Ballew is one man. What can he do?" she implored.

"I know Ballew all his life, and, girl, I could tell you all day what he does . . . and you would not believe. You like baseball?"

"Why?"

"Not important. Ever see how catcher wears his hat?" he asked and watched as Kelli nodded affirmatively. "You watch Ballew . . . if he turns his cap around, stay out of his way . . . and hope it not be you what makes him mad."

"What will he do?"

"To those in his way, a lot. To you, nothing. Trouble is coming. Don't be surprised if it happens."

Ballew returned with an armful of the beautiful oil paintings like the others in the house.

"There be one more, Happy Jak," said Ballew turning

toward the house.

"Who painted these?" asked Kelli.

"Ballew," Happy Jak replied as though she should know.

Only then did she notice the initials on each painting, BD. "Why the comic books?" she muttered.

"The comic books?" asked Happy Jak, and he smiled. "Because Ballew wants to teach himself English. And because he says Spider Man is like him--always getting into trouble when he wants to be left alone. With you here, it seems nothing has changed."

Ballew returned holding a painting depicting life in the swamps. The painting showed huge cypress trees covered with Spanish Moss. The green wet earth covered with decay and a thick mist hanging heavily in the swamp.

"It is beautiful," she said in all sincerity.

"You like?" asked Ballew his face beaming.

"Yes, I like."

Then he handed her the painting, "It be yours. Happy Jak, you don't mind?"

"No . . . let the girl have it. I must go now, Ballew. Be careful."

Ballew nodded and helped Happy Jak load the boat for the return. They watched as he disappeared. It was late in the afternoon and as they returned to the house, they said nothing. Kelli was growing accustomed to Ballew's silence and comfortable in his presence.

Inside the cabin, Richard shrunk into a corner, the effects of the fever beginning to become apparent. Kelli placed the painting against the wall and admired it.

"Ballew, I didn't know you painted," she said.

Flames flickered as the wood stove came to life. Ballew started to heat the herbs, to make a broth to help Richard through the night.

"Who else? I am only one here," he said with a shrug of his shoulders. "Kelli, you must make Richard eat this or he be sick for long time."

The sun disappeared before they finished eating. Kelli had her hands full getting Richard to eat. Already he was delirious, shaking with fever and complaining about being cold.

Ranting and raving, Richard no longer recognized anyone. This enabled Ballew to make bedding for the sick man and wrap him with blankets to break the fever. They could do nothing but wait.

"He be your friend?" asked Ballew as he settled back in his rocking chair and opened one of the new comic books Happy Jak had brought.

"Yes." She watched Ballew open the Comic book and asked, "Can I help you read?"

She watched his face turn red. "I can read!" he muttered in a low tone, embarrassed by the knowledge he couldn't read.

"You misunderstood me. Sometimes the words are hard. If I can help you, let me know."

A few minutes later he asked, "What be this word?"

Kelli went to the rocking chair, and knelt down on the wooden floor, pointed to the word, and told him, "That word is `decided'."

It came as a surprise when he handed the comic book to her, "You read I, . . . I like your voice."

With the comic book in hand, she continued to trace each word with her finger as she read. The eagerness to learn radiated from his face. Then she suddenly understood the difficulty he must have had trying to teach himself. An accurate pronunciation of English would be almost impossible. No sooner did she finish than he begged her to start the next one. After she finished the second one, Kelli declined to read the third comic book offered to her.

Now she tested his ability. Kelli wondered how much his mind was capable of learning. She doubted he knew very many words, so she returned to the place in the book where he had first asked her to read and asked him if he knew the word she pointed to.

Excitedly, Ballew read the word, "Decided, no?"

"Yes," then she paused. "Now **you** read one," she said as she arbitrarily picked a comic book at random.

Instantly he started reading and Kelli noticed he pronounced the words just as she had. Occasionally, he would stumble and she would help. She was astonished when he remembered virtually every word she had read.

After an hour or so, she said, "No more." Then she managed to drag her body into bed and the last thing she remembered was watching Ballew pour over the comic books of Spider Man his mouth moving to form the new words.

Twice during the night Richard's screams awakened her, and each time she rose from the bed only to find Ballew by his side.

Ballew coaxed Richard to drink his strange brew each time, always wiping his forehead with a cool, wet rag.

"He is going to kill me," Richard said hysterically and delirious from the fever as he clung to Ballew.

"You are safe," said Ballew in his heavy accent and the best English he could muster.

"I was going to let them have her," he moaned.

"She safe . . . you save her," Ballew lied.

"I did?"

"Yes."

"Are you my friend?" asked Richard.

"Yes, I am your friend. Now drink this and rest," said Ballew as he forced Richard to drink the dark, hot liquid.

Kelli watched quietly from the door in her room. It touched her heart to see the compassion exhibited by this giant of a man for someone she had said was her friend. She returned to the bed and slept the rest of the night without interruption.

Not until early in the morning did Richard finally settle into a peaceful sleep.

* * *

The sun lit the small frame house but raindrops tap-danced on the tin roof. The sound was soothing to Kelli as she slept, but a shake of her shoulder awakened her. A cup of coffee and a smile from the Cajun greeted her.

"Drink. We leave," Ballew ordered.

Kelli sipped the warm brew and dressed as he demanded. After dressing, she found two rice fritters waiting for her on the table near the kitchen. Richard slept peacefully. Feeling his forehead, she knew the fever had broken. Kelli went to the kitchen. On the counter stood Rocky, waiting. Kelli broke a piece from her fritter and handed it to the pleased raccoon.

The rain had stopped, and outside the Cajun waited. The rising sun heated the swamp quickly, making the air sticky. A musty odor filled the air.

When Kelli sat in the boat, Ballew pushed away from the shore and started rowing. Steam from the morning rain rose from the swamps. Already the heat made the air unbearable. Kelli's shirt was wet and clung to her. She hated the heat and humidity. The Amazon couldn't be this bad, she thought.

"Where are we going?" Kelli quizzed. So far she had done

as Ballew told her, but leaving the house concerned her.

"It be time to play with the swamp rats."

"Swamp rats?"

"Yes . . . it be time to find those what hunt you," he said casually.

"They want to kill me!" came her terrified response.

Ballew looked her in the eyes. "What they want be one thing . . . what happen be another," he said confidently.

Kelli swallowed her arguments and sat silently as Ballew brought the boat to shore on one of the thousands of islands filling the swamps. On the island was a small but much older house.

Ballew tied the boat so it could easily be seen. He slung the old rifle over his shoulder, then they made their way to an old dilapidated cabin.

At the door of the cabin Ballew paused. In front of him on the porch nestled a coiled cottonmouth. The snake reared back and struck out at the two. Although behind Ballew and in no danger, Kelli jumped back. A shrill cry escaped Kelli's lips as she saw the deadly poisonous reptile blocking their entrance to the dwelling. Ballew stuck the barrel of the rifle near the snake and when it struck out. He made a quick motion with the barrel before the cottonmouth could recoil and flung it far from the porch landing near the water's edge.

"Oh God, I wish I was in Kansas," said Kelli with a shudder.

Ballew held Kelli at arm's length. "Wait."

He entered the house to check for unwanted varmints, including men and traps. Ballew had lived much of his life in the old cabin. Few people knew where he really lived--only Belle Rose and Happy Jak. And now Kelli.

When he seemed satisfied, he led Kelli deep into the cypress trees. A hundred yards away, it became marshy and the water clogged with thick, tall reeds. Nearby lay a long board almost a foot wide. Ballew sought the board and when he found it still existed, they returned to the house.

Ballew led Kelli into the house. There they waited . . . for the Swamp Rats.

Chapter 5
Swamp Rats

Without another word, the men climbed into the boats. Delacroix climbed high in the chair of the first airboat with Jerry, Kaja, and one of Kaja's men. The other three terrorists rode with Mamou. The caged props of the airboats coughed to life. Wind from the props laid the reeds flat in the water as they turned to head deep into the swamps.

Delacroix took the lead, since he had an idea where Ballew lived. He felt uneasy, and feared Ballew would find them first. "Ballew Dragun is not human," he yelled over the roar of the propeller-driven airboat, a touch of apprehension in his voice.

Kaja screamed back confidently, "No one has ever beaten us before! He is one man; what can one man do?"

Delacroix had brought strange men into his home, the swamps, but his desire to kill Ballew Dragun overwhelmed his dislike of foreigners and outsiders. Ballew had killed his brother and Delacroix swore an oath that the death would be avenged. When Dragun died, he would be rid of the strangers forever. He was cautious of Kaja, because he knew Kaja was a dangerous man.

The men's ability to adapt to the swamp and their arsenal of weapons surprised Delacroix. Only the man called Jerry seemed out of place, furtively glancing around, suspicious, and tentative.

While Delacroix thought of the men he took in search of Ballew Dragun, both airboats headed to a spot where Delacroix believed he might find Dragun.

Ahead, Delacroix could see the old shed where he thought Ballew lived. A smug smile slowly filled his face as he recognized the old boat. Delacroix's search had paid off. They had found Dragun.

Confidently, Delacroix yelled to Kaja, "Ahead is where Dragun lives. He is there. We have surprised him."

Ballew had heard the boats in the distance and had taken Kelli with him to the edge of the trees. They waited as the two airboats landed and the Swamp Rats approached.

Delacroix and Mamou led the way followed quickly by Jerry and Kaja. They were almost to the shack when a voice bellowed from the trees: "Stop!"

"It be him!" Delacroix said in a low, excited voice.

Before Delacroix finished uttering his words, the Cajun stepped from behind a tree, rifle butt anchored to his hip.

"What you want?" asked the giant.

The size of the Cajun impressed Kaja, "You are Dragun?"

"Yes."

"We want the woman. She is mine. And we want the man."

Ballew laughed and spoke in his heavy Cajun dialect, "I have the woman . . . she is mine. The man is dead--I killed him."

"What did he say?" asked Kaja.

Delacroix explained.

"Good, the agent is dead. It means we only have to kill these two. Tell him we will give him $1,000,000 for the woman," said Kaja.

"You will give him the money?" screamed out Delacroix confusion clearly visible in his face.

"Yes," said Kaja, revealing a sadistic smile, "and when we have the woman, we will slay Dragun!"

The plan delighted Delacroix knowing Dragun would be killed after he took the bait. "They will give you $1,000,000!" Delacroix yelled in Cajun French.

"Let's see the money," came Ballew's reply.

After a few moments, one of Kaja's terrorists returned with the briefcase containing the money.

"Tell him I want to see the woman. Then he will get the money," said Kaja.

Delacroix relayed the message to Ballew, then Ballew disappeared.

Hidden from view he talked to Kelli, "Do as I say."

"You coward. You're turning me in for the money," she

said with extreme anger in the belief Ballew was exchanging her for money. She swung at him in fear and started to run.

"Don't be a fool," he warned, jerking her toward him. "You must do as I say, or we both die. Those men will kill me when they have you. Besides, I have no use for the money."

Kelli sighed, afraid to do what he said but even more afraid not to.

"I am going to pull you out by the hair. I want you to kick, swing and yell. Do you understand?"

"Yes."

Ballew took off the black baseball cap, with the gold New Orleans Saints logo, from his head and ran his hand through his long, dark hair. Then he wound his large hand in Kelli's long, blonde hair and stepped into the line of sight of the eight men.

Kaja and his men watched with delight as she yelled and kicked at Dragun and even managed to slug him in the stomach, much to his surprise.

"The money!" Ballew yelled to Delacroix.

"How do we know he will give us Parsons?" asked Kaja. This was relayed to Dragun.

Some words were exchanged between Dragun and Delacroix. This time Delacroix told Kaja, Dragun would tie the girl to the tree. They watched as he pushed her from sight and wrapped the rope around the tree repeatedly.

Kaja handed the money to one of his best men, "Take the money and when you see the woman . . . kill **him**!"

The terrorist had taken only a few steps with the briefcase when a shot rang out. A bullet smacked the earth, kicking dirt up at the terrorist's feet.

Smoke rolled from the end of the barrel and the clacking of the rifle being cocked could be heard.

Dragun shook his head in a negative manner. "Send Mamou with the money!" he yelled.

After a brief discussion, they sent Mamou to deliver the money. Dragun stopped him short so Mamou could not observe the woman tied to the far side of tree. Still he handed the money to Dragun, then started to return to the men waiting for him.

"Mamou, why do you and Delacroix want to die?" asked Dragun.

The small man only quivered and moved faster. But not as fast as Ballew. Jumping behind the tree, he jerked Kelli to her feet, leaving the empty ropes intact around the tree. They wasted not a moment, running for the marsh and the tall reeds where the board lay. With ease, Ballew lifted the board and laid it perpendicularly to the water's edge. He could sense a structure, hidden by the reeds, as the board made contact.

Quickly, he took Kelli across the narrow board to a wooden platform hidden deep in the reeds.

"Stay here. When I leave, pull the board in with you." Then he handed her the money. "Keep this. I will be back when I finish."

Kelli reached out and grabbed Ballew. Hugging him to her, she pleaded, "Don't leave . . . I'm afraid. Stay with me. They will kill you."

Gently he pushed her away, "Ballew is home. Nothing will happen. You are safe here."

"You don't know them."

A mischievous smile filled his face, "They do not know Ballew Dragun."

Before he left, he again removed his cap and ran his hand through his hair. Only, this time, when he replaced his cap, he reversed the bill to the back, much in the fashion of a baseball catcher.

Ballew ran to the edge of the platform and stopped, "Pull in board . . . I go to hunt Swamp Rats."

* * *

Cautiously, Kaja and his men approached the tree where they expected to find Kelli tied. The ropes held nothing.

A voice speaking in broken English shattered the quiet. It seemed to come from everywhere.

"The money is the girl's. Go home or die," chanted the eerie voice.

One terrorist, Baharam, fired his Uzi in the direction of the voice. No sooner did he fire than a single bullet ripped through his hand. Baharam grabbed his shattered hand and grimaced in pain, dropping the Uzi to the muck filling the swamp floor. Kaja signaled for his men to cease fire.

"Go home . . . Mamou, you are next," came the voice, hidden behind the thick cypress trees.

The small fat man had not intended to die and with a shriek, he ran for the boats. "I'll get him," said Delacroix.

"Forget him," snapped Kaja. "I want you to return to the boats. Watch them! My men will take care of this Ballew Dragun."

Baharam tore apart his shirt and wrapped the pieces around his bleeding hand, while Kaja waited until Delacroix had returned to the boats. Kaja was angry. This Dragun had done something no man had ever done; he had outsmarted him at his own business. For this, Kaja would take great pleasure in killing the man.

Kaja motioned his men behind the trees and from the safety of the cypress, he gave a single order, "If you see him . . . kill him!"

With the order issued by Kaja, they walked slowly and cautiously single file into the marsh. Jerry followed close behind Kaja.

They moved deeper into the marsh, and occasionally tromping through wet areas where they would sink to their knees. An unpleasant odor of decay emanated from the marsh. Once Kaja stumbled in the muck and fell to his elbows. One of his men extracted him from the mire.

"I want him dead," mumbled Kaja. Then he resumed his search through the swamp.

The silence was suddenly broken by Abdul's scream, the last man at the back of the group. It took a minute for the men to get their wits. A few moments before, Salil carried the rear of the advance . . . *now Abdul was last*. Salil had disappeared without a trace.

A man fired blindly into the marsh. Instantly, Kaja pounced on the terrified man, grabbed his weapon and, in their native tongue, ordered the man to stop. Kaja demanded the man gain control. Kaja realized the Cajun had effectively accomplished something at which Kaja himself was so adept.

Kaja barked orders and had his best man placed to the rear. With Nissim at the rear, the Cajun would surely die if he attempted to be so bold another time.

With a semblance of order returned, they again embarked on their mission to find and kill one man . . . the Cajun.

From the safety of the cypress and the reeds of the marsh, Ballew followed parallel and smiled to himself as the men marched in pursuit of the man who at times was within touching distance. Still the men so expert in terror had no indication he watched their every move. Quietly, the Cajun followed, staying closer than their own shadows.

As Ballew watched their useless efforts, he spotted a water snake. Nearly 4 feet in length, the snake closely resembled a poisonous cottonmouth. His face lit up as an idea formed in his mind. Quickly, he gathered the snake and darted through the marsh to a point where the group would cross.

Overhead a series of vines formed a 'V,' where Ballew would put his idea into action. He searched until he found a branch with a slight curve and nearly 12 feet in length. He placed one end through the 'V' and took the irritated and tightly coiled but harmless water snake and wrapped it on the portion of the branch he had extended through the 'V.' Ballew hid behind the thick vegetation. His hand rested on the opposite end of the branch from which the snake hung. Unaware of what was about to take place, the snake rested above the path where the approaching intruders would pass.

Kaja walked beneath the snake first followed by Jerry. Calmly, Ballew waited for the man next to the end.

No one noticed the branch move nor did they see the snake as it fell from above. But everybody became aware of what followed when the angry snake landed on the frightened man's shoulders.

A blood-curdling shriek followed as Abdul jerked at the reptile and in the same motion, pulled the trigger of his weapon, firing a long burst from his automatic weapon as he turned.

More than a dozen shots fired from the Uzi before Abdul pulled the tangled mass from his shoulders. Terrified, Abdul turned, firing his weapon, sure the assailant was the man they pursued. The Uzi was accurate, hitting the target. To his horror, the man lying on the ground before him, with four rounds stitched across his legs from his feet to his hip, was Nissim. Writhing in agony, Kaja's best trained lay on the rotted leaves of the swamp-fed cypress.

Unnoticed by all, the angry snake, uninjured, slithered away to the safety of the thick growth covering the island.

"There he is!" yelled Abdul; "I will finish him off like the dog he is!"

Trying to avenge his accidental shooting of Nissim, Abdul galloped back along the trail pursuing the elusive Cajun.

"Abdul, stop," yelled Kaja, "It is a trap . . . come back." Kaja and the remaining terrorist, Baharam, along with Jerry, followed after the possessed man, but they failed to gain any ground on him.

Kaja sensed a trap, but Abdul failed to hear. Ballew exposed himself only enough to keep the crazed man on the right path. Earlier, when Ballew followed the men, he came upon a timber rattlesnake. To this he led the maddened terrorist. To Ballew's delight the snake remained in the path, so he circled wide and returned to the path, leaving the snake between him and his pursuers. He waited until his pursuer could see him. When Abdul spotted him, he darted down the path and disappeared. He ran in the opposite direction and returned to where Nissim lay in pain.

Abdul heard the rattle first, then felt a shooting pain just behind and below his knee. He turned just in time to see the rare timber rattler strike again in the same place. Though seldom seen, they still existed in the Atchafalaya. Terrified, he shook his leg free and stumbled back, disengaging himself from the growth. In his moment of panic to rid himself of the snake, he had dropped his weapon. He screamed pitifully when he saw Kaja approaching, because he believed it to be the demon Cajun.

Kaja came upon his expertly trained terrorist, Abdul, only to find him ripping at his pant leg, howling in pain. Baharam, along with Jerry, knelt to their comrade's aid.

Baharam took Abdul's belt and used it as a tourniquet, then he took his own knife and cut open the wound. He put his mouth over the wound, sucked the venom out and spat it on the ground. With the wound attended, and Abdul assuring Kaja he would wait for their return, the three men returned to rescue Nissim.

Nissim was nowhere to be found. He was gone! Had the Cajun taken Nissim? Only blood remained; but no sign of Nissim. An uneasy feeling prevailed over the three remaining men.

"This fucking guy is a loony! Let's get the hell out of here," Hyatt begged Kaja.

"What do we do?" asked Baharam.

Kaja slammed his fist into the palm of his hand. Angry at the turn of events he growled, "He will **pay** dearly for this."

"Shit, Kaja, it's us that's **paying** for it," Jerry interjected; "Let's go, before he gets us, too."

They returned to where Abdul waited, only to find he too had disappeared. The Cajun! Obviously the Cajun had returned and taken Abdul. Now they were three.

"We gotta get outa here before he gets us all!" cried Jerry.

"I will kill him!" snapped Kaja, pounding his fist into his open hand again.

Baharam rubbed his injured hand, "He is stronger than we imagined, Kaja. We must return for more men."

Angry with the situation, Kaja wanted revenge for the humiliation. But he reconsidered and decided to make a hasty retreat to the boats. Baharam's idea had merit.

"To the boats!" ordered Kaja with a wave of his hand.

Cautiously, they made their way to the airboats and safety. Every noise made them jump, and the journey was interrupted twice, once by a rabbit and the other by a white-tail deer. Each time, the animals almost tasted death at the hands of the touchy men.

They were nearing the boats when they were distracted by a strange noise coming from behind them. Alerted to the sound, Jerry and Kaja turned, guns in hand and ready to fire. Behind them the last of Kaja's men, Baharam, wobbled on his feet for no apparent reason. They watched as he fell to his knees, then toppled backwards. Blood poured from his mouth and nose. Two of his upper teeth were missing and another protruded through his lower lip and his nose was broken. Hit squarely in the face by a mighty fist, Baharam crumpled to the ground, but his assailant was nowhere to be seen --or heard!

"Oh, shit!" exclaimed Jerry before he turned and ran for the safety of the boats. With his control cracking, even Kaja ran.

When they broke into the clearing, Kaja was in the lead. Abruptly Jerry and Kaja came to a sudden halt. Both men were shocked at the sight near the boats. Mamou--wide-eyed and terrified beyond belief--was bound, gagged, and sitting in the seat of one airboat, as was Delacroix in the other. Tied together in one of the airboats were the three missing terrorists. All of them were unconscious.

Kaja heard a thumping from behind, but before he could turn, he saw Jerry's body fall beside him, rendered unconscious by a blow to the back of the head.

Quickly he spun about, firing his Uzi, determined to kill his unseen attacker. Kaja would end the threat now.

Effortlessly the Cajun grasped the Uzi at the same time his free hand clasped about Kaja's neck, and lifting him like a small child, he tore the harmless Uzi from Kaja's hands.

With both hands free, Kaja tried to pull the massive hand

from his throat, but to no avail. Both feet kicked helplessly in the air.

The Cajun carried Kaja backward against a cypress tree with such force it knocked the wind from Kaja's body. Kaja gasped for air as Ballew lowered him so he could look him in the eye. The vise-like grip remained around Kaja's neck as Ballew brought his knife from the sheath beneath his arm, holding the point against Kaja's shirt. He said nothing as he cut the buttons, exposing Kaja's chest. Ballew turned the blade of his knife over and started tapping it against Kaja's bared breastbone. Each time, it drew blood. He continued this for a few moments until he seemed satisfied. Kaja watched helplessly, filled with utter terror, sure he was about to die.

With a roughness Kaja had never experienced, he was viciously bound and gagged. The Cajun took a handful of wild blue muscadine grapes and crushed them against Kaja's chest, rolling the broken berries until they covered the wounds he had inflicted. Dragun brought the man with the broken nose from the woods, tied him securely and placed him in the airboat.

All of Kaja's men were captured and placed securely within the two airboats. After Ballew checked the men and was content they could not escape, he took the cap from his head, shook his head, then ran his hand through his long, black hair before replacing his baseball cap . . . bill to the front.

Dragun disappeared but returned shortly with Kelli. He said a few words to her in the Cajun dialect and pointed to Kaja. Her face was livid with anger as she approached. She spit full in his face.

Kelli pointed to Ballew, "He asked me if I wanted you killed. I'm stupid not to have you killed, but I can't. Don't ever come back. Go home and leave me alone."

Kaja cursed inwardly. What a weak woman. The man, too, he thought. He would return and kill them both. His eyes turned to the Cajun. Dragun knew nothing of Mustafa or Kidane. When he was free, Kaja would get those men and many others, return, and kill them. Kill them all.

After everyone was secure, Ballew jumped to the boat with Mamou. "I want you to run this one. I will run the other," he said, holding his knife to the frightened man's throat. "We will go to Happy Jak's. If you do anything stupid, I will shoot you. Do you understand?"

Mamou knew of Ballew's ability with a rifle. Mamou had no intention of trying to escape or elude Ballew, so he nodded his assent. Ballew cut him free, then returned to the other boat with Kelli, Jerry, Kaja, and Delacroix.

The Cajun reasoned it was better to have the cause for his inconvenience in the boat with him. It would be easier to kill them if they were with him rather than in the boat with Mamou. He never doubted Mamou would follow his orders. Even so, he held his rifle propped against his leg so Mamou could see.

"Mamou," yelled Ballew, "Delacroix will get you killed one day!" With those final words, he started his airboat and signaled Mamou, who started his.

The two boats made their way through the marsh for Happy Jak's.

Chapter 6
Devil's Island

Late in the afternoon, Happy Jak was ready to close the general store when he heard airboats approaching. He peered from the glass door out across the swamp. First he recognized Ballew, then the woman. They were in the boats the men, Tom and Jerry, had bought from him. Holding his finger in the air, he slowly pointed to each man tied in the boat and counted until he reached eight.

"Ballew, you are a generous man. You let them all live," he mumbled, then burst out in laughter.

One of Happy Jak's workers started to meet the airboats, but the heavy arm of Happy Jak held him back.

"Shouldn't I meet the boats?" the helper asked.

"Of course," said Happy Jak, smiling to himself, "but not this time. I want to watch. Wait until I say."

The two airboats pulled alongside the pier. Ballew jumped from his vessel and tied it to the wooden dock. He stood ready as Mamou tossed his line, which Ballew caught and also tied to the old dock. With this done, Ballew motioned Mamou from the boat. Mamou never hesitated, quickly obeying the command.

"I want you to go inside," he said, addressing the still shaking Mamou, "and when I have gone, you can return to these men and untie them."

Mamou made for the safety of Happy Jak's while Ballew appraised the two airboats. A moment later, Ballew took the men from the airboat he and Kelli arrived in, while Kelli nervously paced the dock. One by one, Ballew removed the bound and defeated men. The last was Kaja, whom Ballew threw unceremoniously to the wooden deck of the pier.

Ballew turned Kaja over and pulled him near so they were face to face for the first time. Calmly, Ballew uttered the words, "Leave and live, return . . . die."

The words were spoken with a cold, defiant confidence Kaja knew all too well. The same way Kaja spoke when he did his work. Kaja was unbeatable, except . . . this time. Assigned a mission by those Kaja held most sacred . . . he had failed. Kaja had been defeated by one man.

Kelli bent down and beat Jerry on the head and shoulders. He was helpless to ward off the blows. "You bastard, you were supposed to protect me!" She continued to hit at him when he failed to answer. "When I get out of here, I'm going to turn you in. Richard will help when he gets well. I hate you for what you have done," she shrieked, almost irrationally. One blow even brought blood from his nose. But what bothered him most was the thunderous headache he had developed from the egg-sized lump at the back of his head. The lump delivered by the butt of Ballew's rifle.

Although he said nothing, Jerry Hyatt was shocked to learn Richard was still alive. Jerry knew his job and life were in jeopardy as long as Kelli and Richard remained alive. But what of this Cajun, the man they had called the Blue Dragun? How could he be stopped?

Gently Ballew grabbed Kelli's arm and pulled her away from the defenseless man, "You told me not to kill them. Was it because you wanted the pleasure yourself?"

With those words, she regained her composure. "You're right."

Ballew motioned her to the empty airboat. When she had clambered aboard, he bent near to Kaja and spoke in a low tone:

"You have caused me much inconvenience." Ballew then waved toward the boat where Kelli waited. "I have always wanted a boat like this one . . . it is mine; I will take it."

Then Ballew knelt beside Kaja and squeezed his collar until Kaja could hardly breathe. He spoke in a cold, matter-of-fact tone. "Do not come back. If you do," Ballew paused and shrugged his shoulders, "you will die!" Those confident words of death sent a cold chill up the spine of the expert of terror. For a moment, Kaja tasted the fear on which he had built his life . . . fear based on stark terror.

Ballew released his hold on Kaja's neck and strode confidently to the boat and Kelli, making no effort to disengage the remaining airboat, unconcerned they might mount an effort to follow. Besides, Ballew had told them if they returned, they would die. He started the airboat and disappeared into the swamps of the Atchafalaya.

When Ballew was gone, Mamou, along with Happy Jak and his helper, made for the seven helpless and bound men. Happy Jak was busy assessing the results of the debacle: one man snake bit, his eyes rolled up; another shot across both legs; blood caked the face of another, his nose broken and his eyes turning black; the American--face bloodied, but alert; the other man showed no signs of distress administered by Ballew.

Mamou cut Delacroix loose, while Kaja screamed for his own release. No sooner had the helper freed Kaja than Kaja pushed him aside. Kaja confronted Happy Jak and demanded help.

"I need boats. I must punish him for stealing my boat!" he yelled.

"Who will you get?" asked Happy Jak. He pointed to the injured men before them, while offering Kaja the wet towel he used in the kitchen.

Ungraciously Kaja accepted, then tore the tattered shirt away and tried to wipe the dried blood from his chest.

With a show of ignorance, Happy Jak tossed his hands in the air. "What man do you seek?" Happy Jak asked, although he knew.

The symbols poked on Kaja's chest concerned him. "What is this?" he moaned.

The berries had stained each cut inflicted by the knife and had acted much as the ink in a tattoo. Two small letters were clearly visible above Kaja's heart. The letters were SM.

Happy Jak could not stifle his laugh, "You have been returned by Spider Man."

"Who is Spider Man?" Kaja demanded in anger.

Delacroix interjected, "It is he who brought us back. Ballew Dragun is Spider Man. Those are the same letters he put on my brother's chest before he killed him."

With a shake of his head, Kaja dismissed the events leading to his capture. Oblivious to the actions of Happy Jak and his own men as they tried to render aid to the critically injured men, his thoughts reverted to revenge and the men needed to capture the Cajun. Kaja, branded by an ignorant man of the swamps, shook with anger. This man some called Spider Man would not die quickly. With great pleasure Kaja would prolong the man's death for his own personal gratification. Ballew Dragun would die slowly, very slowly, and Kaja would enjoy every moment of it.

Kaja knew two men who could destroy the Cajun. Mustafa and Kidane were expert at guerrilla tactics. Kaja was an expert at torture and capturing his victims, but Mustafa and Kidane were in a class by themselves when it came to jungle tactics. They had learned their craft in the jungles of Viet Nam and Cambodia. No one was their equal. These men would defeat and destroy the Cajun. But Kaja himself would administer the Cajun's death.

"Let's go," said Jerry as he interrupted Kaja's thoughts.

All of the injured men were placed in the cars. Time was critical for their survival. Abdul, unconscious from the snakebite was near death and the man he had shot, Nissim, was in shock. For the time, Kaja would have to concern himself with his injured men. Later, when he could organize his men and send for Mustafa and Kidane, he would return. The Cajun was going nowhere, so Kaja had all the time he required.

Happy Jak felt relieved as he watched the men leave. However, his experience over the years told him this was not the end. It would be like Delacroix's brother. They would push his friend Ballew until someone died. He only hoped it was not his friend, Spider Man. That final thought brought a laugh to his lips. The man who called himself Tom, was branded for life by Spider Man. However long that life might be.

* * *

The ride in the airboat so relaxed Kelli, she fell asleep. The engine sputtering to a stop woke her. Her head lay on one of Ballew's legs. Embarrassed, she pushed away and stood erect. They were not back at the small house where Ballew lived. Instead, they were drifting alongside what looked like a small offshore drilling rig. Equipment still operated on top of the low platform. A rusted steel stairway led to the top, 12 feet above the swamp.

Ballew, carrying an empty gas can, scrambled to the top. Kelli followed closely behind. Once on top, Ballew checked a few valves and lines for gas leaks. When he was assured of no leaks, he unlocked a valve on a horizontal gasoline storage tank, opened it and started to fill the can with gas for the airboat. Another similar platform was blown apart by the carelessness of men who had failed to check for gas leaks. All of those men had died.

The remaining abandoned platform was still used by the swamp people. Gasoline and natural gas pumped to storage tanks was used instead of buying butane.

For the first time in days, Kelli relaxed from her never-ending vigil of watching for her pursuers. This one man had accomplished something the FBI had not dreamed possible. Instead of hiding her like the FBI, Ballew had confronted her antagonists . . . and defeated them.

Much like a small boy, Ballew sat on the edge of the platform and hung his legs over the side, dangling them in space. He motioned for Kelli and she did the same. The day brought heat and humidity and even the stiff breeze was hot, offering no comfort. Louisiana was nothing like Kansas, she thought.

"What is that?" Kelli gasped as she pointed to a large alligator-looking fish with fins.

"Gar," was all Ballew said.

Kelli remembered hearing stories about large fish called alligator gar. She had ever seen an alligator gar and never dreamed they grew so large. She guessed the one she saw to be ten feet in length.

Ballew shook Kelli's shoulder and pointed. On the edge of a small island was what looked like a large rat nearly four feet long.

"My God, a rat!" she exclaimed.

"No rat," said Ballew, "Nutria."

As far as Kelli was concerned, the nutria was just a giant damn rat. A few feet from the nutria waited an alligator more than twice the length of the nutria. It made a lunge for the nutria and snapped its jaws closed. But all the alligator caught was air. The nutria was quicker and jumped clear. At a safe distance, the nutria made a strange sounding noise as the hair on its back stood on end all the while looking toward the alligator.

Directly below them, an alligator glided through the water in pursuit of a school of fish. Kelli had not taken time to notice, but life was abundant in the swamps. From her vantage point, she could see things not normally visible. In the distance, she could see a half dozen wild ducks and as many geese resting on the placid waters of the Atchafalaya.

Kelli pointed at the ducks, "I thought they went north for the summer?"

Ballew shrugged his shoulders, "Maybe yes." He pointed to the ducks and smiled, "Maybe no. See them ducks? Sometimes them ducks be sick. Sometimes them ducks be hurt. Maybe next year them ducks go north. Maybe today we eat some them ducks."

A moment later Ballew again attracted her attention. Directly across from them, high in a cypress partially hidden by the Spanish moss, was a black mountain lion. The tail waved in the air, curiosity enticing it to watch the two humans sitting on the old platform. They were being watched.

"It's a panther!" said Kelli and her heart began to race. She clung to Ballew for security. She never dreamed they existed in the wild anymore.

"Puma," corrected Ballew. "You don't have those at home?"

"Of course not," she said with a bit of relief.

"That is too bad. They cause no trouble unless you cause them trouble first." A strange sensation filled Ballew as she clung to him. He could not understand why he enjoyed her touch. Nor could he understand why he could feel his heart beat faster each time he looked into her face. He wanted to grab her and hold her close and found the urge hard to control. Her perspiration soaked shirt accentuated her jutting breasts and slim waist. Ballew discovered he enjoyed looking at them.

A flush covered Kelli's face when she caught Ballew admiring her body. She turned away, almost as quickly as he.

She noticed the small island, for some reason, was different from any of the others. The trees covering the island were taller and thicker. The island was both appealing and terrifying. Like most of the islands in the Atchafalaya, they were all interconnected with shallow marshes. Only the animals knew where the interconnected marshes were, for they traveled between them all.

"That island is so strange," said Kelli.

For a long moment Ballew stared at the island, "Yes . . . have you heard of Jean LaFitte?"

"The pirate?"

"They say the island was his. Many believe treasures are buried there . . . along with his enemies. Some say the devil still lives there. Witches roam at night and perform voodoo. All fear the island and stay away. It is called many things--in the swamps it is known as Devil's Island."

"Do you believe those things?"
"Some."
"Are you afraid?"
"No . . . I have been there many times." His gray eyes stared through her and exhibited no fear. "It is ready," said Ballew as he stood erect and extended a hand to Kelli and helped her up. She stumbled and Ballew caught her, pulling her to him. They stood, staring into each others eyes for what seemed an eternity, but instead, only a few brief moments. Ballew released her and turned to fill his tank. Kelli was finding this Cajun attractive and she wondered at her thoughts of kissing him. Then she quickly dismissed her thoughts to be appreciation for his actions, and she followed Ballew from the rig.

With the tank filled, they were soon on their way. They landed on Devil's Island, where Ballew disappeared into the jungle-like growth for a short time, hiding the briefcase with the money in a safe place. Kelli said she didn't want to know where it was. She took time to observe the island in all its splendor. And yet, she could feel something unnerving about the island.

When the money was safely hidden, Ballew returned--wet to his waist as though he had waded through water. Soon they were on their way, leaving behind the sinister Devil's Island.

Chapter 7

Jambalaya

On the return trip, they stopped at the island where they had encountered the Muslim terrorists. They secured Ballew's boat to the airboat, then continued their trip to his island.

The sun was low in the west when they arrived, and Kelli waited as Ballew tied both boats to shore.

They had only taken a few steps when Ballew stopped. Suddenly he became wary. "Something is wrong." He gave no explanation, just stood and listened. Faintly in the distance he could hear a scream for help.

"Wait here," he ordered Kelli. He broke into a run in the direction of the scream.

The last rays of sunlight were disappearing when he came upon Richard. He breathed heavily and his left leg was swollen twice its normal size. The skin bulged from beneath the pant leg and was ready to burst. The pant leg was covered with white hairy filaments from a plant. Next to Richard stood Rocky, helpless to do anything but watch. Little Rocky seemed relieved to see Ballew. Not so Richard.

Ballew recognized the projectiles from the heat-activated bull nettle. Richard had approached the plant too closely. Not knowing the danger, he had been surprised to see nettles shooting toward his body like iron filings to a magnet. They weren't harmful if proper care was taken, but those ignorant of the toxicity of the fibers might lay paralyzed for days. Sometimes, the skin burst from the swelling.

Ballew had plants in the house he could rub into the skin to treat the swelling, but he had to act now, so he bent quickly over the leg and pulled his knife.

Simultaneously, Richard pulled out his .45, which he had discovered before he commenced his errant journey. "Stop!" barked Richard. "How do I know you won't kill me?"

"If I wanted to kill you . . .," Ballew said, pausing, "I would have killed you already. Kelli says you are her friend, so you are safe. But . . . I don't think you are her friend."

"Well, shit," said Richard as he grimaced in pain. "Here," he said, tossing the .45 to Ballew. Then, as an afterthought, he pulled the clip from his pocket. "Oh, yeah, you need this for it to work," and he tossed the clip.

"Not loaded?"

"Naw. Shit, I felt so bad I was afraid I'd fall and kill myself with it. Hell, man, I think I've got dysentery or malaria. If I don't quit shitting, I'm gonna have to start wearing diapers. Not to mention, you're gonna have to get me some ice for my asshole--it's burning up. I feel like shit and now my leg is killing me."

"Why did you try to run?"

"I've got to notify the FBI. They have to know about Jerry Hyatt. Look, Big Guy, I just wanta get the fuck outa here. Hell, if you'd just had a phone, I could've charged it to my Sprint number."

"Sprint?"

"Never mind. It was a stupid idea."

On the log beside Richard was a row of cigarettes, some broken and all twisted. They were what he had salvaged from his jump into the swamp. He had saved them with the intention of drying them and trying to save the tobacco so he could fabricate a few "smokes" as he called them.

"What is that?" Ballew asked.

Richard looked at the mold-infested tobacco, "It was my last shot at a little bit of relief. I need those damn things in the worst way. Oh well . . . I tried."

"Will you do as I say?"

"Shit . . . I guess so."

Ballew loaded the .45 and tossed it back to the injured man, "You may need this. Now, don't move."

Ballew slid the knife underneath the pant leg and cut it up to the hip. The immediate release of the pressure was a relief to Richard. He didn't mind as he watched Ballew remove the pant leg near the hip.

"Your raccoon has been a great companion. What's his name?"

"Rocky," said Ballew as he stood up and unzipped his pants in front of Richard.

"Hey, what the fuck are you doing?" yelled Richard when it became evident the giant Cajun was about to urinate on him.

"You said you would do as I say. This will relieve the swelling. If not, the skin could split if it comes in contact with anything."

Richard waved his hand as a signal to go ahead and frowned. Then he turned his head, "Hell, I've been shit on by some of my best friends; I see no reason why a stranger can't piss on my leg." It took a great deal of control for Richard to allow Ballew to urinate on his leg, and he grimaced when the sensation of the warm urine flowed over and down his leg. "Oh, fuck."

Just as Ballew zipped up his pants, he heard Rocky chatter. Instinctively, Ballew jumped to one side as the cottonmouth struck. He barely avoided the poisonous snake. Unlike most snakes that dislike human contact, the cottonmouth--when agitated--focused its attention on the helpless person before it.

Richard was unable to move, as he watched the large snake slither in his direction. Quickly, Ballew moved behind the long snake and with his bare hand, grabbed it near the end of its long, slender body.

The snake's body rippled as it turned with open mouth to confront its attacker. Poison dripped from the extended fangs as the mouth neared the hand gripping its body.

In the swamps, Ballew had confronted creatures far worse than the likes of a cottonmouth. The snake was helpless as Ballew twirled the reptile in a circular motion until it stretched straight like a rope. After Ballew had completed a few more rapid circles with the large snake, he slammed it to the ground with tremendous force.

Stunned by the quick action, Richard watched as the snake lifted its head as if to strike. Instead or striking, the deadly head wavered in a drunken stupor. As the head wobbled, Richard noticed the vertical slits of the snake's eyes fill with blood. The mighty head fell to the ground, quivering in its final death throes.

"God damn, you crazy? That fucker coulda bit ya!"

"I have been bitten before," said Ballew with a shrug of his shoulders.

"You have?"
"Many times. More than you would care to think."
"That sonofabitch could have killed you."
"I was small," said Ballew holding his hand 3 feet above the ground, "when I was first bitten. That one almost killed me. Two years ago, I stepped into a nest and was bitten three times." Ballew smiled at the memory and pointed to his belt. "I did not even get sick, and now I wear them."
"Holy shit!"
"We must return."
Ballew pulled Richard to his feet and carried him back to the house. Kelli stood waiting on the porch. Ballew moved past her and helped Richard to the rocking chair, while he went to the kitchen to prepare medication for the leg.
"What are you trying to prove?" Kelli demanded.
Richard laughed. "You heard of people being pissed off?" Then he rolled his eyes. "Well, I've been pissed on."
"What?"
"Never mind," Richard said waving his hand. The swelling in the leg had already gone down and the itching had stopped completely. "Well, I'll be damned," he muttered.
"I saw Jerry."
"Jerry?" asked Richard, the note of alarm evident.
"Yes, Ballew caught him and seven others. I wouldn't have given a prayer for our chances, but he caught them all."
"You shoulda killed the mother fuckers," snapped Richard.
"They'll leave us alone," Kelli assured.
Richard shook his head. "No, they won't. Jerry can't. And Kaja . . . he's a strange man. I have a bad feeling he'll come back . . . and, baby, he won't be alone."
The thought alarmed Kelli but she said no more. A few minutes later, Ballew returned with his homemade concoction, spread it over the leg, then wrapped the poultice with a gauze-type material. Slowly the fever returned and a few hours later Richard became delirious. Ballew cooked some herbs into a broth. Kelli managed to feed Richard some of the broth, and Richard soon fell asleep.
Thunder cracked outside and the wind intensified, blowing the screen door open. Ballew fastened the door and closed all the windows to the storm side, allowing ventilation through the others, so the nighttime heat would be tolerable. Lightning flashed and

thunder boomed. For a moment they stood near the screen door and watched. Although still hot, the breeze from the thunderstorm brought relief from the unabated heat of the swamp.

With the sound of the storm all around them, Ballew and Kelli ate. In the middle of the table, the old lantern continued to emit its light. Kelli mused to herself, "At least the storm would bring no power outage."

Ballew was quite congenial and they talked about the rig and the animals she had seen. They avoided a direct conversation about the terrorists.

Kelli changed and made ready for sleep. Ballew lit a kerosene lamp and placed it on the table beside his rocker. Then he eagerly pulled out one of his many Spider Man comics and began reading. Unconsciously, his free hand rubbed Rocky's neck and when Rocky rolled over, Ballew rubbed his stomach playfully.

Kelli was worried, so she approached Ballew. "Will they return?" she asked bluntly.

The Cajun sighed before he answered, "They always return." An air of confidence echoed from his next words, "But I am here."

The assurance seemed to be all she needed. A few minutes later she fell asleep with her protector in the room beside her.

* * *

Morning brought the sun out over a low, clinging fog hovering 3 feet above the ground. The air was still. No breeze drifted through the swamps of the Atchafalaya, and the damp air made Kelli's hair stick to her face. Already she had kicked the sheet from her body, but the bed felt damp and wet. The smell of the coffee aroused her, and she sat erect, but was not alone in the bed. By her feet stood Rocky, eyeing her inquisitively.

"Well, hi there, Rocky," she said to the small animal. Her pleasant tone and extended hand enticed him to approach her for the neck scratch he eternally sought. After he got his neck scratched, he scampered from the bed and into the kitchen with Kelli close behind.

In the corner sat Richard, weak but alert, sipping on the coffee. "Mornin'." He held the coffee high. "Kinda grows on you." In his lap were the same kind of fritters he had so blatantly refused only the day before.

Ballew brought a cup of the thick Cajun coffee to Kelli, who slowly sipped the eye-opening liquid. With a laugh and a wide grin, he nodded in the direction of Richard and said, *"Ticrot."*

So the Cajun had taken a liking to the sick FBI agent, Kelli thought. The laugh and the Cajun term of *"ticrot,"* which meant little dried turd, was said in a humorous sense.

"What did he say?" asked Richard.

"Nothing you would want to know," she replied.

"I feel like shit," Richard mumbled.

Unable to restrain herself, Kelli burst out laughing as did the Cajun. All of the humor was lost on Richard.

The rest of the morning Ballew spent checking his lines and traps while Kelli and Richard remained confined to the safety of the small island. In the early afternoon, while they waited for Ballew's return, they heard an airboat approach. Even in the distance Kelli could recognize Happy Jak. She approached as he tied his boat.

"How you are, girl?" he asked jovially.

"Okay, I guess."

"Ballew give those men one hell of a day they not soon forget."

"Nor will I."

Happy Jak's boat was filled with supplies and his violin. As he unloaded the boat, the ever jolly rotund man told Kelli he was about to throw together a special meal, "How 'bout I told you how to make one fine Cajun meal?"

"Sure," she said excitedly. "What are you going to make?"

Happy Jak's eyes sparkled and a smile lit his face. He held his finger and thumb to his lips and kissed them, "Come--we make Jambalaya."

Jambalaya, the Cajun dish, was famous even in Kansas. Although Kelli had heard of it many times, she did not know the ingredients. Jambalaya was some type of spicy stew.

"Happy Jak, what do you put in Jambalaya?" she asked as she followed him to his boat.

"Ahhh, Jambalaya!" He laughed as he pulled a large container from his boat, splashing water from the sides of the container. "If it swims, crawls or flies . . . then it be put in the Jambalaya," he said with a laughter fresh and sincere. Then he placed the container on the ground and opened it to show Kelli the contents. Inside were what looked like small lobsters but, in reality, were hundreds of crawfish.

"Crawdads?"

Happy Jak laughed. "Close. These are the swimmers." Next he pulled ham from the boat along with smoked pork sausage. He pointed to the sausage, "*Andouille*, the crawlers." Last of all he pulled from the boat a box full of spices and from this he took a container of salt and poured a portion of it over the crawfish.

"What's that for?" asked Kelli.

"The salt upsets their systems and they purge themselves. Later we cook them." Eyeing the chickens in the pen, he pointed. "Ahhh, the flyers." A mighty arm grabbed Kelli around the shoulders, "Come, girl, let's make with the drink."

They walked casually toward the house, and all the way Happy Jak searched within his bag until he found the bottle of homemade cherry wine.

"I don't know when Ballew will be back," she said.

"Soon, he be back soon . . . and he bring Belle Rose. This is a party for Belle Rose. With you we have even better *Fado*," said Happy Jak, the term *Fado* meaning a Cajun party.

"Who are Ballew's parents?" Kelli asked.

"No one knows. Maybe 'cept for Belle Rose. She not much talk. Some say his parents killed in a hurricane. Others say they killed poaching. I heard even they find poachers and were killed. Many believe Belle Rose is the sister of Ballew's mother. The Atchafalaya tells no secrets."

"Were they from here?"

"Only the swamps know. I never knew them. Belle Rose been here since I can remember. She is like Ballew's mother." Happy Jak laughed, asking the question of himself before Kelli did, knowing what Kelli thought, "Where he is from? He is like the Jambalaya, a little of this and a little of that, but all Cajun."

Taking mental notes for future reference, the reporter in Kelli asked, "Do you believe in Cajun Voodoo?" She still thought of the dolls Belle Rose carried.

"You know of Cajun Voodoo? Papa Das maybe?"

"Some but not much. Belle Rose hangs dolls from her waist; I think they're for some Voodoo ritual."

Happy Jak laughed. "She carries the dolls like a man carries a gun. They are her protection. Many times they save her life. She called Swamp Witch."

"Do you believe?"

"I have seen strange things in the Atchafalaya. Things you would not believe. Ask to yourself, how one man beat all them men what want for you. Some say the Swamp Witch make Ballew Dragun. What you think?"

"C'mon, Happy Jak," Kelli chided.

Happy Jak smiled and looked all around as though someone might hear. "Who dat say the Swamp Witch keep the Dragun alive. Hurt the Witch--Ballew Dragun be your death! No one hurt Belle Rose."

For a moment he paused to let the words sink in, then he continued, "Those dat say Voodoo are hocus pocus. Some dat say it true and live with Voodoo. It is a matter of the mind." He laughed loudly, "The mind say it matter!"

Before they entered the house, Kelli became somber. "Will those men return?" she asked, opening the screen leading to the house.

"Maybe, but it not go so well if they do," he said as he moved his large body sideways through the door.

"What does Ballew expect to do against them?"

"Don't underestimate Ballew. He is an unusual man; he need no Voodoo to beat his enemy." Then slapping his hands together to end the questions he added, "Now, no more of this. Tonight we party."

For Happy Jak the conversation concerning the men chasing Kelli had ended.

Reluctantly Kelli discussed it no further. Soon she was caught up in the contagious festive mood Happy Jak exhibited.

Then Ballew and Belle Rose arrived, just as Happy Jak had predicted. Too weak to help and with the swollen leg, Richard could only watch. But not alone, as Rocky so intrigued with him, tended to stay nearby.

Happy Jak went about the chore of creating his famous Jambalaya. He poured dark wild rice into the concoction of meats and spices. Even the hard-to-please Richard commented on the wonderful smell created by the gourmet cooks.

Outside, Ballew started a fire and filled a large black cast-iron pot with water, brought it to a boil, then poured in the lively crawfish. To this he added corn and potatoes brought by Belle Rose. A large sealed bag of spices, bag and all, was added to the brew.

Happy Jak still worked over the Jambalaya when Ballew, with the help of Kelli, extracted a portion of the steaming contents from the boiling cauldron placing them into a large wooden bowl.

With the deft fingers of experience, Ballew cracked one of the crayfish, expertly removing the tender tail meat. This he offered to Kelli, which she readily took. The shrimp-like creature was spicy beyond even her expectations. Ballew took the head and sucked the yellow fatty matter from its interior. Sucking the head was a ritual true Cajuns believed to be the best part of eating crawfish. Most Cajun cooks saved the fat to create special dishes or to cook other foods. The head of the crawfish was considered a delicacy.

Kelli had watched the procedure. Awkwardly, she imitated Ballew's actions. Though slower and not quite extracting the whole tail of the crawfish, she got Ballew's nod of approval. The favor was returned when she gave the morsel to Ballew. Then she took the head and also sucked the fatty portion.

"Yes!" exclaimed Ballew, "the Cajun way!"

Kelli laughed when Ballew approved of her actions.

They took the bowl with the mixture of corn, potatoes, and crawfish into the house. All partook of the spicy food, while Happy Jak's Jambalaya continued to brew.

Kelli took a small portion to Richard who was nestled comfortably in Ballew's rocking chair reading an old Spider Man comic book. When he saw the food, he returned the comic book to its box.

"You know, that Spider Man guy really has some tough times. He's always in a world of shit," quipped Richard eagerly waiting for the food.

Along with the plate of food, Kelli handed Richard a glass of water, then she whispered, "Richard, this is hot and spicy, that's why I brought the water, so watch what I do. I want you to act as though you like it, even if you don't. These people believe this is the only kind of food to eat. If you do as I've seen you do, it is like an affront to their way of living. Do you understand?"

"Yes ma'am," he said and eagerly followed her example. After he had swallowed the crawfish and bitten into a potato, he grabbed for the water. His eyes were watering and when he spoke, he sounded hoarse, "You weren't just shitting!" Then he dove back in and tore another crawfish apart, "I just didn't expect something that hot. Kinda like shrimp, but definitely the spiciest thing I've ever eaten."

Happy Jak walked near, wiping his hands on a small towel hanging from his waist. The towel, originally white, had long since become covered with the spices and crawfish innards while making the Jambalaya. He picked up a discarded crawfish head. "Like this." Then he sucked the fatty matter from the head.

In shocked disbelief with his mouth hanging open, Richard watched Happy Jak and his ritual. Richard turned the head and looked at the contents inside, "Jesus Christ, it's full of shit!"

Happy Jak roared with laughter. Ballew smiled and Kelli turned red, but she was relieved they saw humor in the words.

Happy Jak bent over and took the head from Richard's hand, then bent down and pointed to the yellow mass within. "It is the best part of the crawfish. It is not shit. I have already purged them of all, as you say, the shit. It takes a man a long time to develop a taste. In time you will learn." He sucked the head, wiped his mouth with the back of his hand and followed it with another laugh.

But Richard's attention was attracted to Belle Rose when she lit her pipe.

"Excuse me, but do you have a smoke?" he asked, pointing to her pipe. Quickly, she spoke in the hard Cajun dialect, but Richard didn't understand the words. "What did she say?"

Kelli laughed and said something to Belle Rose in the same accent. "She says she will give you a pipe if you want."

Richard nodded and it didn't take long for the old woman to fill her spare pipe with the strong tobacco from the small pouch hanging at her side. She offered him the pipe, which he eagerly accepted. He went to the wood stove and took a long slender match stick from a can on the floor near the stove and poked it in the still red hot embers. Instantly it flickered to life and he brought it to the end of the pipe and sucked the flames in the end lighting the tobacco. Smoke poured from his mouth and he released a long, contented sigh.

Belle Rose cackled at the sight, slapped her side, and mumbled something Richard again failed to understand.

"I think I will live," he moaned and took another drag from the small pipe. "Hey, Ballew, do you play?" Richard asked, pointing to the old chess board.

"You know how to play?" Ballew asked and when Richard nodded, he asked, "You want teach me to play?"

"Sure," he said, still clinging to the pipe. Hastily, Ballew pulled the barrel near his rocking chair and Richard. In a few minutes they were deeply immersed in the game.

Kelli took this time to talk to Happy Jak and Belle Rose as

they prepared the Jambalaya. Belle Rose puffed on her pipe while she worked over the red beans and rice.

"Happy Jak, why would other Cajuns help those men to find me?" she asked.

"Oh, no, girl . . . that not what they did. Delacroix wants to kill Ballew. Mamou is foolish and follows like a puppy."

"Why would Delacroix want to kill Ballew?"

"Ballew killed his brother. You have heard of Angola?"

"Portuguese West Africa?" she asked as she cleaned dishes.

"No, not Africa girl," he countered, pausing to wipe his hands on the towel no longer showing any white. He reached in the air, as if pulling for the answer, "Let's see . . . ahhh, yes! You have heard of Alcatraz?"

"The prison? Of course."

"Well, fine lady, Angola is Louisiana's Alcatraz."

"What does it have to do with Ballew and Delacroix?"

"Not so quick . . . let me tell you the story. Once, Ballew leave the Atchafalaya to work. Men steal from company. Ballew told of this wrongful thing what that happen. For that what he did, they fire Ballew. Men angry their friends arrested. Two men go to jail.

"One of those men be Delacroix's brother, Mouton, who swore to kill Ballew when he get released. Mouton get himself sent to Angola. Angola is a strange prison built on the edge of the Atchafalaya. The side what that faces the swamp has no wall because they believe any man who tries to escape into the swamp will die.

"But Mouton escaped and found Ballew. He took Ballew to Devil's Island--"

"I have seen the island; Ballew showed me," Kelli interjected.

"He show you?" Happy Jak said, a bit surprised. "Well, let me continue. Some call the island Legaba or Papa La Bas, the Devil's Island." Kelli smirked, but Happy Jak was quick to respond, "Don't laugh girl! Much of the religion in the swamps be one part Catholic and one part . . . voodoo!"

Then he spoke in English so as not to anger Belle Rose with his words. "That why they call her Swamp Witch," he continued, pointing to the shriveled old woman. "Dat old woman be a conjure of Voodoo!" Happy Jak laughed loudly and continued his story in Cajun French.

"Call it what you want. Those put on Devil's Island do not return. Mouton's curiosity killed him. He go back, make sure Ballew dead. Mouton big, big, but Ballew fast, fast, fast. But it Ballew, who what caught Mouton unaware. Not quick death Ballew offer Mouton. Instead he give Mouton the same as Mouton give Ballew. Ballew never returned to Devil's Island . . . no one see Mouton since.

"For that, Delacroix want kill Ballew." Happy Jak snickered. "Many believe Ballew possessed. See, Ballew left-handed. Cajuns superstitious of people what that are left-handed."

The story intrigued and fascinated Kelli. After what she had seen, she wondered if it might all be true.

"Ballew!" bellowed Happy Jak, "I need more wood for the stove. Maybe six or five logs."

The chess game was interrupted and Kelli went to help. Outside, she stopped. The sun fell in the sky and a haze hung over the swamp. The sky and water washed in a bright gold, through which could be seen the black silhouettes of the cypress with the clinging Spanish moss. The water rippled like liquid gold.

Ballew had to shake Kelli as she stood frozen, absorbing the serene spectacle. "Sometimes, the swamp is belle. Come, we get wood."

"Yes, belle," she whispered and followed behind Ballew to gather the wood.

The sun disappeared and a quiet peacefulness settled over the swamp, save for the eternal droning of the mosquitos.

"It be ready," rejoiced Happy Jak; "Come get de Jambalaya!"

Late into the evening they feasted on Happy Jak's Jambalaya and homemade cherry wine.

When the dinner was finished, Happy Jak started playing his violin, picking expertly with his thick round fingers. The faster he picked, the faster he rocked up and down on his left foot, while stomping his right. Ballew tapped his left foot and clapped, while Belle Rose moved her body back and forth.

Suddenly Happy Jak stopped, "Come Ballew, let's play for your friends."

Immediately Ballew reached for his accordion, and behind him came Belle Rose, reaching for the "thing" that looked like a washboard and the four spoons. While Ballew warmed up on the accordion, Belle Rose slipped the two aluminum straps over her shoulders. She reversed each pair of spoons, put a pair in each hand, and started sliding the handles up and down the corrugations. The sounds blended in beautifully with Ballew and Happy Jak, who were completely into the music. Even Richard started tapping his foot. Everyone was smiling and laughing. Even Rocky stood up and rocked on his back feet.

Hours later, they stopped and yet it seemed to all the music had just started.

As Happy Jak and Belle Rose prepared to leave, Kelli pointed to the instrument Belle Rose had played and asked Happy Jak, "What is that washboard thing called?"

Happy Jak could not suppress a laugh as did Ballew and Belle Rose when they heard the question. He said, "It is a *froittior*. Pretty sounds no?"

"What does *froittior* mean?" she asked.

Again Ballew laughed and Belle Rose crackled.

The question was being milked for all Happy Jak could get. "It means," then Happy Jak burst out laughing. During his outburst he was able to mumble, "Washboard!"

Suddenly he stopped laughing and looked seriously at Kelli, "Seems you know your Cajun instruments well." Again Happy Jak burst into uncontrolled laughter as did all the rest, including Kelli.

A while later, both Happy Jak and Belle Rose were gone. Kelli readied herself for bed while the men engaged in battle at the chess board. For one of the few times in the last month, she felt content. After she fixed her hair, she returned to watch the men play. Richard took his knight and moved it diagonally, putting Ballew's king in check.

"Check," he said.

"Richard, that's cheating," she said, as she admonished Richard for the illegal move. "The knight can't move diagonally."

Richard's face turned crimson, "I was showing him how to modify the game as you play."

"The knight can only move three spaces like this?" Ballew asked Kelli, as he made the motion with the knight.

"That's right," she answered.

When the chess piece was rearranged in its proper position, Ballew took Richard's castle with his bishop.

"Checkmate?" Ballew asked.

"No, I can take him with my queen--"

"Yes, but he can take the queen with his knight and that still leaves the king in check. Yes?" Ballew asked.

Kelli giggled and clapped her hands. "That's checkmate, you lose. Oh, Richard, you're such a wonderful teacher. The student just beat you."

"Well, shit," he said, continuing to study the board and looking for a way to extricate himself from the loss, but there were none.

Chapter 8

Terrorist's Revenge

"Nissim will be okay, but Abdul is dead," Jerry Hyatt said, worried about his present situation. "He didn't have any identity, which is good, but they're asking too many questions. What with one dead, one shot up and near death, and two others looking as if they barely survived a gang fight, I've had hell trying to convince the doctors this was just an unusual hunting accident."

"Do the doctors suspect anything?" Kaja asked.

"I'm sure they do, but they can't prove anything. I doubt if they believe the story, but the men have corroborated me on everything." Jerry contemplated one problem: "If they run a make on the bullets they got out of Nissim and find out they're from an Uzi, I'm afraid we'll have some explaining to do."

"Forget it," snapped Kaja. "We will be gone in a few hours. The men will know what to do if trouble develops. My concern is with the woman and the Cajun."

"Don't forget Staley," interjected Jerry.

"Your friend is of no concern to me." Suddenly Kaja's transformation was like that of a man possessed. "I want the man called Dragun to die. I want to watch him pay for what he has done."

"Me, too," quipped Jerry, rubbing the knot at the back of his head. "But I've gotta get Richard, or it will be my ass."

"I have sent for Mustafa Talas and Kidane. Tomorrow they will arrive with the others--"

"What others?"

"Soon we will be more than twenty strong," Kaja half mused

to himself.

"Twenty? What are you gonna do--declare war?"

"No . . . but I will show him a war like no man has ever seen . . . the Cajun will die, I swear it!" Kaja vowed, his face livid with anger. "Have you purchased the boats and weapons?"

"Piece of cake," said Jerry, reassuring Kaja. "I have some friends in the Bureau who can get me any weapon I need. By the way, I thought you wanted the woman because of that religious stuff, so why the big deal over this Cajun? From what I've heard, he never ventures from the swamp anyway."

Kaja fumed with anger. "The blasphemous woman will be dealt with as I have been instructed by the most high ones, but the Cajun--that is something personal. Because of what he has done to me and my men . . . for that, he will die."

"What if the men in the hospital talk?"

"My men will say nothing. If they talk, they will die. They would prefer life in prison than death at my hands," remarked Kaja.

"Your men will be here tomorrow?"

"Some will arrive today, the others tomorrow. Mustafa and Kidane will be here in the morning. Then we strike," said Kaja.

Also of concern was the $1,000,000 the Cajun took. Real money was necessary to convince the Cajun he was sincere. Never before had he lost any money. He evolved a plan to retrieve the money and keep it for himself. No one would miss the money.

Kaja felt his chest just above the heart. Still swollen, he ran his fingers across the puffs of skin and he could just make out the letters "SM." The Cajun would die if it was the last thing Kaja did. With Mustafa, Kidane, and the others, Kaja would be unbeatable.

* * *

Kelli handed Rocky a piece of rice fritter which he quickly washed with his paws.

"Where's Ballew?" Richard asked.

"He said he had to check some traps," she answered, pouring a cup of steaming black coffee into an old wooden mug and handing it to Richard. She also gave him a plate with two fritters. "That was not a nice thing to do, cheating at chess, last night."

"I was just funning with the big guy," said Richard as he sipped his coffee. "Damn, he learned fast. I'd swear he's played it before and was just suckering me in."

"I don't think he's ever played the game with anyone who

knew how. I also don't think he knows how to read, but he sure did learn fast when I read him the comic books."

Richard seemed surprised, "You're kidding?" But Kelli shook her head. Richard broke off a piece of fritter and handed it under the table to Rocky who was pulling at his leg. "Ya know, this place could grow on ya."

"Well, it's a hell of a lot safer than any place the FBI could find."

"To the FBI," said Richard as he held the Cajun coffee high in a toast, then took a sip. "I'm kinda gettin' to like this strong coffee."

Kelli let out a sarcastic laugh. "Yeah, we might make a man of you yet."

"*Touche*," he said softly. "Guess I deserved that." Richard rose from the table, walked toward the door, and peered across the swamp. "Well, they can't get us here. Hell, I'm getting used to the heat, too."

When able to travel, Richard would return to the Bureau and notify intelligence of the leaks and Jerry Hyatt. He moved across the room and sat lazily in the rocking chair. He was enjoying the peace and quiet.

"Ballew is coming," Kelli said with anticipation in her voice.

Richard listened to the sound of the approaching airboat. Strange, he thought, it sounded like two or more instead of one.

* * *

Kaja wanted to avoid contact with anyone, so he had instructed Delacroix to find a secluded spot where the airboats could be taken undetected. Delacroix and Mamou managed to purchase five airboats for the trip. No questions were asked when they used cash. The boats were tied up and waiting.

Kaja decided to come in small groups. In this manner, they could load and depart without suspicion. The men were told to come in two's or three's. Now they awaited only three men-- Mustafa, Kidane, and Jerry. Jerry had gone to the airport to meet their plane.

The men Kaja assembled were a collection of *killers elite*. Experts in many languages--all knew English. Some of the worst and most successful terrorist acts ever conducted were carried out by many of the men gathered in the swamps of the Atchafalaya at

Kaja's urging. From different parts of the world they had come, and they came quickly. Their accomplishments were varied and far-reaching, but all with the same deadly goal . . . the death of their enemies. Or whoever they assumed to be their enemies.

Abseen and Khayam had worked their terror for over a decade. Both clean cut, average height, and light skin with dark hair, Abseen sported a short, well-manicured moustache, while Khayam's face was covered with a very short full beard. Experts at the German language, they were two of the terrorists who had managed to mix in unnoticed at the Olympics in Germany and kill the young Israeli athletes.

Credit was given to the IRA for the murder of Lord Mountbatten, when, in reality, he was killed by two of the men responding to Kaja's order. Jagat and Bakshi accomplished what a war could not. They killed the great English general. Listed as tourists, they had gone unnoticed in their terrorist work. Jagat was slim and slight of build with a narrow face. Bakshi was just over five-foot-six and bald with a round face matching a round body.

When Egyptian President Sadat tried to make peace, Tahel had the responsibility of killing him, should the air attack fail. His cunning patience as a sniper was rewarded. The bullet from his rifle ended the life of the great Anwar Sadat, and not the attack, as first believed.

Dark skin and hair, along with their short stature and mastery of the Nicaraguan tongue, enabled Raj and Jibreen to find and murder the Catholic nuns in Nicaragua. They had taken a great deal of pleasure in the torture and murder of the helpless women, mocking them and their God, as they died. The two men had even forgotten which side had paid them.

When terrorists had sprayed the crowds in a Rome airport with bullets, two of those men were Fawad and Azad. Somehow, they had managed to escape and continued to spread terror throughout the world. Their dark countenance and slight physique enabled them to pass as Italians unnoticed. What they enjoyed most was their treatment of the Italian women.

Hassan had always enjoyed tormenting his victims before killing them. He had tortured the American Naval SEAL's officer and shot the young American and dumped his body from the commercial airliner. Another terrorist was put on trial, but Hassan had managed the evil deed. The strange code of silence would not allow the one on trial to reveal the truth, that the murderer had been

Hassan.

All of these assassins and others just as malicious had arrived to do Kaja's bidding in the pursuit of Kelli Parsons and the Cajun. But, by far, the worst of the terrorists had not arrived. Kaja waited with eager anticipation for Mustafa and Kidane, his most formidable men .

Mustafa returned from South America where the local Communist government had paid for mercenaries to murder the leaders of a revolt. The democratic revolt was centered deep within the jungles. Mustafa and Kidane penetrated deep into the jungle on the seemingly impossible mission. They succeeded in killing all three revolutionaries, making good their escape, and keeping the Communists in power. Kaja had sent word for his requirements of the mission and both men had responded immediately.

When it came to hand-to-hand combat or the trickery of jungle warfare, there was none better than Mustafa. Kidane was a master of weapons and traps. If Kidane failed with his traps, he could use his brute strength. He was large and powerfully built. Once, he had wrapped his arms about another large man with whom he fought, squeezing him until half his ribs broke and both lungs were punctured. Even the strength and size of the other man had made no difference in the outcome.

No mission had ever failed, proven by the job just completed. They had traveled to a land they had never seen and once there, they had managed to kill the leaders of the revolution. All this was done while the victims were surrounded by their most loyal troops. To fail was to die. The Cajun would certainly be no problem because he was only one man.

Kaja was a planner. Where he had failed, the others would not. His new plan was unbeatable, and Kidane and Mustafa, indestructible.

Sophisticated and brought up in the fine arts, Kaja was as much at home at the ballet as he was cutting a person's throat. A devout and steadfast Muslim, he performed his *jobs* in the name of Allah, but in the end, the financial rewards of a completed project was what drove him. The money taken by the Cajun would be his when he killed the woman.

The Pan Am disaster in England was Kaja's masterpiece. His superiors had wanted to set an example for the Western World to fear, and, if necessary, he was to sacrifice his life in the effort. But, as much as he believed in Allah, he believed in living more.

His ability with the women enabled him to move in on a flight attendant and gain her confidence. He promised to marry her and convinced her to deliver a package on one of her flights. The package, containing plastic explosives, went unchecked--as he expected--and the Pan Am airliner was destroyed in mid-air. The beautiful flight attendant deceived and murdered by the one person she thought loved her.

Now Kaja watched and waited for Jerry's return and the arrival of Mustafa and Kidane before he continued with his plans.

Supplies were carefully loaded aboard the five craft. Nothing would be overlooked this time. All the men wore fatigues, making the small outfit of men appear more like they were going to war against a whole country instead of one single man. Food, water, and guns were stored aboard the boats. Care was taken with the automatic weapons and the ammunition. Along with the food and water were chlorine tablets, should they run low on water. Nothing was left to chance. They were ready.

The sound of men approaching attracted Kaja's attention. Mustafa and Kidane had finally arrived. Kaja explained the situation as the two men dressed and prepared for their new mission. Mustafa was all of six-foot-six in height. The years of training and hand-to-hand combat had sculptured a body rippled with large, powerful muscles.

"Mustafa, Jerry has told you of the man we seek?" Kaja queried.

"It is no problem," Mustafa said with a wave of his arms. "Soon the trouble you have will be dead."

"You know of our first confrontation?"

"You were not prepared," Mustafa said sternly. "You ventured into his land. He knew the terrain. I will kill him for you."

"Not too quick. We must catch him alive. Before he dies, I have things to show him--a score to settle," demanded Kaja.

"Done. It should be easy to catch him . . . and when you finish, we will kill him. Every man has a weakness. I shall find his," Mustafa said with an air of indifference.

Delacroix returned to where the three men were discussing the plan of attack. "I have learned from a man in the swamp the location of Dragun's place. It is not far."

Everything was in order; Mustafa and Kidane made a final check and when they assured themselves all was ready, they set out on their mission.

Led by Mamou and Delacroix, 23 terrorists and an FBI agent, armed and dangerous, set out on their quest to destroy a single man. Terrorists who never failed on a mission. To fail was to die and these specialists of death still lived, spreading the terror they knew so well. The Cajun was theirs for the taking. It would be impossible for him to survive against such insurmountable odds.

Death was their form of revenge. The deadly group of men had only one person on their minds. Ballew Dragun was a marked man for which life would be short. Death in an unknown and hideous form was approaching. His time had come, and it was now.

* * *

Kelli heard the boat stop and after a few minutes she casually approached the door to see what took Ballew so long, only to find herself almost face-to-face with the men who wanted her dead.

"Oh, my God, it's them!" Kelli screamed to Richard.

"Shit!" cursed Richard when he saw what alarmed her. They were moving toward the house slowly and with a great deal of caution. He grabbed Kelli by the arm, "Come on, let's get the hell outa here.

They rushed to the bedroom. As Richard crawled through one of the windows and reached back to lower Kelli, she started out the window, but stopped abruptly.

"Wait, I have to get the painting Ballew gave me," she said, not wanting to leave the gift behind.

"Fuck the painting! Get your ass out here. Now!" he shouted.

But Kelli wasn't listening and ran hastily to where the painting lay. She retrieved it and was running toward Richard waiting outside the window, when the door burst open. Two of Kaja's men, Kamdar and Jibreen, tackled her before she made it to the bedroom window, but somehow, when she lunged forward she tossed the painting through the window.

The scream assured Richard it was too late to help, and he disappeared into the swamp growth. The men who captured Kelli dragged her, kicking and screaming, to where Kaja waited triumphantly.

Kaja squeezed Kelli's face viciously, forcing her jaw apart

until her cheeks touched together. "Where is your savior now?" he demanded, casting a furtive look about the swamps. "He cannot help you now."

Kaja knocked her kick aside effortlessly.

"You bastard!" she cried.

"Burn it!" Kaja said with a sinister laugh as he pointed to the home Ballew had built with his own hands.

"No! You can't!" Kelli screamed.

Helpless and unable to do anything, Richard watched from the safety of the tropical growth.

Within seconds, the flames leaped skyward from the small frame home and haven of security. Kelli watched as the wooden structure surrendered to the hungry flames.

Suddenly, a small creature, its fur smoking, burst from the flames and streaked across the opening. In pain, Rocky ran for his friend, Richard.

"Kill it," Kaja demanded. Four of the men immediately opened up on the small raccoon with their automatic weapons, kicking mud and debris into the air. The bullets traced a path toward the defenseless animal. Somehow, Rocky managed to dance between the projectiles intended for him.

"Stop!" yelled Richard, emerging from the safety of the heavy growth. For a moment he disregarded the danger to himself as he dove for Rocky, scooping him into his arms. Richard managed to turn his back to the invaders and shield the poor raccoon. The bullets stitched a straight line in his direction, narrowly missing.

More bait for the Cajun, Kaja thought when he saw Richard appear. "Hold your fire!" came Kaja's order.

Quickly Richard extinguished the smoking hair. Rocky rolled his eyes so he could look into Richard's. The poor animal was whimpering but grateful.

"Listen, you stupid shit, we're in a hell of a mess, so I suggest you get your furry ass outa here while ya still got one." Then he gave Rocky an affectionate push toward the safety of the trees.

Rocky stopped one more time, casting a quick thank-you in Richard's direction before he disappeared.

"Kill it!" Kaja again ordered.

Bakshi raised his Uzi, but never fired as a quick right to the jaw sent the man sprawling to the ground. Richard leveled the man with one punch. Not bad, he mused, but those were his final clear thoughts as the butt of another gun landed on his skull. As he fell, he managed to maintain consciousness long enough to see Rocky disappear safely.

Kelli screamed in horror. What a stupid but noble effort Richard exhibited. If only Ballew could have seen Richard. But her thoughts were interrupted by Kaja.

"Where is the money?" he asked.

"I don't know," she lied.

Kaja motioned to two of his men. "Kill the man," he said, pointing to Richard, who lay still on the ground.

"No! I'll tell you if you don't kill Richard."

"Done," said Kaja with a sly grin. He had no intention of killing the man, when he could be used to attract the Cajun. How foolish these American people were. Couldn't she understand as soon as he had the money and the Cajun . . . they would all die. Foolish Americans.

"The money is hidden on Devil's Island."

"Where is this Devil's Island?"

Delacroix was unhappy because they did not capture Dragun. "I know where it is. I can take you to the Island."

"Good. We will trap the fool Cajun there." Then Kaja motioned two of his men and pointed to the smokehouse and the chicken pen, "Destroy them."

The Uzi's barked their destruction as the men riddled the two structures. The small chicken pen collapsed under the barrage of bullets and the wooden door to the smokehouse fell sideways, barely hanging on one hinge.

Kaja motioned his men to the boats. With his captives safely secured aboard his own airboat, they started for Devil's Island guided by Delacroix.

* * *

Someone else had seen all the events as they occurred. Ballew gained a new respect for the man Richard Staley. He had seen the smoke from the fire, but he had arrived too late to help his friends and was forced to watch. He heard and saw everything, but remained undetected. The urge to kill and seek Cajun revenge almost prevailed over the reality of the situation and the danger--if not death--his position might have put Kelli. His inward feelings controlled his outward desire and urges, telling him to wait for the proper time to move.

Ballew made plans for his friends' rescue. He would discard the airboat for his own rowboat. This would enable him to reach the island without being noticed. He would go to Devil's Island and rescue his friends. First, he scavenged the burning debris for anything of value in what had once been his peaceful home before the intrusion of these people. While he circled his once beautiful home, Rocky followed closely.

In his search, he found the discarded painting he had given to Kelli. This he put safely in the small outhouse. From the smoker he obtained dried meat, then he filled a leather container with water from the well. In a metal box, within his boat, was a change of clothes he always carried. For some strange reason, he had taken the two Spider Man shirts Happy Jak had given him. Other than his knife, rifle, and bow, along with more than two dozen arrows, he had nothing. The fire had destroyed everything he owned. He hid the airboat so it would not be found, and loaded his small rowboat with all of his worldly possessions. Then he set out to find his friends.

Chapter 9
Snakebitten

The airboats were half out of the water and all the men with their two captives were on the slight rise in the clearing on the Southeast side of Devil's Island. Drooping cypress with hanging Spanish Moss shaded the clearing surrounded with thick swamp growth.

Unnoticed by the two dozen intruders, a twelve-foot alligator, with only its eyes protruding above the water line waited for a future meal to stray helplessly into the waters of the Atchafalaya. On the shore of two nearby islands, a half dozen more watched and waited patiently.

Immediately upon their arrival, Kaja confronted Delacroix.

"Are there poisonous snakes here like the cobra and the asp we have?"

Delacroix shrugged his shoulders, "We have the water moccasin, cottonmouth and a few rattlesnakes."

"Which is the deadliest?" Kaja asked.

"The rattlesnake, but the meanest, is the cottonmouth. He will chase you and bite you for no reason and not let go until you pull him away," Delacroix noted.

"Excellent!" beamed Kaja, rubbing his hands together. "Can you find some now?"

Delacroix turned around, looked at the island, then looked back at Kaja and nodded his head.

"Good, bring me some quickly," ordered Kaja.

A moment later Delacroix, and Mamou, with a burlap bag went in search of the deadly snakes requested by Kaja.

Mustafa confronted Kaja, "Let me and Kidane hide in the growth. We will pick strategic positions where this Cajun will most surely hide when he reaches the island. He should be easy to catch."

"Yes," said Kaja, but as Mustafa started to disappear into the swamps undergrowth, Kaja stopped him. "Alive, Mustafa. Bring this Cajun back alive. I want to see him die. I want to see the fear in his eyes!"

Mustafa nodded to the command and then, he and Kidane disappeared.

For hours the quiet of the swamp was broken only by the relentless questions Kaja forced on Kelli Parsons and Richard Staley. During the questioning, Delacroix and Mamou returned. Delacroix held the burlap bag with its wiggling contents high and nodded toward Kaja, which brought a smile to his lips.

Kaja turned viciously on Kelli and continued. "Where is the money?"

"I don't know," she cried, "I didn't see where he hid it."

Kaja grew impatient with the woman and was ready to kill her. Only his desire to catch the Cajun prevented him from doing so.

"Where is your friend?" he asked Delacroix.

"Dragun come when he wants."

Khayam came near Kaja and whispered in his ear, "Another is on the island . . . I can feel it. Your Cajun is here!"

"Do you think he watches?" Kaja asked.

"He would not be here otherwise. Should I slip away and bring him back?"

"No," said Kaja, gloating to himself for already bringing the trap into place, "Kidane and Mustafa will take care of the Cajun." Kaja pointed to a burlap bag wriggling on the ground, "Delacroix has collected some deadly specimens. They should serve my purpose well."

"If he appears, we will be ready," said Abseen. "But the man would be a fool to show himself."

"Wrong, Abseen. You see, all Americans have the same weakness. They worry more about their friends than they do about their own lives. You will see."

Abseen looked at the burlap bag and understood. "Please Kaja let me take care of the Cajun," he said pointing to the burlap bag. "I have handled snakes before."

"Maybe," said Kaja. He motioned for Raj to bring Richard near. "Hold them both," he ordered. He pulled a small caliber gun from the holster at his side and whispered to Richard, "Let's see if your friend watches."

Without a moment's hesitation, Kaja held the pistol against Richard's leg, six inches above the knee, and as Richard squirmed madly, he pulled the trigger. Richard screamed out in pain and the two men holding him released their grip, letting him fall to the ground, clutching the new wound.

Next, Kaja walked to Kelli, who was held so firmly she could not move. Kaja tore her shirt, exposing her breasts. He jammed the cold steel barrel against her right breast and hesitated. All the while smiling sadistically.

Concealed by the tropical growth of the Atchafalaya, Ballew Dragun moved when he saw Kaja with Kelli. His sudden uncontrolled movement was immediately noticed by Kidane, who lay well hidden only a few feet from the unsuspecting Cajun.

Kidane sprang from the cover, quick as a cat, before Ballew could react. His arms were wrapped around the Cajun, making it impossible for him to fight back. Still, Ballew fought with the tenacity of a cornered animal against a superior antagonist.

For a moment Kidane was surprised when he thought the Cajun was loosening his grip, but before this happened, Mustafa was at his side, helping him with the fighting Cajun.

Kamdar, Haddad, Nouri and Salil, who sat less than two yards from the commotion, scurried for weapons as Ballew was brought back fighting and kicking into the camp with Kidane on one side and Mustafa on the other.

"No!" Kelli cried. "They will kill you!"

Ballew stopped fighting and his chest heaved from the exertion.

Kaja was torn between the desire to disfigure Kelli and his eager anticipation of torturing Ballew. He nodded to Mustafa and lowered the pistol.

Jagat retrieved Ballew's rifle. Moinuddin took the large knife and slid the bow and its quiver of arrows from the Cajun's shoulder and brought them to Kaja, who motioned Moinuddin to hold the Cajun's knife to Kelli's throat.

Delacroix confronted Ballew and spoke in his Cajun tongue, "You are fool and now I watch you die!"

But no fear showed in the blue-gray eyes glaring down on

Delacroix. In his own familiar language, Ballew spoke, "I am not dead yet . . . you will die like your brother."

With those words, Delacroix pulled his knife and came at Ballew. Motionless, Ballew stood before the attack, but, as the knife swung for its target, he struck like lightning, bringing his feet up, catching Delacroix full in the chest, and sending him reeling backwards, tumbling to the ground. Delacroix no longer held his knife.

Delacroix readied himself for a repeat attack but was restrained by Kamdar and Abseen.

"Well done," said Kaja, clapping his hands in mock applause. "But, too little, too late." Then he pointed to Moinuddin, who still held the knife to Kelli's throat. "If you do anything, she will die. Now, you must die, and she will watch."

Kaja gave an arm command and a wave of his head. At the order Khayam and Nouri moved across the camp's small clearing to retrieve those items demanded by Kaja. Kidane and Mustafa released their grasp, but stood at the ready.

With malevolent intent, Kaja stood before Ballew, "Let's see what we have beneath that cap."

Kaja jerked the New Orleans' cap from Ballew's head. He sneered at the cap, threw it down, and stomped it into the ground.

The Cajun said nothing as he ran his hand through his hair. The long, thick, black hair flowed freely.

"Do you believe in your God?" Kaja asked--but Ballew did not acknowledge the question. "I hope so. You see, this is what the whole thing is about. What this woman said about Allah is why you are about to die. It should not bother you . . . that is, if you believe in your God. Do you know how his son died?"

Again, no answer. Kaja expected terror or fear, but he got neither, instead only a defiant stare. He would continue until he had the satisfaction of seeing fear from the man who had so humiliated him before.

"Well, you will soon know."

"Oh God, no!" whined Kelli when she saw what they were building.

Jagat and Nouri fabricated a makeshift cross from thick portions of trees, notched where they crossed. Onto this, they threw Ballew, spread his hands and bound them tightly about each end of the log.

Helpless, Ballew lay tied to the logs. Kaja crept near and

squeezed Ballew's face as he had done to Kelli, "Do you know what they did to him next?"

Kaja kicked Ballew in the side, but he made no sound or movement. When Kaja waved his hands, Khayam came near and he along with Nouri dug a hole so the cross could be placed in an erect position.

The makeshift cross was brought to an erect position and placed into the hole. The cross slid into the hole and came to a jolting stop. Not a word did the Cajun utter.

"This is an unusual man. You must kill him now while you have him," whispered Mustafa into Kaja's ear.

"No!" Kaja screamed hysterically. "He will pay for what he has done. I want his friends to look upon his dead body in the morning." Then he grabbed Richard by his hair and pointed to Ballew, "He can't help you now. Just think of what awaits you tomorrow."

Jerry interrupted, "Kaja, let me kill Richard now."

"What's the matter, Jerry? You worried about what he might do to you again?" Richard challenged, clinging to anything that might irritate his one-time friend. He knew his time was up, and he regretted not being able to kill Jerry. At least he could make him feel miserable.

"Shut up!" Jerry snapped. He stepped forward and slugged Richard in the face, bringing blood from his nose.

"Stop!" Kaja ordered, "They must see the Cajun's death before they die." A look and a snap of the finger brought Delacroix, scurrying for the squiggling brown burlap bag.

As Delacroix brought the bag to Kaja, Mustafa whispered to Kidane, "You did well. I did not see the Cajun."

Kidane had a strange look in his eyes, "I did not see him until he moved. Somehow he crawled past me and I never knew. I think he made a mistake when Kaja held the woman." He gave a sigh of partial relief, "I will feel better when this man is dead."

Mustafa was taken back by Kidane's words but nodded.

Delacroix prepared to open the bag when Kaja stepped up and grabbed the neck of the bag. "Abseen," Kaja said calmly. As Abseen walked forward Kaja looked Delacroix in the eyes, "My friend has expressed the desire to take over from here."

Delacroix shrugged his shoulders and gave the bag over to Abseen, who felt gingerly of the burlap bag until he found what he wanted. Slowly he worked the thing to the opening in the bag.

From the bag, Abseen withdrew a 3 foot water moccasin, which rapidly wound itself around the man's arm. In the process, the snake excreted putrid-smelling yellow feces along the man's arm, in an attempt to gain its release, but to no avail as Abseen continued to hold the poisonous snake just behind the head, with his thumb and forefinger. A sadistic smile crossed Kaja's face as he nodded approval.

The jaws were poised and open, with fangs extended forward, prepared to strike the first thing it touched.

Kaja rubbed his hands together, eagerly anticipating the surprise waiting for the Cajun. Abseen forced a small stick within the mouth of the snake and deadly venom dripped from the fangs as the snake worked the stick with its mouth.

"Now?" Abseen asked.

"Yes," said Kaja, nodding affirmatively. He turned to face the Cajun, "Where we lack the thorns and nails we will use the snakes."

Suddenly Richard and Kelli fully understood the reasons for the snakes. Richard shook his head in dismay and disgust.

Kelli screamed in horror, "No, please! You can't!"

Abseen moved the head of the snake near Ballew's chest, but Kaja momentarily stopped him. "Would you beg for this man's life?" he asked Kelli.

"Yes, please don't kill him," she pleaded.

A hand squeezed one of Kelli's firm breasts. Then Kaja bit at her nipple until it brought blood. She screamed in pain. "Kiss me," he demanded, "if you want your friend's life spared."

She responded, although every fiber of her body recoiled at the repulsive contact of her most assured executioner.

A triumphant laugh echoed from Kaja's lips, "Of course, you will do as I say." One step put him near the helpless Cajun. Reaching to the neckline of the Cajun's shirt, it took one simple motion for Kaja to rip the shirt from Ballew's body, exposing the muscular and tanned chest. Again Kaja nodded to Abseen.

Sadistically, Abseen moved near Ballew again. This time, Abseen would not stop. With the snake poised to strike over the right breast, Abseen let the fangs touch. Like touching a steel trap the fangs sunk deep into Ballew's chest.

Pulling the snake from its victim, Abseen gloated. He peered into what he expected would be eyes filled with terror. Instead, he found only a glare. The cold stare froze him in his tracks. But what terrified him more was the slow smile that creased the Cajun's face. The gray eyes of the Cajun showed revenge; not terror. A look Abseen had seen before, but never by one of his victims. The eyes had an unsettling effect upon Abseen. Then Ballew said something in his native dialect, aiming the words at Abseen.

Abseen turned to Delacroix, "What did he say?"

"He say 'one day the snakes bite you'," Delacroix replied.

"We must kill him now," said Abseen, pleading to Kaja.

"No," snapped Kaja, then demanded, "Again!"

Abseen returned the snake to the burlap bag and withdrew another from the bag of death and repeated the ceremony. Only this time, he used a cottonmouth, letting it bite into the thigh of the Cajun.

Kelli pleaded, unsuccessfully, as Kaja let Abseen continue. Another snake bit Ballew's arm, then the other arm. Again Abseen repeated the sadistic act. Ballew's head drooped and groans could be heard coming from his large frame.

Pleased with what he saw, Kaja stepped to the Cajun, grabbed his head and pulled it back, "This is what happens to those who interfere with Kaja Aboujawdeh."

Ballew managed a smile, "The money is within reach, but you will never find it. Only I know where it is hidden, and I will never tell."

The money! Kaja had forgotten the money in his desire to get revenge. He must find the money before the Cajun died.

Suddenly Kaja yelled, "Everyone fan out. We will comb this island until we find the money."

Kaja pointed to Abseen and Haddad. "Watch the Cajun. If anything happens--kill him!"

Grabbing Kelli by the hair, Kaja pulled viciously, pushing her toward the jungle-like growth. The sadness in her eyes as they turned upon Ballew halted Kaja and again he smiled. Kaja pulled on her arm and shoved her in Haddad's direction. Haddad wrapped his dirty hand in Kelli's hair and pulled her right arm up and behind her back.

Kaja changed his mind. "Abseen, you may continue with the Cajun. I will leave the woman so she can watch him die. If anyone enters the camp . . . kill them both." Again Kaja smiled, "But try to keep the Cajun alive until we return. I want to see his face when we bring back the money."

"I will wait here," said Mustafa.

"No!" yelled Kaja. "We will cover the entire area like a blanket. You will come with us."

Reluctantly, Mustafa followed Kaja's orders and fanned his men out in an effort to find the money. Kaja took the rest in a parallel direction.

"Bring the FBI man," Kaja said to Jerry with a wicked smile. "Should anything happen, at least you will have him."

Surrounded by the security of the others, he pushed Richard, hobbling on his bad leg, along in front of him.

Just that quick the small camp was deserted, except for Abseen and Haddad, who watched the Cajun and Kelli. All was quiet, save for Kelli's sobbing.

Adding to her torment, Abseen motioned for Haddad to hold her head so she would be forced to watch as he produced another snake from the bag. He held it near Ballew's neck, poised to strike. Abseen stood, not moving, so as to prolong Kelli's anguish. He returned the snake to the bag and searched for another. A fresh one more deadly. Soon he found another and held it near the Cajun's chest while he turned his eyes to enjoy Kelli's anguish.

Kelli knew this would mean his death and she wanted to turn her eyes away, but was unable even without Haddad. She watched in shocked disbelief as the Cajun unexpectedly raised his head-- alert, alive, and angry. Muscles in his shoulders and chest flexed and knotted beneath the smooth bronze skin and the board upon which he was impaled started to bend.

Abseen noticed a strange look in Kelli's eyes. Alerted to her eyes he turned too late to the thunderous cracking of wood. The tremendous strength of the Cajun broke the timber in half and two large hands sandwiched Abseen's head between them.

The Cajun knocked Abseen senseless. His limp body fell to the ground. Instantly, Haddad released his hold on Kelli and moved toward Ballew, knife drawn. Ballew was quicker as he spun about, catching his assailant full in the mouth with the edge of the board still tied to his arm. Haddad fell to the ground unconscious, his jaw shattered.

Everything happened so quickly and already Kelli was on her feet to aid Ballew. He appeared to have temporarily overcome the snake venom. But he was not okay. She watched him groan in pain and fall to his knees.

When she reached his side, she could see the venom was

taking effect. Quickly, she untied the boards.

Knowing the extreme danger of the situation, Ballew summoned his strength again. Not a word was uttered through the whole ordeal.

Kelli tried to hold her torn shirt to cover her breasts, which proved a useless endeavor. With a reassuring smile, Ballew removed his thin vest and offered it to Kelli, and she slipped it on quickly. The jacket seemed to restore some of her confidence. No longer exposed, she was ready to leave.

Ballew walked to where his hat lay and, bending over, he removed it from the dirt, returning it to its rightful place. Then he took the burlap bag full of snakes and carried it to where Abseen lay groaning in the marsh grass. He rolled Abseen to his back then sat across his chest, pinning both arms to the ground.

"Ballew, please! Let's leave before they return," Kelli begged.

Ballew did not answer as he continued to straddle Abseen's body. He held the bag of snakes in one hand, and, with the other hand, shook Abseen's mouth to bring him around.

Slowly Abseen regained his senses only to look upon the determined countenance of the Cajun he had intended to kill only moments before. Now Abseen was at the mercy of the Cajun--and he had none.

The gray eyes looked through Abseen and sent a cold chill through his entire frame.

"One day, the snakes will bite you," Ballew said to Abseen. Then he pulled the bag open.

Hopelessly, Abseen tried to wriggle free but could not. Although he was unable to understand the Cajun dialect, he recognized the same words he had heard earlier. The snakes were about to be his. Abseen let loose a hair-raising, terrified, blood-curdling scream, as the bag slipped over his head.

Instantly Ballew tied a knot in the bag snugly against Abseen's neck. Abseen tried vainly to wriggle free. Only then did Ballew remove himself from the terror-stricken man.

Kelli was shocked for a brief moment, but that was all. Screams coming from within the bag seemed to ring of justice.

Ballew retrieved his knife, rifle, and bow, and grabbed Kelli's hand and ran quickly from the scene. He paused only long enough to retrieve the oil belonging to Delacroix. The oil would protect them from the savage onslaught of mosquitoes during the night. Soon the poison from the snakes would weaken him to where he would be unable to continue. In the distance, the sound of men returning to the site of the unnerving yells was obvious. He needed to find a place for them to hide. The same place where he had hidden the money.

Terrified, Abseen scrambled to his feet, pulling furiously at the knotted cord around his neck, running aimlessly about the campsite, screaming. Within the darkness of the bag, the angry snakes lashed out. One snake locked onto his jugular vein, never releasing its hold.

Finally, Abseen stumbled and fell, his body seized with convulsions from the enormous amounts of venom injected into his body. His screams ceased.

The snakes within the burlap bag continued biting at the face of their lifeless victim.

Chapter 10

Escape on Devil's Island

Kaja and Mustafa argued as they directed the men to cover the area in what was proving a vain search for the money. Kaja was about to interject when sounds in the distance made them freeze in place and listen. From the direction of the camp they heard a scream, a scream of terror like none had heard before.

"The camp!" yelled Mustafa and Kidane simultaneously. They broke into a run in the camp's direction, followed closely by the others.

When they arrived, they saw Abseen, still quivering in his final death throes. Nearby lay Haddad, moaning, writhing in pain, choking on his own blood. His lower jaw, fractured on both sides, hung limp on his neck like a hinged bar door. Three teeth were missing and on the right side the bone stuck through his cheek. His tongue flopped in the air, no longer able to find its former resting place. Haddad went into shock. The men rolled him to his side to prevent his lungs from continuing to fill with the blood flowing through the wound created by the bone of his lower jaw.

The Cajun and the woman were nowhere to be found. They had disappeared. And so had Dragun's weapons.

"Impossible! He is near death," said Kaja.

Mustafa sneered, "Maybe you have underestimated him . . . maybe he is still alive!"

* * *

Kelli breathed hard as Ballew pulled her deeper into Devil's Island. Determination pushed Ballew to his destination, but, as to where, Kelli was unaware. Suddenly he slowed, reached out, and grabbed a frail dandelion, pulling roots and all from the ground. Ballew shook the dandelion violently, casting the thousands of soft thistledown seedlings into the air. Again he started to run, and as he ran, he broke the dandelion in half and rubbed its juices over the snake bites. He stripped the leaves casting the stalk aside, shoved them into the leather pouch at his side, and with his hand, worked them into a pulpy green mass. Ballew grabbed another dandelion and repeated the process. In mid-stride he yanked a 4 foot high chicory from the soft earth, breaking away the azure-blue flower's root. The same chicory he used in a mixture of his Cajun coffee, Ballew immediately bit the thick bulbous root. Again he rubbed the sap from the stem onto his wounds. He sucked from the stem and swallowed and shoved more leaves into the pouch, along with portions of the stem.

Kelli knew Ballew was using remedies of the swamp to treat the venom from the snakes. A swamp person's way of healing, but now Kelli was afraid the cures would fail, and he would die.

"You must stop and rest before the poison kills you," she pleaded.

"It is too late. Besides, if the poison stays in the muscle, the muscle will rot," he said as he continued to drag her through the thick growth of Devil's Island.

Abruptly they came to the edge of the island, and before them lay a large expanse of water, dotted by small islands filled with trees and large cypress, from which hung the ever-present Spanish moss. The closest island was separated by more than 100 feet of water, but, growing on the island was a spectacular cypress rising from the water's edge, exposing the massive root system. Ten feet above the water, it split equally in two directions like a giant slingshot.

Ballew leaned his rifle against a tree and searched the nearby growth. For a moment, he wavered and fell to his knees as the snake venom continued to take effect. Again he forced himself to move on. Eventually he found what he searched for among broken branches and decaying leaves littering the ground; a branch straight and long, nearly 8 feet in length. Ballew bent the branch and, satisfied with its strength, he sat on the ground and removed his handmade boots, then laced them together.

"Put around your neck," he said, handing his boots to Kelli. Then he handed her the rifle. "Hold rifle above water."

"Please stop, Ballew. You need to rest."

"Quick!" said Ballew, bending down and motioning for her to ride on his back. She did as he demanded but would have refused if she had known his destination was to cross the expanse of water to the small island with the strange cypress.

"You're crazy, go back before we drown," she pleaded.

"Not drown," he said.

The water rose quickly to his waist. Still, he continued to probe ahead with his new found pole. Suddenly he dropped in the water to his chin but a moment later he walked out and the water was around his chest. Kelli managed to keep the rifle dry and with her free right arm squeezed ever tighter around Ballew's neck. A few more strides and the water was again around his waist.

Cautiously, he moved through the water, feeling ahead with the long stick like a blind man searching the safety of the curb with his cane so he might remain on the sidewalk. Ballew probed with the blind experience and confidence of a lifetime in the Louisiana swamps, searching out the potentially deadly loggerhead turtle. At one point he seemed to find something, and Kelli could tell he felt it with the pole. Slowly, he moved back then around what he found and continued searching with the long stick.

Curiosity took hold of Kelli, "What did you find?"

"Loggerhead," he said.

"A what?"

"You would call it a turtle . . . snapping turtle."

Then her thoughts returned to the huge turtle shell she had seen hanging on the wall inside Ballew's house. "Like the one in your house?"

"Yes."

The suddenness of her legs pulling up above Ballew's waist and squeezing tightly brought an unexpected groan from his lips. "Sorry," she said as she loosened her hold. "Why the stick?"

"So I can feel shell, then I will go behind it."

"You can tell?"

"It be easy, the ridges on the shell point away from its head."

"Was the one you just found as big?"

"Almost."

The information shocked Kelli, "It could bite your toes off."

Somehow Ballew managed a laugh. "That one could bite my foot off if he want."

Kelli shuddered at the thought, and unexpectedly Ballew's body tensed, turned half around in the water, then continued his backward motion in the direction of the small island.

An alligator nearly 6 feet in length, slithered through the water in their direction, and Ballew moved quickly away from the large reptile, no longer concerned with detecting the loggerheads.

The distance between them and the alligator continued to close faster than the distance between them and the island.

Lowering Kelli into the water, he took the rifle and pointed to the small island. "Go!" Then he returned his attention to the present danger.

Ballew raised the rifle to his shoulders, but what he heard gave him pause. Not far away he could detect the sounds of men. Kaja and his men had begun the search. He could not risk a shot, so he reached for his knife. But he quickly rejected the idea. If Kaja's men found the alligator, they would find them. He had to force the alligator away.

All of this passed through his mind before Kelli managed to reach the island. "Here, be quick!" he ordered, throwing her the rifle and turning to confront the creature. He continued to move toward the safety of the island, always keeping himself between Kelli and the alligator.

Time had run out as the alligator came within 2 feet of Ballew. Side-stepping the charge, Ballew slammed a fist between the alligator's eyes. Moving quickly, he clasped his powerful arms about the long mouth of the alligator.

Instantly, the alligator spun in the water to dislodge its attacker. Horrified, Kelli turned to watch as Ballew disappeared beneath the murky waters. It seemed an eternity to Kelli before Ballew's head, with the baseball cap still in place, popped above the surface. He still clung to the alligator. Slowly he wrestled the creature toward the island, as its tail slashed savagely in all directions. Once safely to the small island, he gave a mighty heave, throwing the alligator back into the waters of the Atchafalaya.

Exhausted, sick, and his remaining strength gone, he stumbled to the island, pausing long enough to remove the remains of his Spider Man shirt. He tossed the pieces as far as he could in the direction of another island.

With his strength fading, Ballew collapsed on the ground. Kelli moved to his side and pulled him to his feet, but could see he was disoriented and drained. Now they were stuck on a small island where anyone could see them.

"Where, Ballew? Where do we go?"

One more time Ballew managed to gather enough strength to continue. He said nothing, but pointed to the large tree and moved in its direction, with Kelli close behind.

When they reached the base of the large cypress, Ballew motioned Kelli to place her foot in his cupped hands. He groaned through the pain when he heaved her high into the tree. Kelli reached for the tree where it forked in two directions. She managed to take hold and pull her body into the safety of the cypress. Deformed by lightning, the fork formed a small compartment high in the tree. Time and insects had worn holes, so water drained from the hollow, making it a safe dry hiding place. Instantly Kelli recognized the briefcase containing the money Ballew had taken from Kaja.

Now Kelli's thoughts were of Ballew and his situation below. She watched as he crumbled to the ground on all fours and vomited. Unable to do anything, she continued to watch the effects of the venom on Ballew. His breathing became labored, and she could hear his groans.

Breaths came in short, quick gasps, but he quit vomiting. He tried to stand up, but wavered like a drunken man, then lost his balance and tumbled backwards to the ground. Kelli started down from the tree, but Ballew stopped her.

"No!" yelled Ballew.

She stopped her descent and did as he said. Ballew tried to stand and again could not retain his balance. This time he crawled to the base of the tree and, clinging to it for support, slowly moved up its side toward Kelli and safety. He extended the bow and rifle to her, which she put safely within the tree.

Slowly Ballew made his ascent, once losing his grip and sliding down and another time, pausing to vomit. The snake venom had control, but somehow he managed to near the edge in the fork.

With safety near, Ballew started to lose his hold and slide toward the base of the tree. Kelli reached as far as she could, determined not to let him fall again, and clung ferociously to his wrist.

Kelli clutched his arm and tears fell from her eyes, "I won't let you go. Come on, Ballew, just a little more."

Suddenly the strain of holding his body ceased and she opened her eyes to see a slight smile on his face. Ballew had managed to get a grip on the tree. This time he reached the edge and managed to pour his body into the hold of the cypress.

With care she turned him on his back. His eyes no longer held the strength and power to which she had become so accustomed. For now, Ballew Dragun was as helpless as a baby. She removed the container of grease from about his neck.

Ballew grasped Kelli about the shoulder and pulled her near him so he could whisper in her ear. She did so willingly, for his tremendous strength eluded him, and he was unable to pull her near without her help.

"This," he said, pulling part of the green pulpy mass from the bag at his side. "Rub it on the bites." Then he pulled the stem of the chicory and its root out of the bag, "Squeeze this so the juices go in my mouth." Ballew pointed to the other side of the bag, unable to remove its contents. "Inside."

Inside Kelli found three fruits the size of apples and dozens of berries and a piece of dried meat. She looked at Ballew, and he nodded. "You eat," he said.

"Boat," he mumbled and pointed down below.

Kelli stood and for the first time and saw the boat in which he had first rescued her. Concealed very carefully, she barely discerned the boat's form. From the ground it would go unnoticed.

"If I die . . . "

"No you won't die," she cried as tears came to her eyes.

Gently he wiped the tears from her cheek with his hand, "Belle, don't cry. If I die, you must escape. Go that direction." He made a gesture with his hand and passed out.

Kelli held his limp hand against her face and continued to cry. She slipped the jacket from her shoulders and removed her torn shirt.

Voices alerted her and she stopped her work. A small hole in the cypress afforded her a view of Devil's Island and where they had crossed earlier.

On the bank were Kaja and his men. She recognized Jerry, who pushed Richard before him. The large powerful man, called Mustafa, gave orders to one of his men. The man started to cross the water to where they lay hidden.

Kelli wiped the tears from her face, and with fierce determination, she grabbed Ballew's rifle and checked the chamber. Satisfied, she continued her vigil through the small hole.

* * *

"Find them and kill **her** if you must, but bring the Cajun back to me!" Kaja yelled.

"It is time we killed them all!" Mustafa roared, for he was eager to pursue such excellent quarry. He looked forward to pursuing and catching the man called Ballew Dragun. A formidable opponent, indeed, the man of the swamps. Never had Mustafa hunted and killed a man worthy of the chase. Now something told Mustafa to kill the man and give him no quarter. Something else in him hoped Dragun would recover and make the chase more exciting. Mustafa already had seen the Cajun's capabilities, and he felt Dragun **would** survive.

"I'm gonna kill him," Jerry said to Kaja as he pulled his .45 and pointed it at Richard.

Looking down the barrel of the .45 was nothing new to Richard, but he never ceased to be amazed at how terrifying it was each time it happened. His mind worked quickly, trying to find a way in which he could extend his life. It was a wild shot, but it might be his only chance.

"I hope you do, 'cause when Ballew finds out what you did to me . . . ," Richard looked at Abseen and shook his head. "Hell, Jerry, he'll probably cut your balls off."

"You sonofabitch," mumbled Jerry.

"Stop!" ordered Kaja. "This Ballew Dragun has the woman. He rescued her. It seems reasonable to believe he will try to rescue Staley. If Staley is dead, there will be no reason for the Cajun to come into camp. We will keep him alive for a while. This time we will not be caught off guard."

"We are ready," interrupted Mustafa.

The men divided into three groups--one led by Mustafa, another by Kidane, and the third by Salil, with Delacroix and Mamou.

They spread apart and went parallel to the tracks Mustafa found. They needed to cover the island as far as they could before the sun set. Already the shadows grew longer.

Searching the island was a larger task than anyone imagined except Delacroix, who knew the island, and Mustafa and Kidane, who knew of jungle hunts and death. Men were getting stung, bitten, and lost. Still, they encountered no serious casualties.

While the others found nothing, Mustafa managed to find and follow the Cajun's trail. The clear trail confused Mustafa and he passed it off to the fact the man was injured. Near sunset they came to an opening overlooking an expanse of water dotted by many islands. The trail ended at the water's edge. After a closer investigation of the surrounding bank, one of the men discovered Dragun's torn and tattered shirt.

Some believed the pair to be dead, but Kaja demanded to find proof before they left. Since they held Richard Staley hostage, the possibility still existed that Dragun might return to save his friend. Mustafa also had made a mental note after the incident with the snakes: it would take a few days for him to recover--if at all. Also, if he died, they would detect scavengers picking over Dragun's body. Mustafa knew they must find him while he was weak and helpless.

With keen eyes, Mustafa studied the islands and decided if they crossed, it would be to the island with the cypress shaped like a 'Y.' Mustafa sent Azad and Fawad to that island. The two started to wade across the expanse of water, while the rest watched and waited.

Suddenly Azad disappeared beneath the water, but in an instant his head bobbed above the surface. The men onshore laughed when they realized he had just stepped into a deeper area. Fawad gave him a playful hit in the arm. They continued through the water when suddenly Fawad, who had laughed at Azad for submerging himself beneath the waters, let out a spine-tingling shriek.

A sharp pain shot up from his foot as some unseen force hidden in the swamp jerked at his foot, penetrated the thick leather boot, and pulled him partially under the water. Azad came quickly to his aid, discarding his weapon to help his friend. Because of the commotion created by Fawad, Azad failed to hear the warning shouts from the bank, nor did he see the alligator gliding swiftly and silently through the waters of the swamp on a path toward Azad's unguarded back.

The angry alligator had confronted another similar creature as these two men and lost. This time the alligator would not be careless.

The men tried to alert Azad and Fawad. Azad looked up to see the men waving wildly, so he smiled and waved back. Fawad saw the alligator first, and he screamed in response, then floundered in the water while trying to move back toward the others. The water turned red from the blood of his foot.

Fawad's effort to escape warned Azad of the trouble, but

Mustafa's warning shout alerted Azad to the real danger. He turned too late and found himself staring into the gaping jaws of the thing close enough to touch. In an effort to push the alligator away, he shoved his arm at the alligator's head and, in doing so, inserted his right arm into the wide open mouth.

The jaws came crashing down with such force his arm broke in four places, from his elbow to his wrist. The screams stopped each time the alligator would spin and take Azad beneath the water. Each time he popped above the water, he screamed hysterically, only to be taken below the Atchafalaya again and again. The alligator continued to drown the victim. The vicious motions tore Azad's arm from his body, momentarily freeing him.

His eight comrades were relieved when they saw his head break the water and he stood erect, but what they saw silenced them immediately. Azad just stood in the water looking at the stub near his elbow and watched streams of blood pump into the air. In shock he was unable to move.

Fawad managed to scramble to shore. The end of his boot bitten off, taking the large toe with it. Somewhere beneath the waters, a loggerhead had part of a boot and a single toe as souvenirs. But Fawad was lucky--attacked only by a small loggerhead turtle.

They yelled for Azad to come to shore, but he stood like a statue, staring blankly at the stub where once was an arm. Already, three men, including Mustafa, started wading in his direction in the hopes of cheating the alligator of its meal.

The alligator was not to be deprived of its victim this time, and would not be cheated out of what was his. With one gulp, the alligator swallowed Azad's forearm and returned for the rest. This time the alligator came from below and locked onto Azad just below the waist. Again the alligator started its wild gyrations, trying to drown its victim.

Mustafa halted his men; stunned, they watched as Azad would break the surface each time the alligator completed a roll. Each time he broke the surface, he could be seen swinging the stub at the alligator as though the arm still existed. Suddenly the thrashing stopped, and Azad ceased to surface. Gone. Taken below to be stored beneath a dead cypress until a time when the alligator would be hungry.

A deadly silence prevailed over the men on the return to camp. They found the Cajun's trail but were unable to locate him and still they paid for it dearly. Two men carried Fawad. Azad was dead and Fawad crippled.

The toll: three dead, Richard mused. He fought hard to repress a smile as he kept count.

* * *

When the men retreated, Kelli relaxed and lay down the rifle. Kelli felt the tension release and sheer exhaustion overwhelmed her.

She had felt like cheering when she saw the alligator's victory. What had happened to her? Did she no longer have feelings? The men got what they deserved. How could Ballew, injured, handle the same problems and come away without a mark?

Thoughts raced through her head as she took the bruised poultice and spread it over Ballew's bites. She ate a fruit and a half dozen berries to maintain her energy and strength. The fruit was refreshing and gave her a quick lift.

She barely finished the fruit when Ballew began to shake. First she removed his cap and placed it to the side. Next she propped his head in her lap and rubbed his forehead, brushing his hair with her hand. Softly she spoke to him, knowing unconscious people could hear voices. She wanted to make sure he knew she was near. She smeared the foul-smelling grease on Ballew and herself, preventing the hordes of mosquitoes from attacking. The drone of their countless numbers helped to relax her body and soon she was asleep, dreaming of the cornfields of Kansas.

Chapter 11

Labyrinth

Darkness settled on the subdued campsite when the final group, led by Salil and Delacroix, arrived. They fared no better than the others, led by Mustafa and Kidane. One man held his arm, having cut it on a large cypress. Another was covered in sand and silt to his neck after wandering into quicksand. Except for the fast action of Mamou, who saw the problem and managed to extend the helpless man a branch to pull him free, the deceiving sands almost sucked him below the Atchafalaya.

"What happened?" snapped Kaja at Delacroix. "How did you lead my men into trouble?"

The search had evolved into chaos and not brought the revenge he had sought on Dragun any closer. "I come to find Dragun, not to watch your men. Your men not know how to take care of themselves in the swamp."

"My men are the best," cautioned Kaja.

"If I not here, your men not find way out of Atchafalaya. They get lost, they die in the swamps of the Atchafalaya."

"Stop!" interjected Mustafa, "we need to work together, not against one another." Then looking straight at Delacroix, he said, "It is one man we seek. He bleeds just like the rest of us . . . remember that! Tomorrow we shall start to cover this island and when we find him, we will kill him. The woman will only slow his progress. She will be the weakness that will enable us to find him. So, for now, I want every man to rest. Kidane and I will take the first watch."

"Grease, who take my grease?" Delacroix asked accusingly.

After a long pause, no one came forth. "Do what you can,"

said Mustafa. "The man you seek may have taken it. There is nothing you can do now. Maybe this will make you hunt Dragun better in the morning."

Delacroix slunk away, angry with the turn of events and a little shaken that Dragun managed to escape. He had seen the snake bites. Dragun was in no condition to go anywhere. Not only had he managed to escape, he also had broken the board and removed the large nails from his hands. Was he more than a man? Delacroix tried to discard the last thought and concentrated on a logical place to capture Dragun.

Close behind followed the short and stumpy Mamou. Hearing a sound from behind, he darted to Delacroix's side and checked the path behind. "Do you think he **is** dead?"

"Who?"

"Dragun! You think demons help him?"

"Mamou, watch your tongue. No demons help him escape," Delacroix said as he bent near his gear and prepared his sleeping bag for the night.

"These men bad. We leave now. Something bad happen," Mamou mumbled as he slid into his bag, fully clothed.

"We stay until Dragun dead. If something bad, it probably be another moccasin like last one what sleep with you," mocked Delacroix, remembering the time a snake slithered into Mamou's bag when he slept.

Delacroix heard a zipper as it raced along the edge of Mamou's sleeping bag, sealing him safely inside. Mumbling came from within the bag and Delacroix chuckled to himself, then lay his rifle, cocked and ready, near his head. Soon they were both asleep.

Two men spoke quietly at the edge of the camp, making plans for the next day. "Remember where we ran into the alligator today?" Mustafa asked.

"Yes," came Kidane's answer.

"I believe the man Dragun was near. I want you to find the place and set a trap near where the men tried to cross.

"What kind of trap? Catch him alive?" Kidane asked, pointing toward Kaja.

"He can no longer make sensible decisions. Kaja is like woman. We do not want Dragun alive anymore. I want you to set the trap we used in Angola."

Kidane smiled to himself. "Ah, yes. Make sure it throws him against the spikes. Once the rope snares his feet, he is dead.

If the woman is with him, she might fall into the trap."

"I hope it is not her. I would like to have my way with her . . . before I kill her."

"I would like her also."

"She is yours . . . when I am finished," said Mustafa with a smile.

Both men laughed quietly. Then Kidane disappeared to prepare the trap. A breeze started to blow from the south soon after Kidane departed. A little while later, it started to rain. Lightning flashed and thundered in from the south.

* * *

Drops of rain awakened Kelli from a deep sleep. The droplets were both hated and welcomed. She feared the breeze and the dampness might worsen Ballew's condition, but, for the moment, she welcomed the rain as it increased in force. Removing the vest, she tied two corners to the cypress forming a receptacle for the water. It filled quickly and she drank her fill.

When she finished, she propped Ballew's head against the tree and tried to force the water into his mouth. She was elated when he swallowed and coughed. Twice she repeated it, and he continued to take the life-saving liquid into his body.

Just as quickly the rain stopped, while a breeze from the south stirred the leaves of the trees and the rain-heavy Spanish moss. The limbs of the cypress prevented a chilling wind from reaching the pair. Ballew began to shiver, more from the snake venom than the rain. The temperature had dropped into the high seventies.

With all their clothing soaking wet, Kelli replaced the vest to prevent a direct chilling burst of wind and found her body generated warmth even within the wetness of the vest.

Never had Kelli seen anyone without color in his face--so helpless--so death like!

He started to shiver and she knew she had to warm him. Laying him flat within the large cypress, she began to rub his arms and legs. The tedious chore was more work than her small hands could handle against Ballew's huge physique, then another idea quickly came to mind. Not only would it help him, but it would also warm her.

With his shirt already missing, she opened her vest, exposing her chest. She pressed firmly against his chest and, although chilled, she could feel the warmth of his body. Then she wrapped her arms about him, laying her head near his neck. She pulled her head up and admired the handsome features of his face. Although pale and ghostly, they were handsome nonetheless. Gently, she kissed his cheek, then kissed his lips for a long time.

"I think I like you a lot, Mister Cajun. Kelli Dragun?" she mused. "What an insane thought."

She laid her head near his neck and, still clinging to him, fell asleep.

She neither saw nor heard the man who worked silently and quickly, building a trap across the water separating their island from Devil's Island.

The thin leather gloves Kidane wore enabled him to work precisely and quickly without harm to his hands. Before the sun rose, he had finished and returned to camp, the deadly trap finished and set, waiting for its victim.

* * *

The sun rose over the swamp, bringing steam from the waters of the Atchafalaya. The morning sun bore down intensely on the waking swamp.

A ray of sunlight slid through a small hole in the large cypress, waking Kelli as the beam crossed her face. She stretched and was thankful for the warmth of the sun. She was becoming accustomed to the heat and humidity of the swamps in Louisiana.

Kelli stood within the bough of the cypress and surveyed the area to see if any of Kaja's men remained, or might be hidden. Assured no one was near, she looked about and noticed Ballew's small boat. The thought occurred to her that Ballew might have food or water within the boat. With this in mind, she hung her body over the side of the large cypress and dropped to the ground below.

The search uncovered a leather pouch with water. Thirst was her primary concern and she drank her fill. A metal box revealed pants, shoes, three shirts--two of which were emblazoned with Spider Man--and a small blanket. She found dried meat in a small leather pouch and three rice fritters in a bag sealed with a leather strip.

She broke a fritter in half and ate it, along with a strip of meat. After collecting all the food and clothes, she returned to the tree. To her dismay, she found no way of gaining access to where

Ballew lay. The tree had no footholds and she couldn't jump high enough to reach the intersection in the "Y" of the cypress.

Kelli was stranded, with no way to reach Ballew. For a moment she panicked, then she regained her senses and tried to figure a way she could climb the tree. She returned to the boat and found it tied to the small island by a rope over 8 feet in length. She removed the rope and returned to the cypress. If she could wedge the rope in the "Y," she could pull herself up.

After a quick search, she found a small sturdy branch she hoped would support her weight and tied it to the end of the rope. Kelli threw it near the slit in the tree. It seemed like she would never get the rope to slip into the slot. Finally the rope fell into place. Kelli pulled slowly, until the rope released no more slack. Then she pulled firmly and lifted her body from the ground. The rope held.

Kelli gathered the food and tossed it up and into the safety of the tree. Next, she tied the metal box and water pouch to the other end of the rope. Once they were secured, she pulled herself up into the bough of the large cypress. Soon she had the water and clothes within the tree.

With a tremendous amount of effort, she managed to slip a Spider Man shirt over Ballew's head. Once in place, she covered him with the small blanket. She took the other shirt given to him by Happy Jak and slid it over her shoulders. It felt good to have on dry clothes again.

Kelli ate another fritter, then tried to force some water between Ballew's lips with little success. Finally, he took a little of the water. She relaxed momentarily, but continued her vigil.

Ballew trembled as though he were chilled. Without hesitation, Kelli slid beneath the blanket and wrapped her arms about him to keep him warm. Exhausted from her early morning efforts, she soon fell asleep.

* * *

Morning brought a strange quiet over the camp. At one end were Kidane and Mustafa, and at the other, Mamou and Delacroix; in the middle, the others.

Separating themselves from the others, Mamou and Delacroix drank coffee.

"They are dangerous," Mamou said. "We leave, yes?"

"No," Delacroix said flatly as he sipped the coffee. "We not leave until Dragun is dead."

"Forget Dragun. The men are crazy with to kill. They kill everybody."

"Good . . . when Dragun dead, we leave." Delacroix rolled up his sleeping bag and put it away.

Slowly the rest of the camp stirred, but Kidane and Mustafa were already awake. To the far side of the camp, they had coffee and breakfast started.

"The trap?" Mustafa asked. Kidane nodded as he poured a cup of coffee and sat back on his haunches. "Put out the bear traps when we finish."

Kidane smiled and nodded affirmatively. "If you are right and he is where you think he is, he will be dead before I have to set those traps."

"Maybe," said Mustafa as he ground his teeth and rubbed his chin. "The Cajun should already be dead from the work Abseen administered . . . but it is Abseen who is dead, not the Cajun. We have underestimated our enemy this time. Kidane, I want you to beware of this Cajun."

* * *

When Ballew first opened his eyes, he was keenly aware of the smell and feel of Kelli's hair near his face. Her arms were wrapped about him. With his left arm curled around her, he brought his right arm around so he could hold her. Then he slid his left hand along her back, gently rubbing with his fingers. Slowly he rubbed her neck and ran his fingers through her long hair.

She responded to his caress with a soft sigh. Her eyes flickered and a smile lit her face when she saw that Ballew's color had returned.

"Oh, Ballew! I thought you were dead!" she said as she reached up, kissing him on the face and hugging him tighter than ever. She pushed away, concerned about his condition, "Are you all right?"

"No," he said, barely able to speak, "but I am alive."

As he pulled her firmly toward him and kissed her on the lips, he could feel his strength returning quickly.

"Ballew!" she said, pulling away. But he quickly pulled her near.

"I thought I might die and I didn't want for to worry you for nothing, but . . . " then he paused unable to continue.

"But what?" she asked as she relaxed in his grasp.

"I must tell you . . . I love you, Kelli," Ballew said sincerely.

Kelli laughed, "This is **crazy**; I can't believe it."

"Not crazy!" said Ballew, hurt by the laugh.

It did not take much to discern the hurt in Ballew's gray eyes. "I'm sorry, Ballew. I wasn't laughing at you, but rather myself," she said with a loving smile as she slid her hands under his Spider Man T-shirt, pushing it up and revealing his muscular chest. She kissed him twice on the chest, then looked him straight in the eyes as her heart began to race. "You see, I love you!"

Kelli smothered his face with kisses and he responded. His huge, strong arms pressed her gently to him and for the rest of the morning, they remained in each other's loving embrace.

It seemed like they would never release their hold on each other--as though the love would disappear if one of them let go. Ballew pushed away first.

"Kelli, we must leave. I need real food, if I am to get my strength back," he said, trying to rise on shaky legs.

Kelli steadied him as he stood up. He stretched and his body shuddered. With color back in his face and his strength returning swiftly, Ballew moved about in the tree.

Kelli noticed the loss first, "The boat is gone!" She fell to her knees, crying, "It's my fault. I got the rope from the boat. It must have drifted away."

A quick survey of the area and Ballew understood what had happened. Kelli managed to bring the things from the boat, using the rope to return. In the process, the boat--no longer anchored to shore--had drifted away. He pulled Kelli near and hugged her.

"You did more than expected. For sure we must leave now and try to take one of their boats, or maybe we can find mine," Ballew noted.

Kelli laughed and told him what she had done was nothing compared to the anxiety she felt watching Kaja and his men while Ballew lay unconscious. She told him about the men trying to cross and what happened to Azad.

Ballew knew the alligator had probably stashed Azad's body beneath the root system of a nearby cypress, waiting to use it for a future meal.

"That was a brave thing you did," he said. "Forget the boat; we will return to Devil's Island. Everything we need is

there."
　　His words reassured Kelli, and she ceased to cry over the loss. Ballew lowered himself to the ground. After Kelli lowered everything but the money, she hung from the edge and Ballew eased her gently to the ground.

　　The sun was directly overhead when Ballew, probing ahead with a pole and Kelli riding piggyback, waded across the narrow strip of water separating them from Devil's Island, the same area where one of Kaja's men had lost his life the day before. Their return to the island was uneventful, much to Kelli's relief.

　　When they reached Devil's Island, Ballew lowered Kelli to the ground, then Ballew removed the bow from his shoulder and Kelli dropped the food and water slung over her shoulders. Instead of slinging the rifle about his shoulders, he decided to carry it and the bow in his hands, so his clothes would dry quicker. The decision would save his life.

　　His weakened condition made him oblivious to the trap ahead. They had taken only a few steps when Ballew was jerked viciously from his feet and thrown to the ground. A rope pulled his body, twisting and pitching, along the ground.

　　Kelli screamed and started to run after the man she loved. She had taken a single step when her blood ran cold. Ballew was dragged along the ground, lifted into the air, then flung toward the wooden spikes placed in a position to impale his body and cause his death. Kelli could do nothing but watch in horror.

　　When Ballew hit the ground, he discarded his rifle and bow. Freeing him from the entanglements of the weapons, with the quickness of a cat he responded to the danger, grabbing his knife and reaching for his feet to cut the rope that bound him, but in his weakened condition, he failed the first time. Yet his mind was completely occupied with his imminent death and not his weakness from the snake bites. In another moment, his life would be lost forever if he failed.

　　With a Herculean effort, he bent his body forward, toward his feet, grasping at the rope. As the rope lifted him into the air, he saw the spikes intended for him. Clinging to the rope with his right hand, he lunged forward as far as he could and, with all his strength, swung his knife in a mighty arc. The razor-sharp knife cut the cords, dropping him to the ground, where he rolled to the base of the tree just below the spikes waiting for their victim. Only inches above him projected the long wooden spikes.

No sooner had his body come to rest than Kelli was beside him, her arms wrapped about his neck, and he could hear her sobbing.

Ballew moved to a sitting position and hugged Kelli. "I am okay."

"They are going to kill us. We're not safe," she moaned.

Again the giant Cajun reassured her, "Nothing happen while I am here." It took gentle words and reassurance, but he managed to get her to release her hold. "It just a trap. Next time I will be ready," he said firmly. "Now we must go--before they return."

Quickly, he gathered his weapons and coaxed Kelli along, leading her into the thick growth of Devil's Island. Ballew thought the terrorists might have heard Kelli scream, and on that possibility, he intended to place as much distance between them and the trap as possible.

* * *

Mustafa and Kidane, alerted by the scream, ran quickly in the direction of the sounds. It took a moment for the others to respond, but they were soon following behind the two men who had disappeared ahead of the search party, intent on finding the source of the screams.

Arriving at the trap before the others, Mustafa and Kidane deciphered the clues near the trap set by Kidane the night before. They understood quickly what had taken place.

"How could it be the same man bitten by the snakes only the day before? He would be too weak to have the strength to do what was done here. It cannot be the same," mumbled Kidane, somewhat in awe at what he saw.

"I would agree with you, Kidane," Mustafa assured, "but there is no one else on the island. The only one who could have possibly escaped from your trap is the Cajun." Mustafa could only shake his head and point to the pair of tracks, "The woman is with him. Dragun is more than you and I anticipated. He may be harder to kill than we thought."

Next to arrive were Delacroix and Mamou, followed by Kaja and a few of the others.

Kaja barked instructions to Kamdar, "Tell the others, the Cajun is alive!"

"Be on the alert for the man and the woman," Mustafa interrupted.

"How did they get away?" Kaja asked.
Delacroix held the rope used for the trap, and pointed to the end, "Cut. Dragun escape from trap. We must find him."
"First, we will organize groups to search the perimeter," snapped Mustafa.
"I want them dead," Kaja said.
"So do I, but it would be foolish to follow him blindly. We must prepare and be ready. Send someone to guard the boats. We can't let him escape, just because we didn't have the presence of mind to cover our backsides."
"Yes . . . let's prepare," said Kaja, with a smile on his face. "Send another man to take an airboat and circle the island. Find Dragun's boat and bring it back. When he is strong enough, he will try to escape or free his FBI friend. This island is a maze--he could hide forever. We must force him to come to us."
"I can find him on my own," said Mustafa.
"You have not done well in that pursuit so far," Kaja admonished as he pointed to the cut rope. "Let's return and prepare."

* * *

The island seemed to have no end, running forever. Kelli thought her lungs would burst before they stopped. Suddenly Ballew stopped. Less than a hundred yards from them moved a search party. Pausing only briefly, Ballew took Kelli by the hand and led her in still another direction.
They came upon a small clearing within a cluster of thick growth. Here Ballew hesitated and collapsed to the ground. Falling to her knees, Kelli helped Ballew to his knees. The poison still held Ballew's body, but just the brief pause revived him.
"We must eat," he said wearily.
"Right, you need to eat," she replied with a frown on her face.
He smiled and nodded. Reaching into the divided pouch at his waist, he pulled out two flint stones and a fruit. He ate the fruit, reached back into the pouch, and pulled out the remains of the crushed dandelions and chicory, and rubbed then into the day-old snake bites.
She checked the wounds closely and was relieved when she failed to find any infection and only a slight inflammation.
"Do you want this?" asked Kelli, pulling one of the fritters

from the bag she carried.

"No, but we will need it later," Ballew responded.

Kelli had no idea as to his intentions for the seemingly useless fritters, but she did as he said and placed them back into the leather pouch.

After regaining some of their strength, they started again, this time at a much slower and more cautious pace. Soon they were near the water's edge. Ballew scouted the bank for the proper area and when he found it, he stopped.

"Are you hungry?" he asked.

"Yes, but what is there to eat?"

"Catfish."

"Great idea, but what are you gonna catch it with, your bare hands?"

Ballew smiled, "Maybe."

He removed his shoes which were made from the skins of alligators and snakes, then lowered himself into the water and waded along the bank, in water above his waist. Occasionally he would probe the bank with his feet and then his hands.

Kelli walked along the bank with her hands on her hips, "Okay, Mister Fisherman, how do you expect to catch one?"

This time Ballew managed a chuckle and held his arm in the air. Just then his eyes lit up, "Ah, I have found one."

"I suppose you intend to just grab him," she said with a snicker.

"No. I intend for him to grab me," Ballew said as though it was done every day. Then he dipped his shoulder to the water and groped along the bank. Suddenly his shoulder jerked beneath the water and his body shook. Startled by the suddenness of the actions, Kelli jumped back, stumbling and falling to the ground.

Ballew withdrew his arm slowly. Just above his wrist clung a huge two foot long catfish. It had swallowed Ballew's arm. Kelli struggled forward on all fours to where Ballew stood.

"My God, he swallowed your arm!" came her shocked response.

Ballew laughed, "No, it be me what have caught him."

He shook his arm until the giant catfish slid down his arm, so he could slip his fingers through the gills. Once he accomplished this, he stepped from the water and onto the dry bank beside Kelli.

Somewhat surprised, Kelli stood behind Ballew with her

hands splayed against his back, pushing him ahead and watching what he did. He slid the knife from the sheath and slit the fish's back just behind the head. Now lifeless, the catfish slid from his hand and dropped to the ground.

"We will start a fire and eat," he said.

"Won't they find us?" she asked, doubting her own fears, feeling safer with every passing moment she remained in the Cajun's presence.

With an inner calm always his, Ballew scanned the area. "No, the wind blows toward us. I will know when they come before they know we are near," he continued confidently.

Kelli said no more and joined him in gathering the wood. With enough wood collected, Ballew removed two stones from the pouch hanging at his side. After Ballew piled a clump of dried leaves together, he slapped the stones together a few times. The sparks from the flint caught the leaves, and smoke started to rise from the dried leaves. Bending his face near the smoke, he blew at the base. More smoke poured forth and Ballew piled more leaves on. The small pile burst into flames and to this he added small twigs. The flames spread and he added larger branches.

Deftly, the Cajun gutted and filleted the large catfish. At each end of the fire, he formed supports from the dried branches they found lying nearby. Between the supports and across the top of the fire, he laid another branch, from which protruded many smaller branches and from this he hung the fish.

Kelli supervised the cooking of the fish, turning it with the large knife. While she did this, Ballew disappeared, but soon returned with more of the wild herbs and plants growing abundantly in the swamp. Some herbs he squeezed onto the fish and another he cut and spread across the fish. He offered Kelli some of the wild onions and berries he had found. Both ate the berries and roots while they waited for the catfish to finish cooking.

With his knife, Ballew split a large branch and quickly smoothed the split side with the blade. These he used as plates, placing the finished fish upon the smooth part.

Kelli ate until she could eat no more. She thought the fish tasted delightful. Never had she used wild roots and herbs. Although hungry, she didn't think it prejudiced her opinion of the fish. Ballew propped against a tree and treated the snake bites as he had the day before. Kelli sat beside Ballew, leaned against his shoulder, and fell asleep.

Time slipped away from Kelli, but she awoke refreshed. Time meant nothing in the swamps of the Atchafalaya. She found Ballew's arms wrapped about her as were hers about him. How remarkable his recovery from the snake bites, she thought, and she attributed it to his physical condition and the Cajun remedies of herbs and plants he used. She attributed it in part to his resistance to the snake bites.

Ballew's eyes flickered and he opened them, alert and looking full into Kelli's face. With a slight smile he bent to her and kissed her tempting lips. She sighed and rested her head upon his chest, while he gently rubbed her back with his huge hands.

"What will you do when you leave?" Ballew asked.

"How can I ever leave, with these men following me?"

"They won't follow you forever."

"You're probably right--they'll kill me before I ever get out of this swamp."

"Not while I am here," Ballew assured Kelli.

For some reason she believed him, even in the situation she now found herself. "I suppose I will return to my writing. Why don't you come with me?"

"No. The swamp is home . . . I stay here."

"It's too dangerous here. You'd be safer in civilization."

He shook his head, "Are these men following you civilized? What of the FBI man Jerry. He wants you dead?"

"They aren't all like that," Kelli replied, and she shrugged, wondering if she were telling the truth.

Ballew shook his head. "No, I stay here. I know what the animals do and want. I take what I need and I know when to avoid things dangerous. Your civilization confuses me. I don't understand them."

"What about Happy Jak and Belle Rose?"

"They are my friends. They are not like the men that follow you."

The conversation ended and they gathered their weapons and gear and started to travel along the edge of the island. In the distance, they could hear an airboat approaching and they took cover. Hidden deep within the labyrinth of the Atchafalaya swamp, Kelli somehow felt safe under Ballew Dragun's protection.

Chapter 12

HOSTAGES

"Hey, Jerry, how about a smoke?" Richard asked. He felt death near and if there was one thing he could do before he died, it would be to get one more smoke and pester Jerry at the same time. All morning he watched what transpired and knew something was about to happen. Surely it concerned the Cajun, but, for the world, he couldn't understand how he had survived. Kelli still hadn't been found--of that he was sure. The fact he was alive proved Ballew lived. If he could just get one more smoke.

"Come on, Jerry, just one smoke?" he asked as he eyed the bulge in Jerry's shirt pocket revealing the pack of cigarettes.

"You want a smoke?" Jerry snapped as he grabbed Richard by the neck and blew smoke in his face. "Then smoke this," he added as he slapped Richard in the face, knocking him over onto his side.

Richard recovered and regained his sitting position. "I can feel the Cajun watching somewhere out there. If he saw you, you're a dead man, Jerry." He watched Jerry cast fearful glances in the direction of the jungle-like growth of the island. Richard smiled to himself when he saw evidence of the fear in Jerry's eyes.

Jerry was about to retaliate on Richard when Kaja interrupted, "I want you to watch him closely and make sure nothing happens. He will draw the man Dragun near again."

"That crazy Cajun doesn't want Richard!" Jerry snapped, grabbing Richard's shirt at the neck. Jerry pulled his gun and placed it at Richard's temple, "Come on, Kaja, let me kill this sonofabitch, and we'll have one less problem."

"No!" yelled Kaja. "Let him go."

Jerry hesitated, then threw Richard to the ground and holstered his gun.

Kaja returned to discussing plans to capture the Cajun with Mustafa, Kidane, Jerry, and Delacroix.

"You should kill Richard now. Dragun doesn't give a damn whether he lives or not," Jerry repeated.

"There are those Dragun would die for to save, but you don't need this man," Delacroix said with a sneer on his lips.

The statement caught Kaja's ear, "Who?"

"Old woman we call Swamp Witch. She is like mother to him."

"Anyone else?" Kaja asked.

"Yes, his friend, Happy Jak."

The name was like a prayer answered. "Happy Jak," Kaja mumbled. He could use Happy Jak as a hostage, capture Dragun and kill them both. How easy it would be.

"Can you find this woman?" Mustafa asked Delacroix.

"Yes."

"Good. You bring her back, and I will get Happy Jak," Kaja said and he turned to Mustafa. "You and Kidane watch the camp. And don't let the Cajun get this man as easily as he escaped your trap," he added with a touch of sarcasm.

Mustafa nodded, but the anger was evident as the muscles in his face twitched uncontrollably. Delacroix departed to find Belle Rose, while Kaja waited for the late evening so he could capture Happy Jak after the bar closed. For now, he waited. Soon the trap would be ready and the Cajun would be his again.

* * *

Strength returned to Ballew with every passing minute. Previous encounters with venomous snakes had built up antitoxins in his body and were quickly ridding his body of the last remains of his encounter the day before. The familiar remedies of the swamp also aided in his recovery. The fish, along with the wild roots and berries, brought him along very quickly. Before the sun rose another time, his body would have brushed aside the incident entirely. Where most men would have died and those who survived would have taken weeks to recover, Ballew would be back to normal in less than two days.

Kelli observed the astounding recovery with each stride. "Where are we going?" she asked.

"It will be dark soon and we need food. Do you still have the fritters?"

"Yes, but will it be enough?"

"No. We will use the fritters to get food," said Ballew with a confident shrug of his shoulders.

They walked along the edge of the bank skirting the outer perimeter of Devil's Island. Ahead lay a horseshoe-shaped inlet, where many ducks and geese searched the water for tiny fish. Some rested in the sun along the shores of the shallow inlet.

The birds took to the air at the sound of their approach. Ballew made directly for where the geese lounged in the safety of the inlet.

Near the area where the geese had flocked, Ballew withdrew his knife and excavated two holes a half foot in diameter and a little more than two feet in depth. He took the fritters from Kelli, crushed them in his hand and spread the tiny pieces near the opening of the two holes, dropping more than half of the fritters deep in the holes. He nodded at Kelli and they moved from the area.

"I thought you were hungry," said Kelli as she followed him through the thick undergrowth. "Why would you feed those ducks what we have?"

Ballew shook his head and smiled, "You see. Tonight we eat geese. Two geese."

"You can't shoot them."

"I know. They be there when we return."

"You expect them to wait? They'll just fly away, like they did when they saw us the first time."

"You are wrong . . . they wait," he said with a sly smile.

"Sure, I bet. I suppose they will eat the fritters and be so full they can't fly. Kinda like putting salt on their wings," she teased.

Instantly, Ballew came to a stop and turned to Kelli. "What do you have to bet?"

She thought for a moment. "You can have me," she said with a bit of arrogance.

After a moment of looking her over and weighing the prize, he rubbed his chin, "Is that all?"

Her response was quick and angry: "Is that all! What do you mean, is that all? Let me tell you--"

"Enough," he said, raising his hand to quiet her, "I take

you."

"What do you mean, you will take me? What do I get if I win?"

Ballew shrugged his shoulders, "You not win. Now, gather roots and berries I showed you. I gather the wood and start fire."

"Well, of all the arrogant, pig-headed . . . " Kelli mumbled, but she said nothing more as she went about gathering the roots and berries now so familiar. Ballew's sure attitude irritated her and she failed to see how he intended to capture the birds.

As she searched for the foods Ballew taught her were edible, she wondered how anybody could fail to survive alone. She never dreamed food was in such abundance everywhere they went. Things she had tromped upon all her life could have sustained her indefinitely. There was no need for the geese--they would be extra if Ballew captured any, because they had plenty to eat. She knew he would need the protein from the meat to replenish his energy and heal his wounds. Although not infected, the wounds within his hands were still wicked-looking.

She returned to a crackling fire, where Ballew stood waiting. "Come, let us get the geese."

They returned to where they saw the birds earlier. Kelli expected Ballew to approach quietly, but he didn't. Instead He came upon the birds without any effort to conceal his approach. The birds were already in flight before they came to the opening in the trees.

As she stepped into the opening, no birds were visible, "I told you they wouldn't wait. Now what are you going to give me for winning?"

Ballew said nothing; he only pointed in the direction of the two holes he had dug. Sticking from the holes were the snow white rear portions of two geese. They had become trapped, stuck within the holes, unable to extricate themselves. Kelli was astonished when she realized what Ballew had done. The holes were slightly larger around than the geese and when the geese had reached deep in the hole, they had slipped in wedging their bodies vertically in the hole and unable to move their wings. Now the orange webbed feet waved wildly in the air unable to offer any assistance to the helpless feathered creatures.

"I can't believe it," she said. "My dad won't ever believe this when I tell him. He probably won't believe **any** of this, come to think of it."

Kelli followed behind Ballew as he removed the two birds and snapped their necks. "Now that I think about it, I'm not so sure I believe it," she mumbled to herself.

With the two geese slung over his shoulder, Ballew smiled at Kelli, "You lose."

"You cheated. You knew. It's not fair."

"You lose."

"Okay, okay! Let's go back and I'll think about it."

They returned to camp and, while Kelli prepared the roots on crude wooden utensils, Ballew cleaned the geese and hung them over the open fire. Again he sprinkled swamp herbs over the meat, sliced wild onions and stuffed all deep within the cavity of each goose.

Using a stick, he separated some embers and between these he placed a half dozen wild onions. When they started to burn, he removed them from the fire.

As Kelli ate the meat, she noticed the wild taste she expected taken away by the onions. Again she enjoyed the wonderful taste of the meat.

Ballew extinguished the fire with the setting sun and led Kelli to a hollow high in a cypress tree. It would be their sanctuary for the night.

Within the tree, Ballew spread the lone blanket--then looked Kelli in the eyes. "You lose," he said softly.

Ballew smeared his hands with the thick protective grease. Kelli did the same, spreading the grease on her arms and legs for relief from the mosquitoes. Then she removed her shirt, baring her chest. One mighty hand gently touched full around the neck, then one finger traced softly down the center of her chest between her breasts and hardening nipples until his fingers reached her navel.

With the fingers of both hands, he retraced the path from the navel upwards, until he was just below her breasts. Each hand, thick with grease, followed a different path, sliding under each breast, coming up and over until each nipple pressed firmly against each palm. He made circular patterns covering the entire breast and quickly hardening the nipples with grease.

Kelli smeared grease over the rippling muscles of Ballew's stomach, circling his navel. She responded to his touch, deftly popping the snap of his snakeskin belt. A slight touch released the button on his jeans and pulled the zipper apart as she slid her grease covered hand deep in the front of his jeans. When she found what she wanted, she returned a devilish smile toward Ballew.

His huge chest heaved and he bent forward until their lips met. Her fingers came slowly, enticingly upward and wrapped tightly about his neck, pulling him closer. Quickly, his hands encircled her, sliding down to the small of her back and inside her jeans.

He pulled her gently down upon the blanket. Four hands wandered eagerly and passionately, casting the clothing aside in anticipation of further exploration. Grease-covered, they rolled on the blanket, touching, caressing, satisfying each other's hunger.

Together they became lost in each other's tenderness and touch. A tenderness Kelli did not expect from a man such as Ballew. Yet, this was the same man who was gentle with animals and showed kindness to Richard and to her. She was wrong in being so quick to judge. Although not what she had expected--it was what she wanted. Together they stayed through most of the night. Kelli had lost; she was his.

* * *

A little past midnight the last patron of Happy Jak's stumbled outside, found his old rusted pickup and with a great deal of effort on his part eventually started it and rumbled down the dirt road.

Four men watched impatiently for the driver to disappear, then they stole through the shadows of the night to the entrance leading to Happy Jak's. One guarded the door while the other three entered the empty bar.

"Sorry, I'm closed," said Happy Jak, casually glancing toward the men who entered. "Hey!" he yelled when two of the men grabbed him roughly by the collar and threw him to the floor.

One man pulled Happy Jak's arm behind his back and lifted him from the floor. With an arm tightly about Happy Jak's neck and his arm pinned behind his back, he was turned around to face the man responsible for the attack. Before him stood Kaja gloating his pleasure at Happy Jak's discomfort.

"We are closed. Leave!" Happy Jak continued defiantly.

Kaja pulled his shirt open, revealing the letters SM carved on his chest, "Remember this? Now you will bring the Cajun to us."

"I die first."

A snicker came from Kaja, "Yes, that you will. But now,

you are my bait. Then I will let you have your wish and you can die--after the man Dragun is dead." Kaja laughed, then slugged Happy Jak full in the face.

Semiconscious, Happy Jak was dragged from the store. An approaching car unexpectedly interrupted them in the dusty parking lot. The local deputy was making his nightly rounds and Happy Jak's was his normal stop every night before he returned to the sheriff's office.

At the sight of the men carrying someone, the deputy stopped to offer his assistance.

"Trouble?" the deputy asked as he stepped from his car. Then he recognized Happy Jak. "Hey, what's de matter with dat Happy Jak?"

Unaware of the intentions of the men, he approached and was confronted by Kaja, "No problem, officer . . . he just had one too many."

"Not likely, dat Happy Jak out-drink any man I ever see. I want to check him," he said, trying to push past.

The officer never knew what happened. As he walked near, brushing the stranger, Kaja grabbed the deputy by the shoulder and slipped a long steel blade just below the sternum, jerking it quickly upward and to the right, penetrating the heart and killing Happy Jak's unsuspecting friend.

Happy Jak was faintly aware of what happened, but was unable to aid his friend. Quickly, Kaja and his men pulled Happy Jak to the waiting airboat. The men loaded the dead deputy into one of the airboats, pulled his police vehicle into a normal parking area and locked the car. Kaja was sure it would be days before anyone would figure where the deputy and Happy Jak had disappeared.

Once aboard, they returned to Devil's Island, where Delacroix waited with Belle Rose. On the return trip they deposited the deputy's body in the murky Atchafalaya.

When they arrived at Devil's Island, Delacroix already had the argumentative Belle Rose tied up, but he failed to seal her mouth. The feisty old woman continued to give a verbal Cajun tongue lashing to Delacroix. It was good none of the terrorists understood her babblings, or they might have killed her. Delacroix gave no thought to her idle threats; his concerns were dealing with Dragun and the revenge driving him to whatever means it would take to see Ballew Dragun dead.

Bound tightly, Happy Jak was escorted to where Belle Rose and Richard awaited the new captives' arrival.

"I hate the circumstances, but it's nice to see someone I know," said Richard, managing a feeble smile after Happy Jak was thrown unceremoniously to the ground.

"These men will pay," said Happy Jak. All traces of humor the jolly man had always shown were gone.

"Hate to bust your bubble, but I'm afraid we're dead men," said Richard in a humorous tone to break the tension.

"Not while Ballew is alive. He will make them suffer," vowed Happy Jak, vengeance on his tongue and in his eyes.

The hostages were together, unaware of Kaja's intentions, although Happy Jak and Richard surmised the reason and the probable outcome.

Kaja smiled slyly to himself. The bait was ready, now to set the trap. He would sleep peacefully with the knowledge his nemesis, Ballew Dragun, soon would be his captive again. This time, the Cajun would not escape. This time, the Cajun would die. Dreams of torture and death danced merrily in his head. Kaja slept peacefully.

Chapter 13

TRAP

The first rays of sunlight sliced through the long shadows of the tall cypress, and the new day found Ballew and Kelli with a stolen moment of peace.

The smell of Kelli's hair filled Ballew's nostrils when he awoke. Fresh and alert, he nuzzled his nose deep within her thick hair. His lips searched for her soft neck and once they found the sweet treasure they sought, he kissed her again and again.

A slight moan came from her throat as her hand slipped behind her back, searching for his hand until she found it. Then she pulled his hand in front of her and kissed it. Gently, she slid his hand down and around her breast. As he caressed it slowly, Kelli sighed with desire. He rolled her over and kissed her passionately as they explored each other with searching tongues. In the peace of the swamp, beneath the peeking sun, they made love again. Exhausted and happy, they fell asleep once more.

The sounds of guns awakened them both from their morning sleep. Their temporary peace shattered.

Kelli grabbed the blanket and shrank back. It had taken only a moment and Ballew was on his feet, with his rifle ready. He knew there was nothing to fear, for the shots were far in the distance. He noticed the shots came at precise intervals, as if they were signaling someone.

Ballew understood. The shots were a signal . . . a signal for him.

"Get dressed," he said as he pulled Kelli to her feet. "We go, see what it is." Drawing her near, he kissed her passionately one more time.

What was it Kaja used to lure him near? Ballew would be wary of traps this time.

Cautiously, they moved near the spot where Ballew was almost killed only two days before. Hidden safely behind the thick growth of the island, they gained a vantage point as near as they could venture without being observed. In the middle of the clearing, huddled close together were the reasons for the shots summoning Ballew to the campsite: Richard, Happy Jak, and Belle Rose. Ballew and Kelli, concealed by the heavy vegetation, watched quietly, helpless to do anything.

Kaja, Mustafa, and Jerry stood near the three victims and were making plans to lure Dragun into the opening, so he could be captured again. They had done it before.

"What makes you think Dragun will venture near us?" Mustafa asked.

Mustafa continued to search the jungle for the man he was hired to kill . . . the same man who, in a very short time, Mustafa came to admire for his cunning and strength . . . a man Mustafa would enjoy killing.

"I know his weakness. He will risk his life to save his friends," Kaja said.

"And when do you expect him to arrive?" Mustafa asked sarcastically.

"He will come . . . he did before," Kaja assured.

"The Cajun will not come again--he knows death awaits." Mustafa smiled, knowingly. "He is out there now. He lays hidden and even now he watches us. It is time to do it, if we are to capture him."

"What of him?" Jerry asked, pointing to Richard.

Mustafa only shook his head. "He is crippled by the wound to his leg. He will be no trouble to us. What we must do will be done to those two," he said, pointing to Belle Rose and Happy Jak. "If we can anger Dragun, we just might draw him out of hiding."

Kaja snapped his fingers and pointed to Belle Rose. At Kaja's command, Khayam and Jibreen marched to where she lay tied and cut her bonds. Quickly she grabbed a chew of tobacco and bit off a piece before the men knocked it from her hand. The men held Belle Rose securely on each side as they returned to where Kaja and Mustafa waited.

"Now to hook the bait so we can catch the big fish," mused

Kaja to himself as he looked into the cold eyes of the small old swamp woman. "So you are the Swamp Witch? Take her shoes off," Kaja ordered Jibreen and Khayam. Delacroix and Mamou moved near to watch.

Obediently, they wrestled her to the ground and removed the leather bindings from her feet and legs. As they did so, Salil brought a small plastic box containing a pair of pliers and dozens of single fish hooks, each straightened into a single straight shaft. Kaja opened the box and fingered the small barbs until he found one to his liking.

While trying to hold Belle Rose, Jibreen and Khayam removed her leggings and struggled to keep her immobile. Kaja took the box of straightened hooks and motioned Salil to hold Belle Rose's feet.

Once Salil locked her feet beneath his arms, Kaja knelt to the ground. Kaja ran his fingers along the calloused underside of her foot. Finding the soft white arch, he squeezed the barb between the jaws of the pliers. Abruptly, he shoved the small barb viciously into her foot.

Belle Rose let out a shriek when she felt the stabbing pain. With all of his strength, Kaja yanked hard, pulling the fishhook from her foot, tearing the tissue as the barb was removed in the opposite direction. Tobacco drooled down Belle Rose's chin as she wavered.

The agonizing scream shook the swamps, forcing a flock of ducks, feeding nearby, to take to flight.

"Let me apologize," smirked Kaja. "The hook is not supposed to be removed in such a fashion. It should come out the other side." With a smile on his lips, he took the dripping crimson barb and again shoved it deep within the woman's foot. Kaja shoved hard and could feel the shaft as it scraped the bones in her feet. Slowly, the skin bulged on the top of her foot, then the hook burst through the skin. In rapid succession, he buried two more barbs. Then, he took the pliers and twisted them back and forth until the exposed portion of the hook broke, leaving the barb and a small segment of the shaft buried within her foot.

Defiantly she yelled something in Cajun and for a moment broke free from the men. She grabbed one of the dolls at her side, pulled the long needle from it, mumbled a chant toward Delacroix and Mamou and plunged the needle through the doll.

Mamou moaned and Delacroix tried to smile.

"What did she say?" demanded Kaja, as his men subdued the leathery old woman.

Delacroix nodded his head. "She say she protect Dragun and you not catch him. She say Dragun have for you fate worse than death. She say we all die."

"How for we die?" moaned Mamou.

"Stop your tongue or I kill you myself," snapped Delacroix.

Hidden from sight, Ballew restrained Kelli and controlled his own emotions of running to the old woman's aid. Ballew knew such a hazardous move would mean their death. He watched silently as the torture continued and his anger intensified at the sight of his friend's torment. Revenge filled his thoughts.

The same procedure continued with the other foot until all they heard were Belle Rose's piteous moans.

"Stand her up," said Kaja, with a gleam of pleasure.

The men did as they were ordered, then released Belle Rose, so she could carry her own weight. She screamed in agony from the pain and crumbled to the ground. She crawled helplessly until finally managing to get to her knees. Her breath came in short gasps. Part of the chaw dangled from her mouth and their juices ran down her chin and throat.

"Where is your Ballew Dragun now, Swamp Witch?" Kaja asked as he flipped the pliers in his hand.

Belle Rose managed to catch her breath and suck part of the chaw back into her mouth. Through the pain, her voice cackled to Kaja in heavy Cajun, "Spider Man have his way wid you. You regret coming to Atchafalaya. Spider Man save best for you--you die many times. You die **last**!"

Delacroix relayed the message to Kaja who laughed at the absurd threats.

After the translation, Belle Rose spat the remains of her chewing tobacco full in Kaja's face.

So outraged was he by the old woman's insult, he swung the pliers viciously in an arc, striking her across the face, breaking her nose and rendering her unconscious. Kaja tore at her shirt, using it to wipe the tobacco from his face. After he cleaned his face, he motioned for Jibreen and Khayam to take Belle Rose away. Jibreen wrapped his fingers in her long gray hair and pulled her broken body to where Happy Jak and Richard watched in stunned silence.

His fury evident, Kaja pointed to Happy Jak. "Now I want him!" he bellowed.

Again, Jibreen and Khayam carried out Kaja's orders without question and soon Happy Jak stood before the angry terrorist. A knife flashed in the brilliant sunlight. Kaja moved near Happy Jak with the knife held high.

"I have a surprise for you," growled Kaja, pulling his shirt open, revealing the letters SM cut into his chest. "I think you should have something cut on your chest--before I kill you!"

No longer could Richard remain silent. With all the effort he could muster, he managed to stand on his one good leg, even though his hands were tied behind him, "Hey, asshole, why don't you leave him alone!" As soon as he uttered the words, he realized the futility and the stupidity. When he grasped the error of what he had done, he mumbled to himself, "Well, you stupid shit, you've done it now."

"What was that, my friend?" Kaja asked, momentarily casting his attention toward Richard.

Richard flashed a big grin, "Nothing, really. I was just wondering if you could get me some place with A/C, cause it's hotter'n hell out here. You know a guy could get sick in a place like this."

"A/C?" Kaja asked.

"Yeah. You know . . . like, air conditioning," said Richard to a chorus of laughs from Kaja and his men. "Well, I don't think it's funny. I'd like some water and with ice, too; no, make that a gin and tonic."

Kaja moved nearer to Richard and now stood in front of him. Unexpectedly he brought his knee up and between Richard's legs. The knee found its target.

Richard crumbled to the ground groaning, unable to breathe and doubled over in an effort to ease the pain.

"Quiet him," Kaja ordered Jerry.

The order brought a smile to Jerry's face. In a moment, he was pounding Richard in the face, knocking him senseless. "How you feel, buddy?" Jerry asked as he continued the onslaught.

"Stop!" Kaja commanded. "You can kill him after we have the woman and the Cajun."

Jerry hit Richard one last time, wiped the blood from his hand on Richard's shirt, and shoved him backwards onto his bound arms. Richard lay on the ground motionless, but swore, if the opportunity arose, he would get even with Jerry. The anger enabled him to overcome the fear of death.

With knife in hand, Kaja stood before Happy Jak, "I think I have the perfect letter for your chest--D. It will be for your friend Dragun and for what you will soon be--dead!" Slowly and deliberately, Kaja poked on Happy Jak's chest while his men subdued the straining man. Other than anger, Happy Jak showed no emotion. Kaja wasted no time completing the letter.

"Not bad." Kaja smiled. Then he yelled, "Dead, is what they will all be!"

The men all chorused in behind Kaja, "Dead!"

"Dead!" yelled Kaja.

"Dead!" roared his men again. A blood fever prevailed and the excitement of killing started to take hold of Kaja's men.

"Death to the Cajun!" Kaja yelled excitedly.

"Death to the Cajun!" came the unified response.

Spinning around triumphantly, Kaja turned to Happy Jak, but he was not greeted by a look of fear; instead, a smile covered his victim's face.

"What are you smiling at?" Kaja asked. "You are about to be a dead man."

Even through the pain from the carving on his chest, the smile remained. Happy Jak shrugged his shoulders. "For everyone, there is a place to die . . . you are luckier than most."

"What?" Kaja asked, confused and curious by the words uttered confidently by Happy Jak.

"You are luckier than most," Happy Jak repeated with an obvious smile.

"Why?"

A knowing grin flashed across his face, revealing the spaces between his teeth. "Because you know where you will die . . ." Happy Jak paused and made a sweeping motion of the swamps, keeping his eyes on Kaja; "You will never leave the Atchafalaya alive."

"Fool!" bellowed Kaja as he motioned his men to throw Happy Jak to the ground. "Kidane!"

The large and powerful Kidane came forward. Logs were placed under Happy Jak's right elbow and wrist. Kaja pointed to the arm. Without pausing, Kidane raised his leg and brought the heavy boot crashing down on the unprotected portion of the arm. A sound like dried branches snapping, mixed with a cry of pain, filled the clearing.

To the pleasure of all who watched, Happy Jak withered in

pain. The arm was bent in an unnatural "V" shape. When Happy Jak lifted the arm, it flopped over like it didn't belong on his body. He tried to rescue the broken appendage, all the while crying in pain.

The smile had vanished, Happy Jak wobbled to his feet and controlled his cries of pain so he could confront his would-be killer and spoke directly to Kaja: "He watches. Even now, he takes your measure. You have make big big mistake--you have followed the snake into its hole. For you, there is no turning back."

Flushed with anger at the man's courage, Kaja retaliated by hitting him in the stomach and knocking him to his knees. "Where is your hero now? Why does he leave you for me to do as I please?"

"Maybe I die . . . but soon it will be dark," coughed Happy Jak. Again he coughed and grimaced at the pain in his arm, "They say he can see in the dark, that he has the eyes of the owl."

Kaja laughed. "I have more than twenty men. What can he do?"

"You do not have enough. It would be safer for you to swim in a nest of water moccasins," Happy Jak muttered hoarsely.

Mustafa interrupted, "The Cajun will be a dead man if he enters the camp."

The talk ended and the three captives were herded together and thrown into tents. Then the camp made preparation for the intruder they expected in the darkness of night.

* * *

Far removed from the camp's preparations, two figures slunk away into the depths of the swamp.

Following close behind Ballew, Kelli mumbled, "You can't leave them."

His sudden stop caught her unaware and she walked into him, "Tonight I take them from the camp. Then I teach Kaja the way of the Cajuns."

"You can't go into the camp; they will kill you," she pleaded.

There was no answer--the Cajun only shrugged his huge shoulders. But Kelli saw his eyes. The fire in his eyes made her tremble.

Ballew resumed his path and she followed silently behind him.

Chapter 14
SPIDER MAN

Only a few hours had passed since Kelli and Ballew witnessed the torturing of Kaja's captives, and they wondered if Belle Rose was even alive. Kelli watched as Ballew prepared items for his venture back into the enemy camp, where only days before Ballew had met with certain death.

Methodically he checked his bow, stretching the cord to its full length. The bow was ready. He checked his old rifle and found it to be in working condition; however, he had only five rounds of ammunition left. He made sure the belt holding his huge hunting knife was secure.

They retraced their steps until Ballew found the spot where they had crossed to the small island and hidden in the giant cypress. Ballew scanned the water's edge, hoping to find the body of the man Kelli told him was eaten by the alligator. If the alligator was full at the time of the attack, the body would be stuffed beneath a log, saved for a time when the alligator became hungry again. If the alligator had not become hungry, then Ballew had an idea.

A shirt or cloth of some type floated near the surface, showing the likely spot. Only a few yards from shore was a partially hidden tree just below the waterline where the cloth floated.

Against Kelli's pleading, Ballew removed his boots and waded near the spot where he hoped to find the body. He groped beneath the murky waters and beneath the log. The first thing he felt was the grisly end of Azad's missing arm. Still, he felt along the body and, to his immense pleasure, he found the body still intact, but now bloated to twice its size.

His plan was beginning to take shape. After he returned to where Kelli waited and had strapped his boots back on, he put the rest of his plan into action.

Cautiously he searched the banks along the island until he found a resting cottonmouth. From beneath an overturned log came an angry cottonmouth over four 4 in length. Kelli could handle many things, but she never became accustomed to snakes. All her life she had tried to overcome her fear of snakes, but had never quite succeeded. Kelli retreated from the snake and watched as Ballew deliberately sought the deadly reptile.

Unlike most venomous snakes, the cottonmouth would not try to escape when angry. Instead, it pursued Ballew with its head flattened in a triangular shape. The snake struck lightning quick, but Ballew moved quicker. He sidestepped the snake and grabbed its tail with his hand.

Before the snake could turn and strike, Ballew had begun to swing it in a circular motion above his head, keeping the snake from curling toward his hand. Just as quickly as he had caught the snake, he jerked it in a whip-like motion behind him and forward again. When the snake stretched to its full length in front of him, Ballew flexed his wrist. The snake moved in a whip-like manner, then came a strange snapping noise followed by a pop.

Kelli watched, appalled at what she saw, as the snake's head became disengaged from its body and floated harmlessly to the ground. The body of the snake jerked spasmodically in Ballew's grasp. Before it even stopped the death throes, Ballew cut a small slit at the point of the missing head, caught the corner of the skin with his fingers and with two quick, experienced pulls skinned the snake.

"My God, what are you doing?" she asked.

Ballew turned, fire in his eyes, "It is my way!"

She said no more. Whether a custom or something he wanted to do, she had seen people determined and their minds set. Ballew was one of those, so it was time to watch and ask no questions. She was relieved when he spoke to her in a kinder tone and told her to follow.

Ballew repeated the ritual two more times. Now he had three heads and three skinned snakes. The snake heads would be used as signs. He would leave them in Kaja's camp to show them his power. Delacroix and Mamou would know. The terrorists would understand.

When they found a safe place, Ballew started a small fire, being careful to select older dry wood to prevent smoke from rising. With the sight of the three snakes roasting, Kelli realized Ballew intended to eat the reptiles. He took care in the cooking to spread the herbs and squeeze the wild onions he collected on the roasting carcasses. Kelli had eaten many things on her numerous reporting ventures, but snake was not one of them.

When the snakemeat was finished cooking, Ballew offered Kelli a snake, which she accepted. Though she had lost the desire to eat, she decided to make an effort to sample the meal. To her astonishment, it tasted more like a wild sausage with the texture of fish. She managed to down her entire portion of meat.

"What are you going to do?" she asked.

Ballew took his "Saints" cap off and placed it beside him while he ran both hands through his hair and sighed. It was one of the few times she had seen him without the old and worn cap. She noticed how handsome he was with his thick, black hair.

"I will go into the camp and get them out. You will come with me. I will show you where to hide. Once they are out, I will teach Kaja and his men about the swamps," he added with a calm finality.

Kelli said nothing--she knew it would be useless to try to stop him. He already had overcome many obstacles and if he believed his friends and Richard could be saved, she had no business stopping him.

The fire started to die as darkness set in.

"No more fire," said Ballew. "It is getting too dark."

They set off on the trail. They did not go far before a clash of steel teeth bit into Kelli's ankle, leaving her with a stabbing pain as she fell to the ground. She tried not to scream but the pain was unbearable. Around her ankle was a bear trap. She was sure it had broken her ankle.

Ballew said nothing as he bent down to check her ankle. With a reassuring smile he said, "You are lucky."

Kelli flashed a weak smile and groaned, "Yeah, I guess I could have stepped into two traps."

"No, look at this," he said, pointing to a branch lodged in the massive trap. "This trap was intended to break your ankle, but the branch is lodged in here so it didn't break."

"You say! Even so it hurts like hell."

Ballew smiled. "When I release the trap, pull your foot out."

With all of his strength, Ballew pressed down on both ends of the trap. Kelli immediately pulled her foot from the trap. Carefully, Ballew set the bar in the trap, making it ready for another victim. He put it to the side, then attended to Kelli's ankle. The wound was not deep and had not broken any bones. After binding the injury, he told Kelli to wait, then he took the trap and moved it up the trail in a position where someone would cross.

To the side of the trail, he searched until he found a branch chest high. He bent it in an arc and released it. Satisfied it would catch anyone who moved across the trail, he took his knife and sharpened a perpendicular branch for about six inches, turning it into a deadly spike. He found a long thin vine, tied it near the end of the branch, pulled it tightly, and bent the branch back in its arc configuration. Satisfied the branch would serve its purpose, he ran the vine around a small tree, across the ground and through the trap. Beside the trap, he shoved a stake into the soft ground and tied the end of the vine to it. Taking some fallen leaves and brush, he covered the vine and the trap very carefully so as not to release the trap. With the new trap completed, he returned to where Kelli waited anxiously.

"Can you walk?" he asked.

"I think so," she said.

Ballew helped Kelli to her good leg. Slowly she shifted her weight to her injured ankle. Although painful, she moved along with only a slight limp.

They went on for a while and when Ballew was satisfied, made camp. He checked Kelli's ankle one more time, now rubbing on some ever-present dandelions and chicory. Kelli was sure Ballew used all of these as medications--they worked and they all grew abundantly in the swamps.

"Why does Belle Rose call you Spider Man?" she asked.

"I show Belle Rose the picture books. She say I am like him because Spider Man is always in trouble," he said with a shrug of his shoulders.

"You mean, because of what happened with Delacroix's brother?"

"Yes--and because Spider Man never has a woman."

"Oh," she said casually, "well, you have me."

Ballew broke a twig in his hands and threw it into the shadows, "But one day you will leave . . . I will miss you, Kelli Parsons."

Something about the statement bothered her. She was no comic book buff. Although she occasionally had seen the comic strip, she tried to remember something about it, but it kept eluding her.

She crawled on all fours to where Ballew sat, "I'm here now." Then she put her arms around his neck and kissed him.

In response, he wrapped his arms about her small waist and held her firmly to him.

Near midnight, they set out on their venture. She could see the light from the campfire when Ballew stopped abruptly. He skirted the bank until he found a large cypress with a hollow in the center a little more than 6 feet off the ground. With firm orders to await his return, Ballew left Kelli alone and safe within the hold of the tree.

The time for business was near. Ballew checked the bag with the three snake heads. They were still secure, so he proceeded to where the airboats were tied. The guard, Reyshari, was asleep. Among the airboats he found his own boat. Silently he removed his boat from the moorings. Once out of sight of the guard, he tied his boat to the bank.

Silently he crept along the edge of the camp, searching for his friends and trying to find out where the others slept. Another guard slept at the edge of the fire and two men guarded the perimeter of the campsite. Quickly and quietly Ballew searched the tents until he found the ones holding his friends. Happy Jak and Belle Rose were in one tent while Richard and Jerry were in another. The path to both was guarded by Kaja's men.

Cautiously he moved around Kidane's tent, giving him and Mustafa a wide berth not wanting to take a chance of rousing either of the men.

Behind the tent containing Happy Jak and Belle Rose, Ballew withdrew his razor-sharp knife and made an incision along the base, large enough to admit his body. Before he entered, he clasped his hand over Happy Jak's mouth.

Startled by the hand, Happy Jak jumped but stopped when he recognized his friend. A broad smile filled both men's faces. No words were exchanged, but both understood. Happy Jak pointed to the front of the tent and Ballew nodded. After he gathered himself within the tent, Ballew crawled to the opening where the guard rested. He held the blade firmly in his hand and with one quick move, rendered the guard unconscious with the thick bone handle. Belle Rose stirred, her eyes opened and she smiled when she saw her Spider Man, but she was still too weak to move.

Quiet as a cat, Ballew pulled Belle Rose from the tent, with Happy Jak following quickly behind. Ballew lifted the frail old woman to his shoulders and carried her. Promptly they reached the safety of the large cypress where Kelli remained hidden. The reunion was short, then Ballew returned to the camp again. But this time, Kelli didn't wait alone.

Soon Ballew returned to the camp and again the hilt of the knife found its mark. Ballew could easily have killed the guard but he had a plan--and he didn't want to risk his friends' freedom. This time, Ballew entered the tent from the front. He had to subdue Richard and in the process woke Jerry, but, with a quick backhand motion, his fist sent Jerry back into his own dream world.

Ballew raised his finger to his lips and motioned Richard to follow. As Ballew cut through the rear of the tent, Richard retrieved his .45, checked the full clip, and slid it back into his shoulder holster. With a nod of his head, Ballew indicated the time to go.

But Richard had another idea when he reached over Jerry and removed Jerry's .357 Magnum from its holster. Again, Ballew motioned for Richard to follow.

"No, wait," whispered Richard.

Richard had no reason for removing two rounds from Jerry's gun, but he always hated the way Jerry would brag about how he could outdraw anyone on the force. It seemed amusing to Richard to remove the two rounds. He laughed to himself and thought how funny it would be the next time Jerry pulled the trigger only to find out it wouldn't fire. If only he could be there when it happened!

A smile lit up his face as he crawled from beneath the tent. He started to rise, but Ballew shoved his head down. Richard never dreamed he would be so happy to see the huge Cajun again. A man he had dealt nothing but trouble to, had returned to save his hide. Suddenly, Richard was overwhelmed with an urge to kill Jerry, but the desire to put as much distance between him and the terrorists prevailed. Before he crawled out of the tent, he grabbed the rifle that belonged to Jerry and took it with him.

Richard was thankful when Ballew allowed him to stand. Limping was easier than crawling, however his wound was sufficiently healed for him to hobble around exceptionally well.

With Richard safely away, they found the other three and quietly rejoiced, happy all were safe and still alive. Kelli hobbled toward Richard and hugged him around the neck.

Richard smiled as he held Kelli at arms length, "We all look like shit. What happened to your leg?"

"Nothing. You've had more problems than me. We should just be thankful we're alive," Kelli said with relief.

"Look at this guy," Richard said, pointing to Ballew. "He should have died from all those snake bites."

"He almost did. It has to be the immunity he's built up through the years or the things he uses to treat the bites. Maybe both. Still, he almost died anyway," Kelli added, remembering the incident and her own fear Ballew would die.

Ballew then ended the short celebration, telling them to be quiet and to wait until he returned.

Again, Ballew returned to the camp, and this time, he found the tent concealing Mamou and Delacroix. He gained easy access as neither bothered guarding their tent, which was set away from the others. Inside the tent, he dispatched Delacroix with a blow from the knife handle.

Mamou awoke to a vise-like grip over his mouth and words being whispered into his ear: "Move and die. Do you understand?"

With a positive nod, Ballew released his grip on the terrified man, knowing Mamou would not yell.

Ballew pulled Delacroix quietly from the tent and lifted him effortlessly from the ground, draping him over his shoulders. He prodded Mamou with the tip of his knife, forcing him into the lead. When they came to Ballew's hidden boat, he forced Mamou in, laid Delacroix in the bottom, and took to the oars.

Relentlessly, Ballew rowed to his destination. He rowed for a quarter of an hour before he landed the small boat on a far-removed island. He pulled Delacroix from the boat and placed him on the island.

Ballew took a leather cord and slid it through one of the snake heads. Then he slipped the cord around Delacroix's neck and tied a knot.

Mamou trembled and knew. The snake head was a sign

Ballew controlled Delacroix, a sign Delacroix could never escape.

"Are you going to kill us?" whined Mamou.

"Whether you live or die be up to you. I will leave you here. You must do what you must do," Ballew said.

"You can't leave me here."

"Mamou, you follow Delacroix. One day Delacroix be the death of you. Maybe this that day." Ballew turned to Delacroix and shook him to consciousness.

Delacroix rubbed his head where the handle of Ballew's knife had rendered him unconscious and propped himself onto his elbow. "Do you kill me?" sneered Delacroix.

"No," Ballew replied, and he smiled as he dropped the man to the ground, "I am going to do to you what your brother did to me. You know what to do. Maybe you live . . . maybe you die."

Ballew backed away from the men and stepped into his boat, taking an oar and pushing it free from the island. He took the oars and rowed quickly away, always watching the two men until he disappeared. On the return, he stopped and retrieved the money from the fork of the cypress where it lay hidden.

Before Ballew returned to his friends, he needed to do one more thing. He rowed to where the body of Azad lay hidden in the water under the huge fallen tree. The swollen body took a great deal of effort to dislodge from beneath the tree. When Ballew did free the body, the swollen mass of flesh bobbed to the surface. He tied the body behind the boat and rowed slowly toward the terrorists' camp with the body in tow. When Ballew drew near the camp, he tied the body to the shore. Once secure, he rowed to where his four friends waited.

The group waited anxiously for Ballew's return. The only one seemingly unconcerned was Happy Jak, but he knew the ways of the swamp. Kelli clung to Ballew, refusing to let go.

"Delacroix?" asked Happy Jak when Ballew returned.

Ballew nodded at the question. "You must leave now. Richard, can you row?"

"Yes, I think so, but I haven't got the faintest idea where the hell I am."

"Happy Jak will show you."

"Aren't you coming with us?" Kelli asked.

"No."

"They will kill you! Please come with us," Kelli pleaded.

"I must stay. You will go with the others," Ballew said

flatly. "Happy Jak, the sun will soon be up. Tomorrow when the sun goes down, return for me."

"But they will be here," Kelli said.

"No," said Ballew and she could see that the fire had returned to his eyes, even in the darkness, "No, they not be here."

Happy Jak understood and put his good arm around Kelli's shoulder. Ballew lifted Belle Rose and placed her gently in the boat all the while looking at her black eyes.

Ballew laughed and pointed to her eyes, "You look like Rocky."

Instead of a laugh, it was more of a cackle: "You do favor, Spider Man. I want you fix dem for me." Ballew nodded.

Happy Jak held his arm, as he climbed into the boat.

Richard started to get in but paused and turned to Ballew. "You know, I was gonna give Kelli to them for the money," Richard said. Again Ballew nodded. "I'm no different from them."

With a twinkle in his eyes, Ballew smiled slightly. "You learn much, *Ticrot*. Now you talk truth. I see you yesterday when you help Happy Jak. I see you risk your life for Rocky. I call you a brave man." Then he pointed to the case with the money. "Take care of it--for you and Kelli. You are my friend now and I trust you with their lives."

They shook hands and Richard tried to say thanks, but the words seemed to stick to his throat. He wiped his eyes and tried to act like he had something in them, even though he didn't.

Richard picked up the money. "I cheated at chess."

"I know," Ballew said with a smile.

Happy Jak laughed and slapped Richard on the back as he placed the money in the boat, "Ballew never lose at chess. No one in the swamp will play with him."

"What?" When Richard turned to ask, Ballew was gone. Now it was his duty to take care of the other three.

With a heavy heart, Kelli still clung to the rifle Richard had taken, and she was ready.

Richard asked Happy Jak, "What is *Ticrot*?"

Happy Jak laughed as did Kelli.

"Maybe you tell him what it is?" Happy Jak asked Kelli.

Although her thoughts were on Ballew, she explained, "*Ticrot* is an affectionate term for a friend. It means 'little dried turd.'"

"Wonderful," Richard smirked.

"Spider Man fix 'em," snorted Belle Rose.

Kelli had no doubt Belle Rose was correct in her assumption. She had not taken her eyes from him when Happy Jak and Richard were talking to each other. As the two men had talked, Ballew had smiled at her and held his hand out to her. Before he had turned to leave, the fire and determination had returned to his eyes, and, just before he disappeared, she saw him remove his Saints' cap and turn it around. Then he was gone. Kaja and his men had trouble coming their way. They had made the ultimate mistake; they had angered the Cajun and he wanted revenge.

Chapter 15

The Hunted Becomes the HUNTER

Richard started to climb into the boat, but he hesitated, then turned to face Kelli. A strange look filled his face, "Say, Kelli, you like Ballew, don't ya?"

Her blush was all the answer he needed as she looked down at the ground. "Well . . . "

"He's a hell of a guy. I've never seen more of a man packed into one person in my life. I thought ya liked him, but . . . " Richard hesitated and kicked at the ground, "before we go, I'd like ya to do one favor for me."

Her soft hand touched Richard's arm. "Sure. What do you want?"

Richard felt like a small schoolboy, "Well, I'd kinda like to hug ya real tight . . . and if you would . . . would ya, well . . . give me a big kiss?"

"Richard!"

"I'm sorry--ya don't have to," he apologized.

"Richard . . . " She smiled, when he looked into her eyes. "Of course, I will."

He stepped forward and hugged Kelli, "Boy, ya feel a lot better than I imagined," he sighed. She took his face in her hands and planted a kiss full on his lips . . . a kiss he would never forget. When she released his face, he stepped back and his arms fell limp at his sides. "Jesus!" he muttered as if he had lost his breath. "Say, you wouldn't ever think about gettin' serious over an old FBI agent, would ya?"

Kelli smiled. "I'll never forget what you've done for me, but I love Ballew."

Richard tightened his lips and shook his head. "Kinda figured that. Ballew's a lucky guy. Hell, you sure got soft lips." He turned quickly and climbed into the boat.

Kelli gave the boat a slight push, and started to jump in the boat, but hesitated. Ballew could not possibly hope to deal with so many alone. She looked at the rifle, then at the three, injured in the boat waiting to row to safety.

"Hurry girl," urged Happy Jak.

"Come on Kelli, let's get the hell out of here," begged Richard.

Foolish thoughts, foolish actions. Kelli pushed the boat hard, and remained on the island. She let her heart rule, instead of her head as she waved the rifle in the air. "Ballew needs help."

The small boat drifted quickly away. Far enough so that Kelli would soon have no option, but to remain on the island.

"Come girl!" demanded Happy Jak.

"Goddamn it Kelli, you can't help him. Get in the boat!" Richard ordered.

Whether love or the perpetual anger Kelli harbored at being belittled by men and ordered around by them, the defiance was evident in her face when she snarled between clenched teeth, "No!"

She turned and was quickly swallowed in the brush.

Richard was shocked when he realized what had just happened. "Oh, shit--Ballew's gonna kill me."

Shaking his head, Happy Jak said, "Stupid woman. Stubborn woman." He sighed, then quickly smiled, "Kelli must be part Cajun. Ballew, he has good taste in women. No?"

"What do we do?" begged Richard.

With a shrug of his shoulders, Happy Jak noted, "We can do nothing. We must leave, now."

"Shit," mumbled Richard as he sat in the boat and began to row away from Devils Island. "Ballew's gonna kill me."

Happy Jak smiled, "Maybe I talk to Ballew. Maybe he only beat you up." Although he made light of the situation, he also was worried about Kelli. If she had been with Ballew, he would not have worried, and for as strong of a woman as Kelli was, she knew nothing of the Atchafalaya.

Richard didn't answer he just started to row.

* * *

When Jerry came to, his head hurt and Richard was gone. To tell Kaja was to feel his rage, so he stole from his tent and, alone, attempted to find Richard. With the camp still cloaked in darkness, Jerry set out in search of Richard. Immediately, he headed for the boats. All the airboats were accounted for and he was about to head elsewhere when he noticed the boat they had found belonging to the Cajun was missing.

He ran along the shore trying to spot his escaped captive. Almost immediately, he was rewarded when he sighted the boat. He pulled out his gun, but the boat was too far away to hit. More than one person occupied the boat, and, assuming they had the money, he came upon a brilliant plan. If he could follow them and find the money, he would kill them, hide the money, and tell Kaja they had fired on him, and he had to kill them. When everything blew over he would return and the million dollars would be his.

So he wouldn't be detected, he took the Swamp Witch's boat, which was at the far end of where all the boats were tied. He was just thankful Delacroix had towed it back when he had found her. The guard Reyshari held a pole he used to torment alligators at the water's edge. Jerry smiled to himself at the incompetence of Reyshari, unable to detect the boat far out in the water, or him as he untied the boat. With very little effort, he managed to shove the boat away from shore and start rowing after Richard and the others. He followed at a distance, always keeping them in sight.

* * *

When Ballew left his friends, he set off in the direction of the body once hidden by the alligator.

The bloated body was easy to find, still bobbing in the water. Before Ballew continued with his plans, he would need to silence the man left to guard the airboats, and the two perimeter guards he passed. He disabled the two unsuspecting guards with ease.

The airboat guard, Reyshari, was no longer sleeping as before when Ballew stole away with his boat. Reyshari stood near the water, prodding alligators that ventured near the craft. He continued to turn the hideous creatures away from the shore. Every time he saw one, it made his skin crawl. He was oblivious to the attack and the swift blow from behind rendered him temporarily unconscious.

Silently and with astounding quickness, Ballew dragged

Reyshari to a stump at the water's edge. With a nylon cord from an airboat, he tied Reyshari tightly to the stump. Ballew found a rag and shoved it into the unconscious man's mouth. Another piece of cord kept the rag in place and immobilized the guard's neck to assure he couldn't escape. Ballew wrapped the cord around the mouth, the neck, back over the mouth, and again around the neck, each time circling the stump. Twice he circled under each of Reyshari's arms.

Something made Ballew stop and he paused on the shore. Belle Rose's small boat was missing. With no time to guess what had happened or who might have taken it, he just hoped Richard would be ready when the time came.

Special care then was directed to each airboat, with all but two disabled. He removed the rotors from the distributors and flung them deep into the darkness of the swamp. A quick check of the camp told Ballew the two guards dispatched earlier were still unconscious.

The last remaining guard squatted near the fire, unaware of what was happening around him. Calmly, Ballew strolled to the center of the camp, and sat beside the man near the fire.

The guard never even looked up, but, instead, just cast a glance in the direction of the man. "Kaja is crazy, we should leave," said Jibreen.

The man beside Jibreen only grunted confirmation.

"Do you think the Cajun would be fool enough to come into the camp tonight?" Jibreen asked his companion.

"Yes, I believe so," came the reply.

Instantly he recognized the voice and the accent and the words sent a chill up the guard's back. Jibreen grabbed his rifle and spun quickly, only to see the wild look in the man's eyes and the cap, turned backwards. The last thing he saw was the hilt of the knife catching him between the eyes.

The guard was tied securely near the fire. Exercising special care, Ballew dragged the swollen mass of flesh--Azad--near the fire. A small tarp made the effort easier. Ballew laid the tarp in the water and floated the corpse over to and up onto the tarp. He managed to pull the body from the water without damaging or puncturing it. Little by little, he inched the body closer, until it rested near the fire, opposite the unconscious Jibreen. He then used rags so as not to burst the watertight skin and propped Azad in a sitting position. Around the neck of Azad, he hung another snake head.

Ballew searched the camp for matches and anything used to start fires, then destroyed them. Next he emptied all the water containers and filled them with swamp water, being careful to place them in their original positions.

Cautiously, Ballew searched the tents. Finally he found the one he sought--Kaja! He made an incision in the cottonmouth's head and through this inserted a long, slim, leather cord. Taking time and care not to awaken Kaja, Ballew slid the cord under Kaja's neck and tied it together at the ends. He placed the head of the snake, mouth open and fangs extended, on Kaja's chest in a position so it would be the first thing he saw when he awoke.

Everything was complete. Confidently, Ballew strolled across the campsite to the airboats. He gathered his weapons and placed them in one of the two remaining airboats still operational. He found a pole and stepped aboard the airboat, casting a furtive glance toward Reyshari, who was now conscious.

The terror in his eyes appealed to the Cajun for mercy. Helplessly tied to the stump, Reyshari moaned and quivered with fear. His left boot was missing, taken by an alligator he managed to thwart away one more time. But the alligators were getting closer. Reyshari's eyes pleaded for help, as Ballew pushed away with the pole.

Everything was finished. Now Ballew would wait for the sun to rise to put the rest of his plan into action.

* * *

With the rifle at the ready, and confident in her ability to find Ballew, Kelli charged through the thick undergrowth of Devils Island trying to find Ballew. The charge moved all of twenty yards before she stopped bewildered. Ahead was a path but where? She turned completely around and could see no path, not even the one she had made. She looked at the ground and could discern no visible path. With Ballew there had always been a path, but she could find none.

Suddenly she felt as she had when she jumped off the bridge into the Atchafalaya. Kelli Parsons was suddenly terrified. She had forgotten what fear was like while Ballew had been around.

Surely Ballew must be just ahead, she thought. She started to yell but fear strangled her voice. The others will hear, she thought.

Happy Jak and the boat were her only hope. Quickly she retraced her steps, only to see them far from the island. Again she started to yell--and again she stopped.

Kelli kicked the matted vegetation, and she started to sob.

"Damn you, Kelli," she said to herself. "How stupid can you be. Now you're in real trouble, stupid." Suddenly she laughed, and wiped the tears from her eyes, "It looks like you can be real stupid. Well stupid, you better do something and quit crying, cause there's no one to help you outa this one."

She looked in all directions, finally her eyes settled on the cypress where Ballew had hidden her, while he found the others.

Kelli climbed up and back into the cypress to hide. Terrified, every noise made her jump, she was afraid to move. Afraid and alone, Kelli could only hide and wait.

* * *

The first rays of sunlight brought a clear and crisp, but humid, morning. The gentle drone of birds and insects settled upon the peaceful serenity of the Atchafalaya. Animals on the island scurried about searching for food. A possum and a dozen mice quietly roamed the campsite of the terrorists, searching for discarded morsels of food.

Suddenly, a scream of terror broke the tranquility of the new morning. A dozen men dashed from their tents, screams bringing them from a restful night's sleep. Others scrambled to find clothes before exiting from their tents. Even the possum ran from the camp, leaving behind the food he had found.

Men rushed toward the screams. Lost in the terror-stricken screams was Kaja's yell of terror. Startled by the noise, he awoke only to come eye to eye with a snake head staring back in his face. Jumping to his feet, he pushed at the snake head in a futile effort to escape its fangs. Not until he stood up did he realize the snake was dead and tied about his neck. Unable to break the leather cord, he scrambled from his tent and toward the commotion.

Most of the men were still fastening their pants or trying to reach into the sleeves of their shirts as they hurried to the center of the camp, to where the screams continued.

With guns readied, they neared the man with hastened strides. Mustafa and Kidane approached with caution, weapons ready, as they scanned the jungles for unusual signs. Even Kaja moved across the campsite cautiously.

Already, men congregated about the terrified terrorist, while the first man to reach his bound comrade pulled a knife to cut Jibreen's bonds. The frightened stare alerted the men as they, too, looked in the direction of Jibreen's terror. Shrieks came from three men who turned to look upon their former friend, Azad, now swollen beyond recognition. The days stashed beneath the log of the Atchafalaya had swollen him to twice his size. Only the torn tattered clothes and the stub for an arm, lent any recognition of their fellow terrorist.

In the abrupt scramble to escape from the hideous creature, Fawad stumbled and fell into the body. The sudden impact caused the taut, swollen membranes to rupture, sending a fountain of putrid liquid into the gathering and saturating those gathered in too close in proximity. One man, overcome by the nauseous smell, threw up immediately, while two others turned and gagged.

The smell was overwhelming, even for Mustafa and Kidane, who thought they had witnessed everything. Kaja pulled his shirt over his nose and backed away with the rest.

"Give me your knife," Kaja demanded of Mustafa. "Look what he did," added Kaja, cutting the cord from his neck, then handing the snake head to Mustafa. "What does it mean?"

Across the campsite Azad's body seemed to laugh back, a similar snake head hung from his neck.

Mustafa pointed at Azad and the snake head. "This Cajun is trying to tell you something. I guess he wants you to know you are a dead man like Azad. It seems he wants to play with us." Mustafa laughed, "But you--you must have something special coming."

Showing no outward sign of emotion, Kaja stiffened and trembled inside, the inner anger displaced with fear, when he fully understood what the Cajun had accomplished.

Nouri interrupted the two to show them two marks on his forearm, surrounded by redness the size of a silver dollar. Kaja took his arm and instantly recognized the marks; a spider bite. He had no way of knowing the bite had come from a deadly recluse spider.

"It is nothing more than a spider bite; you will be fine," said Kaja, giving it no more than a casual glance.

"The boats!" interrupted Mustafa, anticipating the logical next move of the Cajun. Breaking into a run, Kaja, Kidane, and the others followed Mustafa.

Mustafa came to a sudden halt near the shore. Tied to a stump was the remains of Reyshari, the guard who protected the boats. The men stopped near Mustafa, immobilized by the new horror they saw. Only a grisly portion of Reyshari remained. The rope around his neck held what remained of his body, from his left shoulder across to the right side of his chest and his arm down to his right elbow. Everything below was chewed and torn away by alligators during the night. Reyshari had known what happened to him, but the gag, still in place, had kept him silent and made it impossible for him to yell and have his friends come to his aid. In death his eyes remained open, frozen by what he had seen, reflecting the horror of knowing he was being eaten alive.

Mustafa and Kidane remained still for a moment. Swiftly they checked the airboats, only to find the boats sabotaged and one missing.

"By Allah, damn this Cajun," mumbled Mustafa.

"I brought you here to stop the Cajun!" yelled Kaja, voicing his rage. "Are you not able to defeat one man?"

"You could not stop the placement of the snake head. This is no ordinary man," snapped Mustafa, "and for this, he will pay with his life, I swear it!"

"Mustafa, this one is operational," Kidane interrupted, relieved with the discovery one boat was operational. "It has not been touched."

Almost immediately they heard the approach of an airboat. Just out of range of their guns the airboat stopped, as though inviting any who dared come near. At the controls was a large man wearing a cap much like that of a catcher.

"It is him," whispered Kaja. "Kill him!"

They watched as Ballew pulled slowly away. Kidane started the airboat in response, but just as quickly Mustafa moved to his side, stopping him.

"No," he whispered to Kidane. Then he yelled to his men, "Who wants the honor of killing the Cajun?" While the invitation aroused the men, he pulled Kidane from the boat.

Angered at watching their friends die, five men volunteered and scrambled aboard the ready airboat. Salil was first and led the armed and angry men as they departed. In the distance they could see Ballew and aimed in his direction. Salil had a score to settle, from the first time they met, when Ballew had knocked him out. This time, Salil would not be so careless.

"Why did you stop me?" Kidane asked Mustafa.

"Don't you see?" Mustafa asked. Without waiting for an answer he continued, "It is a trap. If Salil can kill the Cajun, fine. I need you here to help me set traps for Dragun. He must not escape us this time."

"What makes you think it was a trap?"

"Think, my friend, think! One boat was missing, the one he took. The others were sabotaged . . . all save one. Why? So he could lead a group he could control into a trap he has prepared."

"Ahhh."

A few yards away, Mustafa saw Kaja questioning his men about the disappearance of the FBI agent, Jerry Hyatt.

"I only regret Kaja did not volunteer," Mustafa muttered. Then he motioned for Kidane to follow. "Come quickly; we must prepare for the Cajun."

* * *

Ballew was careful to keep some distance between him and the pursuing airboat. He came around a turn in the island and only 100 yards ahead was the same platform he used for fuel. This time he had a plan for the platform, but not like ever before. The terrorists were hidden from view, giving Ballew the opportunity to swing close to shore, directly across from the platform.

Jumping from the seat, he grabbed his bow, quiver, and rifle, tossed them to the bank, then returned to his seat and headed for the platform. While the boat was still moving, he threw a rope around a bollard along the small landing platform leading to the main deck. He pulled the large knife from its sheath and, with one swift movement, cut the fuel line of the airboat, allowing it to drain into the swampy waters. With the terrorists in clear view, Ballew disembarked from the derelict boat and charged to the top of the platform.

Once on top, he raced along the platform, started the pumps and opened all the valves he could find. Shots rang out, ricocheting near him. He ran for the far side of the platform.

Ballew fell to the deck, crawling along the thick wooden decking toward a large valve controlling the flow of gasoline. Safely hidden from view of the terrorists, he turned the valve until gas flowed freely. He crawled toward the edge of the platform, farthest from the terrorists.

While still lying flat he extended his body from the waist up over the edge, bent down, and looked beneath the platform. The underside was criss-crossed with steel bracing. He pulled himself back up, rolled over on his back, removed his cap and stuffed it in the front of his pants. When he heard the men clamber to the dock, he pushed his body over the edge of the platform until he hung by his waist. Reaching as far as he could, he took hold of one of the webs of bracing below. With his hand gripping the steel, he pulled his legs from the platform.

The muscles in his arms and chest bulged as he released his right hand, and swung his body around in the opposite direction. Like a gymnast, he moved easily from brace to brace beneath the platform. He made sure to avoid the gasoline dripping between the thick wooden deck above.

One man remained, guarding the airboat. The guard had an excellent view of the underneath side of the platform, and the man spied Ballew hanging from the bracing below. He swung his rifle to his shoulders and fired, but he hit nothing.

When Ballew saw the rifle, he released his hold, dropping to the water below. As he fell, he removed his knife from its sheath, clinging to it tightly.

The terrorist aimed his fire at the water where the Cajun had disappeared, but the murky waters of the Atchafalaya swallowed Ballew. The terrorist waited for Ballew to surface.

With his knife in one hand, Ballew swam beneath the water, in the direction of the island. Ballew swam until he thought his lungs would burst, then he swam some more. A passing alligator bumped him, and he was thankful the alligator either was not hungry or thought he was another alligator.

Underwater Ballew was not the splashing, slashing prey the great alligators sought. Brushing alongside their tough hides, he became one of them. He held his breath until he could hold it no more and when he was about to surface, he felt the bottom rise sharply. He reached the bank on one breath.

He popped to the surface only to confront an alligator--and its gaping mouth--resting on the edge of the bank. The alligator jumped at Ballew, slamming its jaws shut. Ballew dodged the powerful jaws by slapping the blade of his knife across the snapping teeth, shoving them aside and at the same time grabbing the large snout with his free hand, preventing the alligator from opening it again.

Just when he had the alligator under control, he heard a yell from the platform, as a terrorist started firing his Uzi in Ballew's direction. Ballew dropped his head below the surface as bullets ripped along the bank, tearing the alligator apart. He felt the creature go limp in his hands, pulled it below the water and released his hold. He held his breath and waited until he no longer heard shots being fired. Then he coiled his body beneath the surface and sprang from the water to a chorus of gunfire. As he hoped, the suddenness of his action caught his pursuers by surprise, enabling him to roll behind the trunk of a large cypress.

His weapons rested a few yards away. Cautiously, he crawled in the direction of his rifle. Just as he reached his weapons, the gunfire ceased.

From the top of the deck, Salil screamed orders because he fully understood the dangerous situation he and his men were in. He was trying to get his men off from the top of the deck when Ballew cocked the lever-action rifle and fired one shot in the direction of the fuel storage.

The concussion from the thunderous roar knocked Ballew from his feet. The whole platform became a ball of flames mushrooming into the sky. The guard near Ballew's airboat was showered with droplets of fire. His body aflame, he ran screaming from the dock and plunged into the waters of the swamp. Three small explosions followed in rapid succession, killing all but one. The only remaining terrorist thrashed vainly in the waters, with burns so severe he would not survive.

With deceptive power, and agility, alligators launched their great bodies quickly into the water, guided by the commotion created by the floundering man. Two alligators reached the screaming half-burned man, ending his pain and anguish forever as they pulled him below the surface of the water.

Salil and his four men were no more.

The explosions leveled the small storage platform in just a few minutes. The swamp gobbled up all traces of the platform and the five men. Only a sheen from the unburned oil and fuel remained on the water and the smoke quickly dissipated. It was as though it never existed. Again, the swamps were silent, except for the comings and goings of its own predators.

Ballew removed the cap from his pants, returned it to the catcher's position, slung the quiver over one shoulder, the rifle over the other, and retrieved his bow. He paused long enough to split a cactus-type plant with his knife and suck its sweet liquid. A few feet away was a wild onion he extracted from the ground and ate quickly, washing it down with more of the cactus plant. After plucking a handful of berries, he moved into the island, returning his attention to the fourteen remaining terrorists.

* * *

Kaja barked commands to his men. The two men previously guarding the tents of the hostages were now conscious and alert, as were the two perimeter guards. Mustafa and Kidane made plans to trap the Cajun. All three men were running short on ideas and nerves.

"What can we do to stop him?" Kidane asked.

"He is but one man," snapped Mustafa. "We were too confident of our victory over the man. I will be prepared for him this time."

After he set the men about their duties, Kaja ambled over to where his two strong men conversed. "What do you plan?" he asked.

"We should spread out in two's, staying in sight of each other and cover the island. No one should go alone. If we are careful, we will capture the Cajun," Mustafa told Kaja as he bent over to the water container to pour a drink. The cup barely touched his lips when he immediately stopped. He paused and sniffed the liquid, cursed, and tossed the contents to the ground. Then he yelled so everyone could hear, "Don't drink the water; it has been contaminated. Check the rest of the water containers."

"You have done a fine job, Mustafa," Kaja said sarcastically. "One man has defeated you single-handedly."

"I have not yet been defeated," came Mustafa's response from between gritted teeth. "But **you** already have been beaten by this man!"

"Come--we must trap the Cajun," said Kidane, feeling the tension between the two.

"Send eight men," Kaja ordered, "We will wait here for Salil's return."

No sooner did Kaja finish his words than the jungle shook from a horrendous explosion. In the distance, they could see many explosions.

"Ahhh, Salil has rid us of the Cajun," said Kaja, with a confident smile on his face.

"Maybe . . . maybe not," cautioned Mustafa. "If he has, it

will not hurt to send the men as a precaution. Remember, Salil had no explosives."

The accuracy of Mustafa's words haunted Kaja. "You are right. Send the men."

Mustafa selected eight men and cautioned them to search in pairs, but to remain close to the others, to prevent anything from happening to them. He asked which of those who had remained behind, drank the water. In the back of his mind, he kept count. Fourteen men were left, assuming Salil and his men were dead. Of the eight in search of the Cajun, only one had drunk the water. Mustafa knew those who drank the contaminated water would more than likely become ill.

With eight gone in search of the Cajun, only six remained in camp. Kaja, Kidane, Mustafa and the three, who were soon to become ill, were the only ones remaining in the camp.

Mustafa assumed Jerry, Mamou, and Delacroix were all dead. But how? How had the Cajun managed to remove the men from the camp?

Chapter 16
Wyatt Earp

A light haze covered the water. Richard continued his non-stop rowing and felt more at ease with the rising sun.

The three neared the island, thanks to the guidance of Happy Jak. His knowledge led them directly to the island where Ballew's house was but an ashen memory.

They could see the island and the charred remains of Ballew's former home.

The peace was suddenly disrupted by the faint sound of a distant explosion. They looked in the direction of the echoing sound. Far removed from where they were, they could see a cloud of smoke rise above the Atchafalaya Swamp.

"Ballew!" said Richard.

A hand of comfort rested on his shoulder, "I would not worry so much about Ballew as I would worry about the safety of those men." Happy Jak laughed. "Tomorrow night we pick up Ballew. Now don't you worry."

"You don't know those men," said Richard.

"You don't know Ballew Dragun."

Tired and battered, Belle Rose's voice crackled at the back of the boat, "They not get Spider Man . . . but what say you we watch who dat follow us."

"What? Where?" Happy Jak asked.

Belle Rose pointed and in the distance, a boat and its lone occupant could barely be observed, "There he be."

"We be followed," said Happy Jak, also pointing to the boat in the distance.

Richard doubled his efforts, "Happy Jak, when we reach shore, I want you to take Belle Rose to where Ballew said he left his airboat. Get outa here. I'll take care of whoever is following us."

"Don't be a hero," said Happy Jak.

"I haven't been. It's about time I acted like one."

"Don't be foolish, boy," Happy Jak added.

"It's time for Wyatt Earp to protect the lady. They got the drop on him once, but it won't happen again," Richard said firmly.

The boat started to drag bottom just before it hit the shore. It came to a sudden halt and all three disembarked. An unexpected visitor waited when they landed.

Standing before them on the solitude of the island, with his paws outstretched, stood Rocky. If ever a raccoon was excited to see humans, it was Rocky. Without hesitation, he headed directly for his friend, Richard.

"Hey, little guy," said Richard with a smile as he tied the boat to shore. Rocky tried to reach into Richard's pant cuff and climb his leg in search of some tidbit waiting for him. "Sorry, I don't have anything."

With the approaching boat far enough away, Richard helped Happy Jak and Belle Rose to the edge of the trees. He brought the money back with him and gave it to Happy Jak.

Happy Jak turned to Richard, "Come with us. We can beat him in the airboat."

With a smile and a shrug of his shoulders, Richard said, "Hey, it's only one man. After all the shit we've been through, one man will be a cake walk. Besides, I can see him. If we take the airboat, he will just follow us. I've got to take him here if the three of us intend to get out."

"You don't have to prove anything."

"Wrong. I have to prove **everything** to myself," Richard said flatly.

Happy Jak frowned.

"Oh, don't worry, I'm a coward at heart," Richard added with a smile.

"Go," said Richard, the tone of urgency apparent in his voice. He looked over his shoulder at the boat, with its single occupant, closing upon the island. Every stroke brought him closer to the three trying to escape to freedom. He hurried them away and when they were at the edge of the trees, turned so he could watch

the approach of the boat.
   Happy Jak tried to support Belle Rose with his good arm and shoulder.
   From the safety of the trees, Richard watched as they stumbled in the direction of the concealed airboat. Hidden from view, he waited as the pursuer neared the island. He checked the clip of his .45 and, finding it full, returned the clip and slid a live round into the chamber. With his free hand, he rubbed Rocky's neck and continued his surveillance of the rapidly approaching boat. He crouched close to the ground to avoid detection and continued his vigil.
   The boat was near shore when a slight smile crossed Richard's lips. It was Jerry who stroked the oars at a fever pitch! Patiently, he waited as Jerry disembarked and set about on the trail of his companions . . . a trail that would lead him to where Richard lay hidden.
   Richard lay motionless until Jerry passed a few steps beyond where he lay in wait. When the element of surprise was on his side, he stepped from the undergrowth and onto the trail. Jerry was only a dozen paces ahead.
   "Hold it, Jer," he said confidently, "don't turn around too fast, or you'll force me to shoot ya. I sure would hate to do that, seeing as how you and I have been through so much. Oh, yeah, don't reach for the gun, either, or I'll shoot before ya. Now turn around."
   Jerry jerked at the last statement and his hand came to a sudden halt. He was already making a move for his gun, but, instead, he lifted his hands over his head and turned slowly around to face Richard.
   "You wouldn't shoot me like that, would you?" he asked, while lowering his gun to his side.
   But the thoughts running through Richard's mind were of Jerry smashing him in the mouth when he was tied . . . and visions of his fellow FBI agents and friends', Del and Ralph, meeting death at Jerry's hands on the dark bridge crossing the Atchafalaya swamps.
   "Yes, Jerry, I would. I'd shoot ya without blinking an eye."
   "The money! Where's the money?" Jerry Hyatt pleaded. "Look, there's a million dollars in that case. You can have half of it, if you help me get it. It's more money than you'll ever see as an agent."

"If I did have it, we'd have to kill the others so there would be no witnesses."

"Right. Then we'd be in the clear," he said eagerly.

Richard only shook his head. "'Fraid not. Don't think I could sleep well at night if I did that."

"Don't be a fool!"

A chuckle escaped Richard's lips, "Wyatt Earp wouldn't do it."

"You're stupid. You can have it all with that money."

"Sorry, Jer."

"Give me a chance."

Again Richard laughed. "You wouldn't have a chance against me."

"Let me draw," begged Jerry. He remembered Richard's interest in drawing his gun on others when they were at the Academy. He hoped Richard would be foolish enough to try it one more time. Jerry always won, no one was faster.

"You'll lose."

"I want that chance."

"Okay . . . but remember, I warned ya," said Richard, sliding the gun snugly into the holster beneath his left arm.

Immediately, an aura of confidence prevailed over Jerry. Now he spoke with an assured arrogance, "You fool! You never beat me at the Academy; what makes you think you'll win now?"

Richard crossed his arms in front of his chest and shrugged his shoulders, while a sly smile filled his face. "Ya can't teach young dogs old tricks."

"You old fool, you've even got that backwards."

"Jerry, I want ya to put your gun down, so I don't have to kill ya," Richard said in all seriousness.

"You're a dead man!" yelled Jerry, and with lightning speed, he pulled his gun from its holster before Richard could unfold his arms.

Jerry pulled the trigger, but the sound of the empty chamber turned his blood cold. Again, he pulled the trigger only to hear the same sound. For a moment, he knew real fear.

Then came the loud report from a gun and a bullet quickly found its mark. Stunned, Jerry staggered back, then crumbled to his knees. His hand tried to stem the flow of blood pumping from a small hole just below his heart.

Shocked, eyes open wide, he stared blankly at Richard,

"How? How?"

"In the tent, when I escaped. I told you not to draw, or I'd have to shoot ya," said Richard, still pointing his gun at Jerry as he moved closer. He removed the gun from Jerry's grasp.

Jerry's eyes blinked increasingly faster and he gasped, "You cheated! It's not fair."

"Tell Del and Ralph about fair," snickered Richard. Then, with a mock laugh, he added, "Look at the bright side; you're still faster than me."

"Yes, I'm still faster," he agreed and then started to cough blood uncontrollably.

"No doubt about it."

"You've killed me."

Richard tightened his lips and nodded his head, "Bingo again, Jer."

Slowly Jerry's eyes rolled up, then he pitched forward on his face into the soft earth. Air rushed from his body and, after a moment, he lay perfectly still in death.

Richard put his gun back in the holster. "That's for Del, Ralph, the lady . . . and me."

With the present danger over, Richard went in pursuit of Happy Jak and Belle Rose. They would need his help to return to Happy Jak's place on the edge of the swamp.

They were almost finished loading the airboat, hidden by Ballew, when Richard arrived. Both breathed a sigh of relief when they saw Richard emerge from the trail. When the shot had sounded, they had redoubled their efforts to escape.

As they made their way from Ballew's island, their thoughts were of Ballew and how Jerry followed them. If Jerry managed to escape, was Ballew still safe? Were the terrorists about to escape from Devil's Island?

Richard wondered how they dared return to the island the following night. He wondered how Ballew could hope to overcome such overwhelming odds.

Chapter 17 *→ Righteous!*

Cajun Justice

Devil's Island was as familiar to Ballew as any person's backyard would be to them. He ran through the thick undergrowth of the island with a confidence only years on the island could instill. But even an unfamiliar island would not have made much difference in his actions or his plans. The swamps were his, especially the Atchafalaya. Raised in the harshness of the swamps all his life, the Atchafalaya was the essence of life. Now he searched for the men who put a bounty on the life of the woman he loved. The time had come to find them and put an end to their reign of terror.

Ballew searched the island for the things he would use against these modern terrorists. If he could not use the swamp to destroy them, he would do it himself. There were many ways to die in the swamp, and Ballew knew most of them.

The men approaching Ballew never detected him, but he heard them long before he saw them. He guessed there to be at least a half dozen. Silently he melted into the swamp, then in and around the unsuspecting men. He counted eight, and assumed the others still waited in camp. Ballew turned his Saints cap around.

The sun beat down unmercifully on the island, and the humidity hung heavily from the surrounding cypress trees as the eight men plodded blindly along the trail, searching for the lone man who had spread chaos so completely through their camp only hours earlier.

"Look!" yelled Jagat to his companions. "He has come this way."

The men congregated around the tracks. "When?" asked

another.

"Not long ago," said Tahel, examining the man-made tracks more closely.

Moinuddin trembled, surprised at the sign. "He is here! We have passed him and didn't see him."

The men readied their guns and scanned the surrounding area. "Spread out," whispered Jagat. They fanned out and started to retrace their steps.

"There he is!" shouted Hassan as he fired a quick burst from his Uzi and ran toward the movement. When he separated the brush, all he found was a dead rabbit. No Cajun.

"Ah!" laughed Bakshi, his companion. "You have saved us the trouble of finding dinner."

Hassan was not at all pleased to hear the words as he watched his companion attach the rabbit to his belt with a short cord.

Jagat yelled, "I see him!" He, too, shot a burst from his automatic weapon and ran in the direction of what he had heard.

The men split away from one another and no longer had each other in sight.

Safely hidden away, Ballew watched as the men became separated. The two men farthest ahead would be the first to feel the wrath of the swamp. Ballew made himself a target just long enough to continue luring the men in his direction. Not far ahead of him was an angry male brown bear, disturbed by the noise of the guns and ready to mate. Ballew smiled because he knew, when the two men who followed him came upon the surprise he had waiting, all hell would break loose.

Another burst from Jagat's Uzi brought a roar from the undergrowth. "I got him," said the terrorist excitedly.

"Wait," said his companion, Moinuddin, unable to slow Jagat's careless charge in the direction of the unhuman sound.

Jagat's foolish charge brought him bouncing into the furry body of the angry brown bear. Annoyed by the noise of the Uzi and the sting of a bullet in its leg, the bear stood erect and caught the shocked man in its outstretched arms.

The giant brown bear squeezed Jagat, bringing a blood-curdling scream from the terrified man. To silence the man, the bear closed its jaws about Jagat's head, grinding the skull with its huge teeth.

Unable to use his weapon for fear of hitting Jagat,

Moinuddin rushed to the rescue.

The bear ripped Jagat's left ear from his skull and the long teeth penetrated the left eye. With ease the bear tore the lips and nose from Jagat's face.

As Moinuddin reached the bear, he heard the sickening crack of bone as the bear fractured Jagat's skull in its jaws. Moinuddin hit at the bear with the Uzi, finally placing the cold steel barrel against the body of the bear. Before he pulled the trigger of his weapon, the brown bear released its hold on Jagat and turned its attention to the new attacker. A swift motion of its huge arm caught Moinuddin in the shoulder, sending him more than ten feet into the air, breaking his collarbone and upper arm.

The sound of more men approaching sent the brown bear scurrying from the scene of the incident. The bear was anxious to escape from these noisy human creatures that stung his body.

Tahel and Raj were the first to arrive on the scene, followed closely by Hassan and Bakshi. Moinuddin lay on the ground, moaning. Not far from him was Jagat, or what they assumed to be Jagat. His face torn away, bubbles popped through the flow of blood, from where his nose should have been. His left eye hung from its socket. A large lump formed to the right side of his head where the skull had fractured. The pressure on his brain continued to increase and could not escape. Jagat was dying.

Tahel and Raj attended to Moinuddin, when Hassan announced Jagat was dead. No sooner did he make the announcement, to the stunned silence of his three companions, than Jibreen and Khayam arrived on the scene. They, along with Hassan and Bakshi, returned to the quest of the elusive Cajun, leaving Tahel and Raj to care for Moinuddin and follow along later.

Ballew watched what happened from a distance. Hassan passed within a few feet of the Cajun, but never detected his presence. Now Ballew set his sights on the two who stayed behind, Tahel and Raj.

When Moinuddin regained consciousness, he told Raj and Tahel of the events. The pain was too much to bear and Moinuddin screamed as Raj set the arm. Raj took the shirt from Jagat and, along with a sturdy branch he found, fabricated a makeshift splint to immobilize the arm.

"We must return Moinuddin to camp," said Tahel.

Ballew had not remained idle. Once the other four men disappeared, he circled Raj, Tahel, and the injured Moinuddin. It would be necessary to put these men out of action before they returned to camp. He found a clearing to his liking. At the edge of the clearing, he found a tree to suit his plans. A large limb extended itself high over the clearing. Ballew removed an arrow from his quiver. Behind the special barbed shaft was tied a strong nylon cord he used to reel in the unruly alligators. But today he would use it on a different, and more violent, two-legged creature. He tossed one end of the long cord over the high limb, moved a distance from the tree, then hid his bow from sight, at the edge of the thick undergrowth surrounding the clearing. Then he returned to where the two men prepared to return Moinuddin to camp. On the return, Ballew passed near a heavy outcropping of bullnettle and this made him smile with pleasure--the same plant that had afflicted Richard's leg.

Raj was leading the way when he spotted the Cajun in their path. He did not fire spontaneously like the others. Instead he turned to Tahel and whispered, "I see him. Stay with Moinuddin. I will get the Cajun."

Quietly Raj moved after Ballew. Ballew kept his distance, but each time he showed himself to Raj, he made sure he was closer to view.

Like luring candy before a child, Raj began to taste the imminent capture of the Cajun. When he caught a glimpse of Ballew enticingly close, he was only a few yards from the nasty bullnettle plant. With the anticipation of the capture almost assured, be broke into a run and headlong into the bullnettle.

The heat-activated plant sent its hundreds of spines in the direction of the unsuspecting man, much like a porcupine flings its quills. Raj screamed in agony as he tried to back away from the hostile quills, his arms and legs covered with the hairy spines of Bullnettle.

The screams alerted Tahel and he, along with Moinuddin, proceeded cautiously. Soon they came upon Raj moaning, his body covered with the tiny quills. Tahel was about to help when he saw the Cajun cross the path not more than thirty yards ahead. He cried out an obscenity in his native tongue and broke into pursuit, against the pleading and begging of his two companions.

Once Ballew knew Tahel pursued, he continued to the clearing and his bow. Ballew broke across the clearing and retrieved his bow. He placed the arrows within the quiver, slung the bow over his shoulder, and went to the tree where he would wait for the terrorist who followed. Directly overhead was the vantage point he needed to accomplish his part of the mission.

Stretching from a nearby tree was a large branch, more than four feet above Ballew's head. This was the vantage point he wanted to reach. Carefully, he gauged the distance, moved his arm back, bent slightly over and let the muscles of his legs unwind, sending him up and toward his target, where he grabbed for the extended limb. With a firm grip about the sturdy branch, he lifted his body effortlessly as a trained gymnast, curling his legs up and over the branch. Pulling himself into a crouching position, he fitted the arrow with the cord in his bow. Patiently he waited for his quarry to come to him.

Breathless and wide-eyed, Tahel broke into the clearing, Uzi in hand and ready for action. Something caused him to pause, so he continued cautiously. The color caught his eye first. Something white hung from a tree across the clearing. Unsure of what it was, he ventured closer. Not until he stood directly beneath the tree could he discern some type of rope or cord.

His eyes followed the cord making him turn sideways. The position was exactly what Ballew waited for. He stood, took careful aim, then let the shaft fly.

Tahel's eyes met those of the Cajun's just as the arrow came in contact with his kneecap. The barbs split the kneecap and embedded in the joint. Tahel shrieked in pain, released his hold on the Uzi, and grasped the area of pain in his leg.

Ballew took in the slack and jumped to the ground. The force of his weight jerked Tahel viciously from the ground. A continuous scream mixed with pain and terror came from Tahel as he dangled from the tree by the thin cord attached to the arrow embedded deep in his leg.

With the other end of the rope wrapped around the tree, Ballew made a hasty departure, in pursuit of the remaining four.

The hideous screams made Raj and Moinuddin hesitate before they entered the clearing. Suddenly they froze. Screams of pain emanated from Tahel, who had raced ahead intent on capturing the Cajun; instead, Tahel hurried into the trap and now dangled from the end of a rope.

Only agonized gibberish could be heard from Tahel as he tried vainly to pull up on the rope and ease the pain of the arrow embedded in the joint of his knee.

Moinuddin and Raj discussed circling the clearing to avoid

what surely waited for them. Raj was consumed with pain in his quickly swelling leg and was forced to cut his pant leg to alleviate the excruciating pain caused by the quills of the bullnettle. This plant was seldom a problem when encountered unless it went untreated. To Raj the plant was as foreign as the swamps of the Atchafalaya. Raj did nothing to treat the quills and the painful swelling continued.

Hesitating, mostly in fear of the Cajun, they cautiously entered the clearing. With each step, Raj groaned painfully, his legs continuing to swell.

Moinuddin and Raj tried to hold Tahel while they cut the rope, but neither could. The rope was tied beyond their reach. Moinuddin's shoulder made it impossible for him to climb and Raj was barely able to move his legs. Finally Raj cut the rope with a quick burst from his Uzi. Neither of the injured men was capable of softening Tahel's fall. The fall rendered Tahel unconscious. Unable to do anything, they waited for Tahel to come around.

When Tahel regained his senses, they discussed plans for a combined effort to return to camp. Moinuddin, using his good arm, tried to remove the shaft from Tahel's knee, but failed. Raj watched helplessly, while the bullnettle continued swelling his legs. His arms became numb, making both useless. Moinuddin forced the other two to their feet, making them return to camp. Slowly they limped along, dragging each other closer to the safety of their comrades and farther from the nemesis who had brought them such misery.

The false belief they were escaping the Cajun gave them the strength to continue.

* * *

Hassan and Bakshi, flanked by Jibreen and Khayam, searched for signs of the Cajun and found none.

Jibreen had a personal score to settle, after being tied by the fire the night before. The first thing he had seen was the swollen and disfigured body of his friend, Azad, and his screams had awakened the camp. Now he hoped to rid his friends of the Cajun forever.

The four separated enough so they could still keep each other in view, but none of them noticed Ballew making his way quietly around them. From a vantage point in front of them, Ballew quickly planned his next trap.

Far ahead, he found the area covered with quicksand. It was as he remembered. A few yards to the left of the quicksand, he stopped, and using the tip of his bow, he separated the reeds before him. It gave the appearance of dry land when, in reality, it hid a marsh-like area that opened into a small lagoon. An unwary traveler might step headlong into the reeds. The shock of the water would be disturbing to most, but not as bad as the nest of water moccasin nestled quietly at the water's edge. A slight smile came to Ballew's face as he released the reeds and moved quickly down the shore.

Nearly 200 yards beyond lay the bear trap that had caught Kelli. A quick check showed the trap set and ready. With the trap still operational, he returned to the water. Most would not have noticed the two large alligators, more than 10 feet in length, residing along the edge of the water, so well did they blend into their surroundings. Between the alligators was a strip of water no more than 4 yards in width.

There was only one way to pass the alligators safely and that was to do it quickly. Intentionally, he ran headlong on a path directly between the two large alligators. At the water's edge, he planted his feet and hurled himself across the narrow expanse of water.

The alligators, taken by surprise, reacted quickly. One jumped at the object hurling past, but the jaws snapped thin air, missing its victim by only a foot. The other alligator fared better. The tail, capable of killing victims wandering too close, scraped Ballew as he flew by, but it came too late.

On the other side, Ballew did two somersaults and bounded quickly to his feet. The alligator only grazed his leg, but the rough skin opened a small wound.

Ballew took a few moments to gather some berries and rub them into the wound. He had no time to waste if his plan was to work. It would be necessary to separate the men.

Hassan and Bakshi were the first to spot him. They warned Jibreen and Khayam, then set out in pursuit of the Cajun. Hassan and Bakshi had disappeared when Jibreen sighted the Cajun.

"Khayam, stop!" he whispered. "The Cajun is over there," he said, pointing in a perpendicular direction to the one taken by Hassan and Bakshi.

"Are you sure?" Khayam asked.

"The Cajun is smart. He is leading them in the wrong

direction, but I saw him. Follow me quickly," he said, moving after the Cajun.

They had not traveled far when Jibreen warned Khayam to silence. "Look," he said, pointing to an area of reeds.

"What makes you think--" but Khayam was interrupted.

Jibreen pointed to a cap hanging on the reeds . . . a black cap with gold lettering.

"He will die," a smiling Jibreen vowed.

Jibreen pulled a long knife from the sheath hanging at his side. With the knife ready for instant action, he took a few quick strides, then hurled himself in the direction of the reeds and on top of his anticipated victim. Still in mid-air, he cut through the narrow barrier of reeds and came within full view of the death that awaited him below. A scream of terror came from his lips as he clawed helplessly at the air as though he might grasp something to stop his forward motion. Nothing helped and he crashed among the angry water moccasins.

Close behind came Khayam, but the scream made him freeze and the hair rise on the back of his neck. He checked the Uzi and moved slowly forward. It sounded like two men wrestling in water and, as he separated the reeds, he saw the reasons for the commotion. Before him, clawing at the reeds, eyes opened wide in terror was Jibreen--*covered with snakes*! One had a hold of his cheek, while three clung to his neck as he tried to scramble from the water. Jibreen was covered with so many snakes all Khayam could see were his arms and head.

The sight so unnerved Khayam he stumbled backward, lost his balance, fell to the ground and dropped his Uzi. Moving on all fours, Khayam crawled quickly backwards upon the ground. Jibreen emerged from the reeds with a dozen poisonous vipers still clinging to his body. His eyes shone with terror, as he reached one hand in Khayam's direction.

Khayam rose to his feet, and turned to run. Four strides and his feet locked in mud, or what seemed like mud, and he started to sink. Each time he tried to extract one of his legs, the quicksand pulled him under further. He continued to watch as Jibreen fell to his knees and started to crawl in Khayam's direction. A few snakes continued their death hold on Jibreen, while the others released and returned to their nest.

At the same moment, both men noticed the lone figure squatting nearby--watching! Arms crossed, holding onto his rifle, the Cajun watched.

Jibreen attempted to reach the Uzi dropped by Khayam. When he made his move, the Cajun rose from his squatting position and slowly moved toward the Uzi, arriving simultaneously with Jibreen. Jibreen's hand clasped about the weapon just as the Cajun's foot came down on his hand. Effortlessly, the Cajun bent over and removed Jibreen's hand from the weapon, then squeezed his jaw and turned Jibreen's head in his direction. He shook his head, picked up the Uzi, then cast it into the water.

With the barrel of his rifle, Ballew casually flipped one of the snakes away. Then he resumed his squatting position and watched. Jibreen groaned and started to quiver as the poison acted quickly. The spasmodic motions stopped, and he ceased to move.

"Help me!" begged Khayam, quicksand to his chest, and still sinking.

"No," Ballew said, continuing to watch.

"You can't let me die," Khayam pleaded, the quicksand now around his neck.

Righteous!! "You killed yourself when you came into my swamp."

"My friends will kill you!" Khayam threatened.

Ballew shrugged his shoulders, "They will die soon . . . as will you." He continued to squat, never moving, continuing to stare with his unrelenting blue-grey eyes.

The sand reached Khayam's nose and he tossed his head about, gasping for air. The thought of rescue vanished, and death was assured as his eyes slowly sunk from sight. His last horrifying vision: that of the Cajun calmly watching his death.

* * *

"Hassan, did you hear that scream?" asked Bakshi, fearful of every movement around him. "We must go back," he pleaded.

"No," said Hassan, his eyes glued to the trail. "The Cajun has gone this way," he said, pointing along the trail.

The screams ended and, with every step, Bakshi regained his lost confidence. They searched into the early morning and saw very few signs suggesting the Cajun even existed. If Bakshi had not seen the Cajun, he would have sworn they were on a wasteful search for a man who did not exist. Bakshi had seen the man, when he was bitten by Abseen's snakes. He had seen the horrible body of Azad. Yes, they searched for a man who truly existed and was ever elusive. He was relieved when they came into a clearing and he could see the water's edge.

The skies suddenly darkened and the winds came briskly from the south. Thunder rolled in from the Gulf of Mexico, as a common summer afternoon thunderstorm formed rapidly. Large droplets of water splashed sporadically. The wind whipped the dry leaves and dirt into the air.

"There," said Hassan, pointing to the water, "he went in that direction. We will follow."

"Let's return before the storm hits," Bakshi suggested. "We will not find the Cajun."

With renewed enthusiasm, Hassan assured, "We will find him. I can feel it."

Other men already had died when they failed to be cautious, but caution would lead to Hassan's death. He reached the shore, followed closely by Bakshi, but failed to notice the pair of large alligators lining the path to the other side. The winds kicked up quickly and a streak of lightning could be seen in the darkening southeasterly skies. The alligators went unnoticed.

With lightning speed, one alligator, jaws opened wide, made a lunge in Hassan's direction. His defensive actions saved his life, when he reacted by shoving his Uzi in the direction of the alligator. The weapon jammed in the massive jaws and Hassan stumbled backward, but, as he turned to escape, the huge tail of the second alligator caught him across the middle of the back, breaking three ribs and tossing his body through the air.

Bakshi screamed out in horror and cowered back from the scene unraveling before him.

Even with the pain in his side and back, Hassan's reaction was of self-preservation. He pushed himself up from the ground, but his legs failed to respond, and he crumbled to the ground.

Hassan bent down to see the damage the alligator rendered. Neither the rib sticking through his side nor the blood he spit from his mouth telling him his lung was punctured registered on his brain. What made him tremble was watching the alligator approach and knowing he could not move. Hassan's back was broken, he was paralyzed. No longer could he move his lower extremities. It was as though the useless appendages that had supported him through his life belonged to another. Never more would his legs be ready when he needed them and he needed them most now. For a moment, he glanced skyward. The skies had become as dark as night, while streaks of lightning lit the surrounding swamps. Still, the rains failed to fall.

The beauty of the afternoon storm on the Atchafalaya Swamps was lost on Hassan, who was absorbed in his own personal hideous terror. Quickly he turned on his stomach and used his arms to pull himself away from the approaching horror. His legs flopped uselessly behind his body like a rag doll.

"Bakshi, quick--help me!" Hassan pleaded.

Bakshi could stand no more and turned and ran, screaming as he went, leaving Hassan to his imminent death in the jaws of the huge alligators. Hassan cursed under his breath--there was nothing more he could do, but he swore if somehow he escaped, he would kill Bakshi with his bare hands.

The moments dragged by agonizingly slowly as Hassan used all his strength to pull his body through the mud and away from the alligators.

He was stunned when he looked ahead. Before him a man squatted watching--the one they pursued and were hired to kill! The Cajun sat on his haunches and watched quietly, offering no help as the alligator crawled nearer and nearer.

Eluding the pursuing jaws of the powerful reptile was impossible. The large alligator closed its powerful vise-like jaws about the paralyzed man's legs.

Hassan was unable to feel the rows of long, sharp teeth lining the alligator's mouth as it clamped about his legs. Suddenly Hassan jerked wickedly backwards as the alligator started toward the murky waters of the swamp.

For an instant, Hassan had a vision of Azad's swollen and putrid body as it lay before the campfire and he envisioned his own grisly fate.

"Aaayyyiii!" screamed Hassan. "By Allah! Help me! Don't let me die," he pleaded, in his Arabic tongue. He held his hand out to Ballew in a sign of mercy. The blinding flash of lightning and simultaneous blast of thunder, followed by a torrential downpour, was Hassan's answer. There would be no help from the Cajun. Hassan was alone to fend for himself.

Ballew only watched, never answering as Hassan pleaded for his life. He understood none of the words spoken by Hassan, but he knew well what the man wanted. The look in his eyes was the same frantic pleading as that of Khayam before he disappeared beneath the quicksand. The men all came to kill him and the others. They showed no mercy in their dealings with him or his friends. If Ballew showed mercy to these men, as before, when Kelli asked them to be spared, he knew they would return again and again until they accomplished what they wanted. For this reason there would be no mercy, no compromise--only Cajun justice.

Ballew was determined to play the life/death struggle to its bitter end . . . until the terrorists were no more, or until they killed him. He would give them no quarter, as he knew none would be given him. The only thing he would receive at the hands of the terrorists would be a slow, painful death.

Terrified by what he understood was taking place, Hassan groped about, reaching for anything to stall the inevitable. The terrain around him was a quagmire and still the rains gathered in intensity. At one point, he managed to grasp a limb from a nearby fallen tree. His tenacity and strength were proportionate to his fear and terror. Fear held to the branch where no mortal man could. And the alligator surely would have torn him in half had not the branch given way instead.

Fingers plowed the mud in a futile effort to stop the alligator's retreat. The unhuman screams and pleadings could be heard until he disappeared beneath the surface of the water. Heavy rain covered the trail and its pounding upon the waters of the swamp obscured the path where the alligator took its meal. In moments, every existing trace of Hassan had vanished.

Hassan was gone. Now Ballew turned his attention to the next terrorist--Bakshi.

* * *

Bakshi's mad ravings could be heard as he ran headlong through the thick growth of Devil's Island. Darkness, surrounded by rumbles of thunder, only added to his terror. With each blast of thunder, Bakshi feared he had met death by the gun of the Cajun. Mumbling and crying, he stumbled blindly along the path, determined to reach camp before the Cajun reached him. Still the tropical downpour continued, unabated. Bakshi's thoughts were on the other six men who had accompanied him and Hassan. He was extremely afraid a similar fate as Hassan's waited for him and the others. Visions of Hassan began to play games in his mind, and he redoubled his efforts.

Suddenly, lightning wrapped around a tree, following a path to the ground, not 20 paces to his right. The blast filled the air with shrapnel of bark from the tall tree. Never had Bakshi felt anything with such force, so close. The natural blast knocked him from his feet and the instantaneous deafening roar left his ears ringing. Bakshi knew he was going to die.

Bakshi ran and ran. No longer did he know the direction he traveled, nor did he know how long he had run blindly in the swamps. Still the rains fell. Once he slipped, sliding down an embankment. Quickly, he scrambled to the trail and continued his chaotic charge. The specter of Ballew Dragun, the Cajun, suddenly loomed before him directly in his path. With a scream of terror, he rushed in the opposite direction. He ran blindly into a small opening and stumbled across a log. He turned in the mud and crawled to the log to see if he could spy the Cajun following. What he reached was not a log. Instead he was greeted with Jibreen's death face and wide-open eyes. Instantly Bakshi was on his feet, running wildly.

Again, the Cajun showed himself and again Bakshi changed directions. As he ran, his lips trembled and moans, tinged with fear, came from deep within all the while his thoughts magnified his fears. Where was the Cajun?

But his thoughts were savagely interrupted by the sound of gnashing steel followed by a wrenching pain in his left foot, jerking him to the ground. As he fell, a branch cut through the air, slapping at Bakshi, stinging him in the neck and face. He pitched forward, half-burying himself in the mud. In vain, he tried to wipe the mud from his eyes, but it only became worse with the mud and decaying vegetation covering his hands.

Blinking his eyes rapidly, trying to rid them of the particles of grasses and mud, he managed to see, through his blurred vision, the bear trap holding him secure. The trap had broken his ankle, but his rapidly returning vision filled his heart with despair. He turned his head slightly to the right to get a better look at what he thought might be movement in the trees. To his immense horror, the movement was blood, shooting through the air. The blood coursing through the air was his own. The ankle was all but forgotten as Bakshi slapped his hand over the severed artery in his neck.

In disbelief, he stared at the branch that caught him in the neck. A thin cord hung from the branch and a wooden stake whittled to a fine point protruded from the branch. It was a trap. A trap set for him by the Cajun!

The Cajun had intentionally exposed himself so as to redirect

Bakshi on his deadly path.

A strange sensation came over Bakshi and he turned about. Less than a yard away squatted the Cajun on his haunches, the black cap on his head turned around. He seemed oblivious to the rain as he watched Bakshi.

With his sanity almost gone, Bakshi spoke to Ballew: "Are you going to kill me?" he asked in broken English. The man he spoke to said nothing, only shook his head negatively.

Bakshi whined like a child as he asked the Cajun, "Are you going to let me live?"

The rains continued the harsh downpour. It seemed to Bakshi the Cajun waited an eternity to answer. Again Ballew shook his head side to side, but much more slowly, never taking his eyes from his victim.

Terror gripped Bakshi, "What?"

Ballew wiped the water from his face with one of his huge hands and shifted his weight to his right leg, continuing to squat near Bakshi. He leaned forward.

"You are already dead," he said, pointing to the mud-splattered neck where Bakshi's hand tried to stem the flow of blood. "You cannot hold your neck forever."

"I can!" assured Bakshi, "I can!"

Lightning hit nearby, making Bakshi jump. Ballew never flinched nor took his eyes off of him.

"The blood goes to here," he said pointing to his head. He shrugged his shoulders and continued, "Soon you will get dizzy."

The words only added to Bakshi's terror and answered the question he had about why he was getting light-headed.

Rising from the ground, Ballew stood erect, "Then you will pass out and your hand will fall from your neck. You will bleed to death." With those final words, Ballew turned and disappeared into the swamp, leaving Bakshi alone.

Valiantly, Bakshi tried to ward off the black veil of dizziness creeping through his every fiber, but without success. He fought against the dizziness. The lack of oxygen to the brain made him feel euphoric. He leaned against the nearby tree in a drunken stupor. Lightning flashed, and Bakshi smiled. His arm grew heavy, and his hand fell to his side. A bright red fluid gushed from his neck, turning the rain-soaked earth of Devil's Island crimson. Bakshi smiled and the darkness took him.

* * *

Less than 200 feet separated the trio from the campsite, but, in the torrential downpour, they had lost their way. Confusion could best describe their plight as they argued over the proper direction in which to continue.

Somehow Moinuddin and Raj managed to support Tahel on the return journey to the camp. The rains made travel precarious for the three injured men. With his legs swollen almost twice their normal size, Raj could barely waddle through the thick muck covering the rain-soaked island. Moinuddin offered his good shoulder to support Tahel but, with each step, he grimaced in pain.

The small incline they tried to traverse, while the heavy rains fell, proved their undoing.

Swollen beyond recognition, pain unbearable, Raj tried to scale the short rise by moving sideways up the incline. They were near the top when the mud gave way beneath Raj's feet, sending him down the short bank in the direction of a large cypress. But as he slid away from the others, Moinuddin's legs were jerked from beneath him, Tahel collapsed and followed closely behind Raj.

Moinuddin spun around and landed hard on the already-broken shoulder, forcing part of the fractured collarbone through his shoulder. The bone pushed farther through the skin as it plowed through the soaked ground on the way to the bottom of the ravine. A sound much like a branch snapping brought a scream of pain from Moinuddin, when the exposed bone caught a root of the cypress, snapping the bone near the base of his neck. Buried beneath the mud of Devil's Island was a four-inch piece of his collarbone. A jagged tear in the skin, from his shoulder to his neck, revealed the position where his collarbone once had been.

Raj managed to stay erect during his perilous slide, coming to a stop with his legs only inches from the rough bark of the cypress. He was set to congratulate himself on his luck when Tahel's body careened into his own. The left leg barely touched the bark covering the cypress, but the contact was all the taut skin on the swollen leg needed. Stretched far beyond its limits, the skin split below the knee and slowly tore down the calf to the ankle. The swollen muscle and tissues no longer remained compressed beneath the skin, as they pushed forth from the open wound when it ruptured like a crimson fluff of popcorn.

Raj screamed in agony and his leg buckled, forcing his arm into the same tree. The swollen arm responded as had his leg, leaving an open gash from his wrist to his elbow, to a width exceeding two of his fingers side-by-side. As he fell to his knees, the leg sunk into the rain-soaked ground, filling the grotesque opening with mud and decayed vegetation.

With their strength dissipated and their determination gone, they cowered beneath the huge cypress, as though some miracle would rescue them from their deadly situation. Shock overcame the three, making it easier for each to withstand his personal pain and agony. No longer did they argue about the correct directions to the camp.

None of the three could rise or continue. The minutes stretched into hours. Fate proved cruel, for they had no way of knowing the camp laid less than 30 yards away. With every passing hour, they became weaker and weaker. Fever wreaked their bodies, and infections set in their open injuries. They became delirious.

Just as quickly as the rains started, they stopped, allowing the final rays of the sun to flicker across the landscape before it disappeared below the horizon. The sun brought no reassurance to the three injured men, who, unknowingly, rested so near the safety of the camp.

But they were not alone--the jungle had eyes; their every move watched by the Cajun.

* * *

The torrential downpour made Kelli shiver. All day she had heard gunfire, men scream, and once someone passed near. An explosion woke her, she dozed, but gunfire, screams, and more gunfire woke her again. She managed enough courage to peek out from her sanctuary, praying it might be Ballew, but when she saw it was one of Kaja's men, she cowered back and held her breath for what she thought was forever.

She reasoned it best to wait, after all Ballew had told Happy Jak to return tomorrow. If she could only make it through the fast approaching night, and if the damn rain would only stop.

Then, as though her prayers were answered, the rain suddenly stopped. As she watched the sun be taken away by night, exhaustion took over and she fell asleep.

* * *

With the rain gone, the last flickers of the sun were disappearing. To the east, stars shone in the sky. Still, it was hot and muggy on Devil's Island, deep within the swamps of the Atchafalaya. But the small group--getting smaller by the hour--congregated about the campsite and spoke in whispers. On everyone's mind was the whereabouts of the eight men in search of the Cajun. They assumed the early morning explosion had claimed the lives of all five of their companions.

A few of the stronger-willed men had thrown a rope about the body of Azad and drug him from the campsite. Now their minds worried about the fate of the eight who had left earlier in the day.

Fawad came running to where Kaja and Mustafa stood discussing the fate of their men.

"Kaja, it seems the Cajun has taken everything we had to start a fire. The rain destroyed the fire we had. We have nothing to start one again."

"You bother me with such trivial things at a time like this!" Kaja snapped.

"Yes, but--"

"No more!" yelled Kaja, holding his hand in the air for the man to stop. "Find something and start a fire."

"Yes," he said, bowing slightly. Turning on his heels, he made a quick departure.

"We should send someone for the men," snapped Kaja.

"Who? We sent eight," retorted Mustafa. "They can take care of themselves. If they cannot, there is no reason to lose more in the darkness. The others are sick and Nouri is feverish from the spider bite." He turned and walked away, leaving Kaja to his own thoughts and anger.

On the other side of the camp stood Kidane, alert and ready for the Cajun. Mustafa made his way toward his ally of so many different ventures.

Kidane glanced over his shoulder when he heard Mustafa approach.

"A strange man, this Dragun. No other have I chased, as elusive as he," Kidane stated, somewhat perplexed at the situation in which he found himself.

"Yes, strange indeed," agreed Mustafa.

"All that we have and it still seems we are at his mercy. Many things have I seen. The jungles of Viet Nam, cities in Israel, Germany, and the unusual things of South America . . . but never have I seen a man better at what I have done all my life. Now I come to a place with many and cannot beat one. He should be dead, but he continues to live." Kidane paused, looking Mustafa in the face as though his thoughts were crazy. "Could this Cajun be a demon?"

Mustafa snickered at the comment, "He bleeds like you and me. The Cajun is no different from us; he can be killed."

A skeptical nod came from Kidane in response, "Aaahhh, but will he kill us first?"

"No!" said Mustafa firmly. "I have a plan. Tomorrow you and I will kill Dragun. Let me tell you how."

The two men discussed a plan that would surely lead to Ballew's demise. The idea met with Kidane's sinister approval, for he would have the initial chance to kill the Cajun. A chance to kill the elusive enemy they sought, and with his bare hands. Something he enjoyed with a passion, to watch his victim's eyes when they realized he, Kidane, was crushing them with his superior strength.

At one point, they stopped the discussion when they detected noise nearby. They dismissed it as an injured animal in the distance.

Little did they know the sounds were three of their comrades withering in pain mere yards away. The sounds created by men dying, not by animals.

Chapter 18
Return to Danger

    A southerly breeze kicked up in force and lightning could be seen in the dark skies to the southwest. The small house attached to Happy Jak's bar was filled with three exhausted and recuperating people. Belle Rose had managed to fabricate a cast and place it over Happy Jak's injured arm. While she took a needle and jabbed her Voo-Doo dolls repeatedly, Happy Jak went to the bar and returned with two bottles of rum--one he offered to Richard, who readily accepted. Then Happy Jak settled himself in his favorite oak rocker and took a big swig from the bottle. It seemed a never ending effort to place his injured arm in such a fashion where the least pain could be felt, but still the arm throbbed. Soon the rum began working its pain relieving powers on his body and his spirits soared. Both men watched and shook their heads as Belle Rose would stab a doll, then cackle with pleasure at her revenge.
    Richard hobbled to the wall directly across from Happy Jak, leaned against it, and slid down onto the wooden floor. He turned his bottle on end and took a large swallow, feeling the warmth of the rum as it made a trail to his stomach. Again he took a drink, looked around the room at Belle Rose, relaxed enough to let his head rest against the wall, and finally felt relieved.
    Happy Jak held his bottle high, "Tomorrow night we return for Ballew. Tonight we rest."
    "How will we keep those men from capturing us when we return? With that?" Richard asked, pointing to Belle Rose.
    "It be no problem--did not Ballew say he get them?" said

Happy Jak, more as a statement than a question.

"I don't see how," Richard mumbled.

With his head bobbing from the effects of the rum, Happy Jak smiled. "We would only be trouble for Ballew. Haven't we already shown we are more of a burden than help? Tomorrow."

With those final words, Happy Jak took another drink of the soothing rum. The pain in his arm was gone. He propped the bottle between his legs and closed his eyes. Almost immediately, he fell asleep. Not long after, Richard's head slid slowly down the wall until it came to rest on the wooden floor. Exhausted by the ordeal, he, too, had fallen asleep, but he still clutched his pistol, just in case.

* * *

The six men huddled in fear, the nearness of the others giving security to the rest. With nothing to start a fire, they congregated close together in the darkness. The Cajun had removed every means with which to start a fire. They had reverted to rubbing sticks together, but unsuccessfully as the recent rains had dampened everything. They could find nothing dry with which to start a fire.

Every sound scrambled the frazzled nerves of the men. Lightning flashed, Nouri screamed, and, pointing to the edge of the camp, he opened fire with his Uzi!

"Stop!" snapped Mustafa, moving quickly to the man to silence the gun. He jerked the gun from Nouri and knocked him to the ground.

"It was him!" pleaded Nouri. "The Cajun, I saw him."

"Control yourself!" Mustafa ordered. "Don't let him use your fears against you. There are six of us."

"Once there were 23 of us," whimpered Kamdar.

"Stop!" Kaja demanded. "I will kill you myself, if you continue to act like a coward."

Ballew smiled. He had accomplished a great deal by revealing himself to the men. Their own worst fears were at work within their minds. Ballew stayed in the shadows, lying in wait.

The lightning increased and thunder came at shorter intervals. The wind swirled through the camp of terrified men and droplets of rain began to fall. Even Mustafa and Kidane found it hard to control their inner fears. The rains returned.

The rains fell harder and Kaja ordered the men to the tents, leaving Kamdar to watch the camp. Soon the men fell into a restless sleep, letting fatigue take over. Kamdar, drenched by the rain and chilled by the stiff southerly winds, crawled into the opening of his tent. His head started to drop, but he pulled himself erect and rubbed the sleep from his aching shoulders, moving his head from side to side. Repeatedly, his head dropped. Finally, it didn't rise as his chin rested firmly on his chest in sleep.

From the shadows, Ballew waited patiently. When Kamdar slept, he slunk into the camp, moving silently to the tent with Kaja and Fawad. Without a sound, he pulled his knife from its sheath and gripped the blade firmly in his hand. One motion rendered Fawad unconscious. Kaja stirred and the hilt of his knife assured he would not move for hours.

A smile lit Ballew's face when he saw the weapon at Kaja's side. The deadly Uzi lay ready, waiting for Ballew to return. He took hold of the strap attached to the gun and slung it about his neck. Ballew pulled Kaja's unconscious body from the tent, swung him over his shoulders, and moved quietly and effortlessly from the camp.

For nearly a half hour, Ballew traversed Devil's Island with Kaja secure over his shoulder. When he reached a point where he was satisfied, he dumped Kaja unceremoniously to the marshy ground. It took just a moment to roll him to his stomach and place the Uzi beside him, the way Ballew had found him in the tent. Again the faint sign of a smile touched his lips. He made a quick jaunt to a nearby pond. Searching, he spied a snake making its way across the pond. It would be just what he needed. A quick motion of his hand and he had the reptile pinned just behind the head. The snake would serve its purpose well. He slid it into his pouch and pulled the cords snug, then returned to where Kaja lay.

He found shelter in the bough of a nearby tree. From his vantage point, he could watch Kaja. Once inside the tree, he sat, then took the old Saints cap from his head and returned it to its normal position. In the dryness of the tree, he curled up and waited for morning.

* * *

The rain stopped and a thick haze prevented the sun from breaking through. A low-lying fog clung to the swamp, hovering no more than two feet above the water. The eerie fog crawled along the island, making everything one. Mustafa awoke first, with intentions of asking Kaja what his plans were for the day. With shock and dismay, he discovered Kaja gone and Fawad unconscious from a blow to the head. Angry, he searched for the guard Kamdar, only to find him asleep in his tent. Mustafa jerked Kamdar from the tent, pulled him to his feet so he could look him eye-to-eye, then hurled him fiercely to the ground. For a brief moment, he disappeared into the fog covering the ground, leaving a swirl as evidence to where he had vanished.

Quickly, Kamdar brought himself to his feet, confused by the actions. "Mustafa . . . What? I--"

Mustafa interrupted, "You slept on guard. Kaja is gone!"

"But I--"

"Enough!" Mustafa admonished. "Another mistake and I will personally take pleasure in killing you." Angry at first, gradually Mustafa realized, with Kaja gone, he could search for the Cajun as he pleased. Now he would capture the Cajun without the irrational decisions of Kaja. Together, he and Kidane would kill the Cajun, once and for all.

The other three were alerted to the situation. The men set a plan of attack. Fawad, Nouri, and Kamdar would skirt the island, searching for signs of the Cajun or Kaja, while Mustafa and Kidane would cut across the center of the island. They collected their weapons and dispersed.

* * *

Kelli awakened to a low-lying fog, patiently she listened for the sounds of men, but none could be detected. She remained frozen as she listened for anything abnormal. With her fear abating, she was determined to go in search of Ballew, albeit cautiously. She could wait no longer.

Content none of the men were near, she checked the rifle one more time, then set out in search of Ballew. How easy it was to see a trail in the light, and with every step her courage and determination were bolstered. The rifle gave her added confidence. After all she had proven proficient when her father had taught her how to shoot on the farm in Kansas. She didn't mind shooting ducks and geese, because they seemed so removed, but she had refused to shoot deer, after nursing a fawn one summer. But this was the first time she had taken a rifle, intent on using it on men if she must. Oh, how she wished she were home.

She walked only a short distance when she came to a small

clearing in the thick growth.

A man to the opposite side of the small opening startled her. Tahel seemed more surprised to see her appear, than Kelli at stumbling upon him.

It was a stand-off until Tahel's eyes found the Uzi lying nearby. He started to make a move.

"Uhnh, uhhh," Kelli said coldly, bringing the rifle to her shoulder.

Tahel looked at Kelli, hesitated, cried in desperation and leaped for the Uzi. He reached the weapon and, bringing his body up on his one good knee, turned toward Kelli.

A single shot sounded and a bullet ripped through Tahel's chest, piercing his heart before exiting his back. The force of the shot lifted him from the ground, throwing him to his back.

A shudder went through her body when she heard the last breath leave his body. She watched in stunned silence as his body quivered, then lay still. Not until then did she notice the hideous sight of the other two men.

A few yards to one side of the small clearing were Raj and Moinuddin. Moinuddin watched, the pain clear and evident in his eyes, and his hideous body seemed non-human. His shoulder sagged so far it appeared his arm extended from his midsection. Moinuddin made no effort to move when Kelli approached, rifle ready. The broken bone had caused the right arm to swell and the tear in his shoulder, created by the missing portion of his collarbone, was filled with dirt and rotted foliage. Already it was infected. A bloody froth bubbled from his half-open mouth, with remnants of blood dried on his chin and neck. The remaining piece of collarbone in his shoulder had punctured his right lung.

Moinuddin's outward appearance was more repulsive than Raj, but Raj was closer to death. Air barely managed to whistle by the swollen tongue forcing Raj's mouth to open wide. The swollen areas in his arm and leg that had ruptured crawled with insects and flies moving freely over the wounds. But he would never know. Already unconscious, he would never know, his face ashen gray and the protruding tongue already blue. Near death, his swollen tongue would soon suffocate him.

Kelli backed away, feeling uneasy as she watched Moinuddin follow her with his eyes. Her body shook as she left the clearing. The visions of the two helpless men, spurred her on in her determination to find Ballew.

* * *

Kidane and Mustafa said nothing after they discovered the brutal remains of Jagat. They walked in silence, disturbed by the horror they had found.

Obviously shaken at finding Jagat like they did, Kidane asked, "Would this Cajun do such a thing?"

The question angered Mustafa. "No! What we saw was done by some animal. But rest assured, the Cajun was responsible."

Kidane cast a very apprehensive look in all directions as they continued their search for the others.

"Forget what you saw. It is done. We must kill the Cajun," Mustafa said angrily.

"We couldn't keep him when we had him," Kidane retorted sarcastically.

"That was Kaja's fault. Now Kaja is gone--"

"Killed by the Cajun, maybe?"

Abruptly, they stopped and Mustafa strained his eyes to see something in the distance, "It matters not. We will kill him this time." Mustafa finally recognized the object in the distance. Another body. "Quick!" he said, breaking into a cautious run.

When they reached the body, they recognized Jibreen. Mustafa bent near the body, rolling him to his back, a look of horror locked on his dead face.

"The Cajun!" Kidane whispered.

"No," said Mustafa, with a touch of irritation in his voice. "The Cajun does not do this," he added, pointing to the many bite marks inflicted on Jibreen's body. "Snakes . . . many snakes."

They did not linger long and were soon on the trail again, but they had not gone far when they came upon the body of Bakshi and the ingenious trap rigged by the Cajun. So far, all they had found were bodies of their fellow terrorists, but no signs of the Cajun.

"How can we catch a man we cannot even see?" Kidane asked, upset at what they were finding.

Mustafa laughed. "We will bring him to us."

"How?"

"Simple. It looks like he has led the others into traps. We will make a trap and let him follow us to his death."

Farther along the trail, they came to an area Mustafa deemed excellent to lead the Cajun to his death. The trail narrowed and at one point would afford no view to a person who followed. At this point, Mustafa put his plan into action. For a half-hour, they sharpened stakes and embedded them into the tree behind which Kidane would hide. Mustafa would continue along the path, luring the unsuspecting Cajun near enough for Kidane. He would use his brute strength to contain Ballew. Once he had Ballew under his control, he would throw him against the stakes. The plan was simple and easy. A plan Kidane looked forward to with interest. No man had ever escaped from him and lived. The Cajun would be no different--when the time came.

All they needed was a reason for the Cajun to follow them. A single shot, coming from the camp alerted them. Both men eyed each other, then nodded, and started for the camp. Again the silence of the swamp was broken by automatic fire from an Uzi in the opposite direction.

Kidane hesitated and started to turn in the direction of the most recent gunfire, but he was stopped by Mustafa.

"It is one of our men," said Kidane.

A sly smile creased Mustafa's face, "Yes, it is one of our men. But we will go to our camp . . . that single shot was not fired by any of our guns."

"The Cajun!" whispered Kidane when he fully understood Mustafa's words. With renewed vigor and anticipation, they retraced their footsteps toward the camp.

Chapter 19

Lost

A haze hung over Devil's Island, worsened by the total absence of a breeze of any kind. Kaja lay motionless on the ground, soaked by the night rains.

The nagging pain in his head overwhelmed Kaja as he regained his senses. His eyes fluttered open and he rubbed the bump on the back of his head. He thought he was dreaming, for no longer was he safely in his tent. Instead, he found himself waking on the cold wet slime of the marsh.

For a moment fear gripped Kaja, when the harsh reality of his situation finally registered in his brain. He reached for his Uzi and when he felt the warm security of the cold steel, he relaxed.

A shot sounded in the distance and Kaja wondered why the camp did not stir. He would have to deal with Mustafa for not being more alert. The pain in his head bewildered him as did his present location when he realized he no longer was in camp.

His arrogant attitude returned quickly, though, and his thoughts filled with revenge as he spread his hands from his body to lift himself from the ground. Suddenly his heart froze and his eyes opened wide in horror--only inches in front of his face was a snake, coiled to strike. When Kaja attempted to escape, the snake struck him in the side of the face.

The first instinct was to turn and run from the snake, which he did. Even more terrifying than the snake was what he saw squatting before him when he came about in the opposite direction.

Crawling on all fours, Kaja confronted the Cajun. The cap he wore in the reverse direction went unnoticed by Kaja as he peered into the cold, steel-blue gray eyes. The bold, emotionless stare sent a chill through Kaja's body. The eyes of a man in control and the all-too-familiar look he used, but had never seen . . . the eyes of a man who brought death.

"I've been bitten!" Kaja shrieked. "I'm going to die."

Ballew continued to stare at Kaja. "You let your fear defeat you. The snake is not poisonous." He paused for a moment, then continued. "The snake will not kill you . . . but today you will die," he added calmly.

Kaja started to shake, then he remembered the Uzi. He chattered incoherently, and like a man possessed, turned and lunged for his weapon. He congratulated himself for his brilliance in leaving the Uzi always ready to fire. In his mind, he could already see Ballew's body lying before him, when he spun about to face the Cajun. The Uzi already had fired death in the direction of the wraith, but bullets didn't come out the end of the barrel, only a click each time he pulled the trigger.

Visions of victory quickly dissipated into visions of fear. The Cajun stood and held out the ammunition clip for Kaja's Uzi. His face showed no emotion. Slowly his expressionless face turned into a smile. He turned around, showing his back contemptuously to Kaja, as Kaja had countless times to others. He slowly walked away and disappeared into the thick jungle-like growth of the Atchafalaya.

* * *

Nouri was feverish and passed it off to the water, but the poison of the recluse spider was working. The skin was dying around the area of the bite. Nouri failed to notice the light red line on his arm moving slowly toward his shoulder. Nouri suffered from blood poisoning and failed to recognize the signs.

"Did you hear that?" Nouri asked.

"A gunshot?" said Fawad, more in question than answer.

"Maybe, Mustafa has the Cajun. We should go back," added Kamdar.

They stopped in the trail to discuss returning to camp. From the words passed back and forth, it was difficult to discern whether they feared Ballew or Mustafa more.

To return with nothing would bring the wrath of Mustafa and Kaja--if he were present. They argued it would also be foolish to continue if the Cajun was caught. Then came the sound of the familiar Uzi. The three men cast apprehensive looks at each other. They decided that the most logical path would be in the direction they heard the Uzi fired. With Kidane and Mustafa behind, they were apprehensive over who fired the shots from the Uzi.

Cautiously, they moved out, praying to Allah they not find the Cajun, and worried they would.

* * *

While Ballew watched Kaja, he was not concerned as to who had shot the rifle. And soon he dismissed it from his mind. From the safety of the jungle-like growth of the swamp, he watched the three men moving slowly in his direction. Nearby was a small lagoon, where many loggerhead turtles nested and waited in their perpetual pursuit of food. A plan slowly evolved and it would need a loggerhead to be successful.

None of the three men noticed Ballew's departure, and soon he reached the edge of the lagoon. The same lack of movement in the air making the terrorists so miserable went unnoticed by Ballew and worked in his favor. The usually murky waters were calm and provided a clear view to a depth of two feet.

The plan was about to be discarded when he spied the top of a huge loggerhead. He estimated its shell to be bigger than the one he once had mounted in his house . . . his once proud home, destroyed by the fire started by the men hunting him.

A few yards away at the edge of the lagoon grew a cluster of reeds. Ballew cut a handful of the reeds, cleaned them, then took two of almost identical size and length, casting the others away. He took one reed and blew through one end, forcing material lodged in the round, hollow shoot out and leaving a clear passage. He repeated the same thing with the second reed.

He removed his Spider Man T-shirt, took one of the shoots and shoved it through the fabric near the neck. With the shirt firmly in place, he took care to find the front of the loggerhead and carefully shoved the reed into the mud near the turtle's head. The reed jerked viciously, then released. Ballew pulled the slender tube back quickly, while he continued to keep his eye on the turtle. It had taken little effort for the snapper to remove the end of the shoot.

Ballew waited for the loggerhead to move, but instead it lay quietly in the same spot beneath the water. The second time, the small reed went unnoticed by the huge reptile.

Again, Ballew repeated the process, using the other reed, this time with a bit more success. The turtle did not approach the reed. The shirt, secure to the reed, floated almost a foot below the surface of the water. All the motion had stirred the water up to its usual murkiness.

Clutching the other reed, he went in pursuit of the three men. A short distance away, he encountered them moving slowly through the swamp. His appearance on the trail startled them, but they recovered quickly and ran in pursuit, firing their weapons each time they saw him come into view. Efforts to catch their elusive quarry were futile. Ballew made sure to present himself to them to insure they saw the reed he carried.

Ballew led them to the bank of the lagoon, where he hid, making sure they would not see him.

Fawad reached the lagoon first, desperate for revenge. Only a few yards away lay the loggerhead.

"Only a demon can disappear like that," whispered Kamdar.

"Search for him. He is no demon," Fawad admonished. "The Cajun is hiding."

"Look!" said Nouri, pointing to the murky waters and the shirt floating below. "There is the reed he carried. He hides below the water," he added. He pointed the Uzi and started to squeeze the trigger.

"Wait!" snapped Fawad, pushing the gun aside. "The water will deflect your shots." A sinister smile covered his face, "Besides, I have not forgotten what he did to Azad. I personally will choke the life from him. I want him to know what it is like to drown."

Nouri and Kamdar smiled their approval. Fawad eased himself into the knee-deep water. He stood only a few feet from the reed poking above the water.

"Die!" he yelled, sinking both hands below the water and toward the base of the reed and the soft neck he expected to clutch in his bare hands.

Instead of the anticipated soft neck, both hands felt a horrendous pain as something clamped about them like a steel vise. The shriek of terror and pain so caught Nouri and Kamdar by surprise, they stumbled back in fear, both falling to the ground.

A normal man would be unable to rise from the water. But the fear and terror Fawad experienced gave him a strength of no mortal man. Somehow, he managed to back out of the water with the huge loggerhead in a death grip on both hands. Although endowed with seemingly superhuman strength, he was no match for the giant turtle.

Ear-piercing screams continued as the right arm came free. The right arm no longer had a hand. Mechanically, Fawad tried to beat off the turtle with the stub of his right arm.

Recovered from their initial shock, Nouri and Kamdar rushed to the aid of their companion. Even their quick actions were not as fast as the loggerhead. Its jaws opened and closed, moving up Fawad's arm, refusing to release its prey. Incredibly, Fawad found the turtle past his left elbow and still moving up the arm.

Shock and the loss of blood made Fawad stumble to the ground. Futilely, he beat the turtle with the stub of his right arm. All three men beat furiously on the turtle with no seeming effect.

With the arm firmly locked in its jaws, the loggerhead backed into the lagoon. Nouri reacted to the new situation, retrieving his Uzi and firing many rounds into the body of the huge turtle. The loggerhead ceased to move, killed by the blast.

Nouri tied a tourniquet around Fawad's right forearm to prevent the flow of blood from the missing hand. Only the excitement of the moment gave Nouri the strength to continue in his weakened state. Not only had he contacted a virus from the water, but blood poisoning spread rapidly up his arm, a result of the bite from the Recluse spider. The fever worsened and his strength faded quickly.

Frantically, Kamdar tried to pry the jaws from Fawad's left arm but his trembling fingers failed to remove the powerful jaws. They had no way of knowing the arm was severed at the elbow and the blood flowing from the turtle was in reality Fawad's.

Fawad chattered incessantly as they tried to pry the jaws from his arm. His breathing accelerated and his speech slurred. Finally, he stopped speaking. Fawad had bled to death.

Kamdar checked Fawad's pulse and shook his head. Silently, both men moved away from the grisly remains of their friend, sitting on the ground staring at the body, stunned by the quickly changing events.

The loss started to register on the two men when Ballew made his presence known to them . . . at a time when anger ruled their judgmental faculties. Ballew would get the men to continue their blind pursuit of him through the swamp and into yet another trap.

Kamdar spotted Ballew and instantly jumped to his feet, forcing Nouri to his, and on with the chase of the elusive Cajun. Blind anger pushed the two men on. Twice, Nouri stumbled and fell to the marsh grass. Each time, he thought he would never rise again, but Kamdar forced Nouri on again and again, not knowing how deathly ill his companion was. Every time they were on the verge of stopping, Ballew revealed himself to continue the chase.

Finally, Nouri stumbled and slumped to the ground, his body racked by convulsions as he tried to throw up, but couldn't. Nothing remained in his stomach as his body squeezed it dry. The now painful heaves continued intermittently, bringing forth only blood. His body shook with chills from the dangerously high fever. The journey ended for he could continue no further.

During a brief interlude in the agonizing convulsions, Nouri put a weak hand on Kamdar's shoulder and, through chattering teeth, said, "Go, find him for Fawad and Azad."

Determined to find the Cajun, Kamdar forged slowly ahead. Again Ballew made his presence known, forcing Kamdar into a mad rush toward him.

* * *

Every sound, every movement put Kaja on edge. He was slowly losing control. For the first time in his life, the master of terror experienced fear. The words continued to be dominant in his mind. "Today you will die," were the exact words spoken by the Cajun. The Uzi trembled in his hands. A low moan would escape from deep within Kaja each time a leaf even rustled . . . from the place deep in a person where fear resides. Even the shadows startled him, and horror slowly took control of Kaja. Cautiously, he searched the jungle to find the others, but all he found were bodies of his comrades, first Jibreen then Bakshi. He stood over Bakshi, horror stricken, when he saw the slight smile on Bakshi's face. Kaja trembled as he searched Bakshi's pockets, being unable to take his eyes away from the smile on the dead man's face. What had happened to make him smile? For some reason Kaja felt like Bakshi was about to reach up and stop him.

His thoughts were interrupted when he found something he could use. Bakshi had a loaded clip for the Uzi.

None too soon, for in the distance Kaja could discern someone's approach. A rapid approach! He fumbled with the clip and thought he would never get the clip in his Uzi, but he finally managed to load and set his weapon. Now he could deal with the Cajun!

Kaja managed enough courage to stand and face the sounds as they came ever closer. He was ready for the rapid advance of someone or something from the thick growth of the swamps. Kneeling in the ankle deep water beside a large cypress, its roots exposed, he braced for the onslaught. As the sounds came closer, he tried to grip the Uzi tighter in his shaking hands.

Kaja responded instantly--just as the thick growth began to part and before the victim came within sight, Kaja started firing. Terror and fear of dying kept his finger locked on the trigger, even when he realized the man he fired upon was not the Cajun, but he was determined to take no chances. The clicking of the firing pin on empty chambers brought Kaja back to reality.

Slowly, Kaja approached the body of the man on the ground, holding the empty Uzi pointed in the dead man's direction. Not until he turned the body over with the barrel of the weapon did he recognize his attacker as Kamdar. It took a moment before Kaja rationalized that Kamdar was not his attacker, but instead his possible savior. Now Kamdar was dead.

"He is dead," came a chilling voice from behind Kaja, so close he could feel the breath on his neck.

Kaja recognized the voice even as he turned. Before him stood the Cajun with the familiar bow slung over his shoulder, arms hanging at his side.

"I will kill you," shrieked Kaja, raising the Uzi and pointing it at Ballew.

But Kaja was disarmed when he heard Ballew laugh and point to the gun Kaja held. "It is empty." Then he walked over to Kamdar's body, bent over, and picked up his Uzi, removed the clip, and threw the Uzi in Kaja's direction, "That one was full."

Ballew stepped to Kaja and took his Uzi as though it were a toy. "You do not have much time. I must go now."

Then casually, as though Kaja were no threat, Ballew moved away silently and disappeared into the swamp. Before Kaja could regain his senses, Ballew was gone.

Kaja was lost and alone--alone to his own thoughts and the terror in his mind. Even the small sounds of the trees and their movements made Kaja jump--and the Atchafalaya never rested!

* * *

Hidden to the side of the trail, Mustafa and Kidane lay patiently, waiting the approach of the person who fired the shot killing Tahel.

They had discovered the grisly site where the bodies of Tahel and Raj lay dead, and surmised Tahel was killed by the shot they had heard. When they arrived, Moinuddin barely clung to life. He died when they reached his side. The trail of Tahel's killer led to the camp. Just outside the camp, they lay in wait for the killer's return.

They were surprised to find the person in camp was Kelli. Surely she could not be alone, they thought, and both cast apprehensive looks, all around, for the Cajun they were sure was near, but as she continued toward both men, they saw no sign of another.

The sound of an Uzi in the distance startled all three, but gave Kidane and Mustafa the edge when Kelli turned in the direction of the gunfire. Mustafa was first to react, springing from the concealment of the thick growth along the trail and wrestling the weapon from the unsuspecting woman.

She kicked, bit and fought, but without success, as the two men overpowered her. Savagely, they threw her to the ground, tying her hands behind her back. Mustafa entwined his fingers in her hair, jerking her head from the ground. He looped a gag over her mouth and around the back of her head.

"Should we kill her?" asked Kidane.

"No," said Mustafa with a sly smile. "The Cajun made only one mistake--to free the woman!"

Chapter 20

Vengeance

Kidane and Mustafa reached the place where the trap prepared for Ballew waited. Both men surveyed the area--nothing touched, everything as it was. The sharpened spikes still remained in the tree.

Mustafa peered back along the trail and smiled with delight. "He will not see you here," he said, pointing to a recess in the ground near the tree with the spikes. "Lay in the hole and I will cover you." Mustafa looked all around, "This is the only way he can pass. When he passes, you know what to do."

"And you?" asked Kidane as he knelt into the hole.

"I will take her along the trail. If the Cajun does what I expect, he will soon be at the camp. There he will discover we have the woman. He will pursue quickly, so you must be ready," Mustafa said, while covering Kidane with broken leaves and branches. "I will wait for you."

Mustafa could no longer see Kidane beneath the cover.

"Come!" he demanded, jerking Kelli to her feet, then along the trail.

But Mustafa had other intentions for the woman. He had creeping doubts about his ability to defeat the Cajun. So he decided, should the Cajun be victorious over him, he would not lose when it came to the woman. When Mustafa finished, the woman would be of no value to anyone . . . even if she were alive.

They came to the edge of the clearing, stopping so quickly Kelli tripped, falling to her knees. Quickly, he pulled her to her feet.

"You are beautiful," Mustafa whispered, his pulse rate quickening. Twisting his left hand in her hair, he pulled her head back and kissed her neck, running his wet, hot tongue along her neck and down toward her breasts.

His offensive breath appalled her. With his right hand, he ripped the shirt from her body, tearing the material as though it were paper, revealing her breasts. He squeezed her breast viciously.

Quickly, Kelli brought a knee to Mustafa's groin, but the move was anticipated and warded off by Mustafa's quickness. He held her at arm's length, laughed, and rewarded her actions with a blow of his own to her midsection, choking the air from her body.

Instantly, the blow sent Kelli reeling and to her knees, falling forward against Mustafa's thighs. He grabbed her face with one hand and threw her on her back. With his legs straddling her body, he sat across her midsection, pinning her against the soft, wet grasses covering the bog. He squeezed her left breast cruelly, while he sucked savagely on the other.

Sitting erect, he laughed at Kelli while he reached behind his back and ran his hand between her legs. When he found what he wanted, he squeezed hard. "You will enjoy Mustafa; all women do," he said with a sinister grin.

Still Kelli defied him, spitting in his face. The back of his hand came across her violently, bringing blood from her lips.

Kelli smiled and squinted her eyes, "Do what you want. It won't matter . . . Ballew Dragun will kill you, like the others."

The grin quickly subsided and Mustafa renewed his attack as he started to remove Kelli's jeans. She fought savagely but hopelessly against Mustafa's superior strength. At one point, she screamed for help, but Mustafa dealt her a crushing blow to the face. Tears crept into her eyes, knowing he would probably kill her. She found herself wishing for revenge and hoping Ballew would kill Mustafa.

* * *

Ballew found the three dead men, Moinuddin, Tahel, and Raj.
At first the signs were confusing. The small footprints made no sense. Suddenly, he realized they belonged to Kelli. He didn't take time to guess how Kelli had returned, and, for the moment, he cursed Happy Jak and Richard for their carelessness in letting Kelli

return to Devil's Island. He knew Happy Jak would not return until evening as Ballew had ordered.

Somehow, Kelli had returned and once again, Kaja's men had captured her. Ballew moved quickly along the fresh trail . . . quickly and carelessly.

He ran silently, gripping his bow in one hand and the quiver filled with arrows in the other. The terrain rose slightly, and just ahead the trail disappeared around a large tree.

Once he rounded the tree, he slowed and stopped. The trail took a strange twist. One set of footprints disappeared. In the distance, a scream halted his heart and in the moment of anguish for Kelli, he failed to hear Kidane's mad lunge toward him from behind.

Ballew turned none too soon, only to meet the full force of Kidane's savage attack. The suddenness of the charge enabled Kidane to achieve the upper hand, clasping his giant arms about Ballew, pinning the Cajun's arms to his sides, and knocking him to the ground on his back.

The impact forced Ballew to release his weapons.

Gloating in triumph, Kidane, never releasing his prey, struggled to his feet. In victory he stood staring at his semi-conscious victim in the eyes.

"Now I will crush you before I kill you," he laughed.

The pain brought Ballew to his senses, but the more he struggled, the tighter Kidane squeezed. Ballew was helpless to free himself.

Kidane sensed his triumph and let out with a sinister roar of approval. "So this is the mighty Cajun Kaja feared. He is but a boy in my grasp." He glanced toward the spikes embedded in the tree. "It is time to die--but, first, you should **suffer** . . . feel **real** pain that will make you **beg** for death."

Ballew turned his head enough to see what Kidane stared at so excitedly. The spikes were intended for him! He redoubled his efforts, but Kidane increased his superhuman effort to crush the life from Ballew.

Unable to breathe as Kidane's arms increased their pressure, Ballew felt one of his ribs snap.

His mind was still clear, even through the pain of the breaking rib. Gallantly, he pulled the muscles within his chest and ribs taut, resisting Kidane's crushing onslaught.

The sudden resistance Kidane felt momentarily surprised

him, and he made a fatal mistake when he looked up into the Cajun's face. Like lightning, Ballew snapped his head down, catching Kidane full between the eyes, and staggering the mighty man, but he failed to dislodge Kidane's grip. In a last desperate effort, Ballew brought his head down face-to-face with Kidane, only this time his jaws clamped like a vise about Kidane's nose.

Horrified that the Cajun had latched onto his nose, Kidane screamed out in pain, released Ballew and clasped his hand to his noseless face, blood gushing between the fingers of his massive hands. All thoughts of the Cajun were momentarily gone.

The slight hesitation on Kidane's part was all Ballew needed. He did not wait to gloat or talk over his victory and Kidane's agony, but instead took advantage of the moment and acted swiftly.

This time Ballew pinned Kidane's arms to his side and, without wasting the advantage, he rushed Kidane, shoving him into the spikes intended for him.

Kidane released a blood-curdling scream, one of a man who knows he is dead. He struggled briefly, trying to pull himself from the spikes, but his breathing quickened and blood ran from his mouth. The Cajun stood before him, watching silently. When Kidane failed to struggle any longer, and only watched Ballew with blinking eyes and hastened breath, Ballew spit the portion of the nose from his mouth and into his open hand. Slowly and deliberately, he moved forward while Kidane watched helplessly. Then to Kidane's sheer horror, Ballew separated Kidane's jaws, and shoved the grisly portion of the nose into Kidane's mouth.

Kidane struggled ever so slightly, trying to spit the bloody mass from his mouth, but he could not. For a brief moment, he saw everything clearly before he died.

Ballew had not hesitated, stopping only long enough to retrieve his weapons and continue on the trail in search of Kelli.

* * *

Mustafa heard the eerie scream. In an instant, he scrambled to his feet and retrieved his pants. He was angry at the interruption because Kelli had proved to be more of a fighter than he had anticipated and he had been unable to complete his desires. But when he finished the Cajun he would finish what he had started with Kelli. No sooner had he secured his pants than another scream could be heard, more uncanny than the first.

The Atchafalaya echoed with the terrified agony of a dying

man.
It seemed to take forever to complete the simple task of fastening his pants. He fumbled with the buttons of his shirt, while Kelli lay moaning on the ground. It would be better to move on and prepare for the Cajun and learn later that Kidane had triumphed, than it would be to wait and find the Cajun victorious. For some reason, he doubted Kidane succeeded.

Mustafa jerked Kelli to her feet. She retaliated by kicking his leg. Viciously, his right hand knocked her to the ground, then he moved toward her, bent on further punishment for her acts. Although he heard nothing, the look of relief in Kelli's eyes warned him. Turning quickly, he saw the reason for her excitement. At the edge of the clearing was his nemesis, Ballew Dragun.

Ballew took in the scene immediately and found it hard to contain his anger when he saw Kelli lying on the soft, moss-covered ground. He initiated a full attack on Mustafa.

With astonishing speed, Mustafa sprang to his feet to meet the onslaught. Moving with cat-like speed, he grabbed the gun laying beside him. Never had Mustafa failed, nor would he now. No one had ever escaped his expert marksmanship. In one motion, he turned the weapon and, with deadly aim, squeezed the trigger.

Quick was Mustafa, but quicker yet was Ballew. Not missing a stride, he saw Mustafa retrieve the gun. At the same instant he reached across his body and in one smooth, swift motion, slipped his large knife from his sheath and threw it with the speed and accuracy of an arrow in Mustafa's direction.

Metal clanged as the knife met the Uzi. The force knocked the weapon harmlessly to the side as Ballew's charge caught Mustafa, knocking him to the ground and the Uzi yards away. Both men rolled free and were immediately on their feet.

Slowly they circled each other like two cats ready to spring. Mustafa smiled confidently to himself, for as long as he could see his adversary, he knew he would be victorious. His only fear was when the Cajun remained hidden in the heavy undergrowth. The Cajun had no contact with civilization, this Mustafa knew. Likewise, he had no knowledge of hand-to-hand combat. With Mustafa's superior knowledge of martial arts, the Cajun would be easily defeated.

Kelli regained her senses enough to crawl to the edge of the clearing. She could only watch in awe, unable to help.

The two combatants moved ever closer, all the while circling each other, waiting to gain an advantage over the other. Ballew moved cautiously with his legs bent, arms spread wide, and hands open. Never had he seen a man fight with his hands flat and fingers closed closely together. He thought it curious Mustafa fought with no intention to clasp and wrestle to the death as had Kidane.

Swiftly, Mustafa swung his right hand in the direction of Ballew's head. Ballew moved under the blow and it appeared to him Mustafa had lost his balance when his left leg rose in the air. The swiftness of the left leg caught Ballew off guard as the left foot dealt a crushing blow to his already tender ribs.

The impact sent him reeling and somersaulting across the thick, dead vegetation. Pain filled his side and he found it hard to breathe as he came quickly to his feet, turning to catch the onslaught of Mustafa. Another foot came flying in his direction, but Ballew managed to deflect it. Never had he seen such manner of fighting. He marveled at the speed of the feet, then a fist caught him full in the face. Staggering backwards, he tripped and fell to the ground. Rolling over, he managed to get to all fours in an effort to regain his feet.

"No!" screamed Kelli.

Ballew heard the scream at the same instant a foot caught him full in the stomach. The force sent him reeling. No sooner had he rolled over, readied in anticipation of another swift kick, than an elbow caught him just below the neck, almost knocking him out. His arms failed to respond as he tried to lift himself from the ground. Again, a foot caught him in the ribs. Stunned and unable to move, he felt Mustafa atop his back with a strategically placed knee below his shoulders. A hand clasped about his chin and Mustafa slowly pulled Ballew's head back to break the neck.

"You bastard!" Kelli screamed as she stormed over to Mustafa in a frenzy of biting, scratching and hitting.

All unsuccessfully as the mighty Mustafa pulled her around with his free hand and hit her full in the stomach with his fist. She fell to the ground like a rag doll, groaning, gasping for air and semi-conscious. Aware of what had happened, she could do nothing.

With sadistic pleasure, he went about his work again, clasping his hand under Ballew's chin and pulling his head back, waiting for the sickening snap that would bring about an end to the Cajun's life.

He bent near Ballew's ear for one final pleasure and

whispered in his ear, "When you die, I will have my way with your woman. I will strip her, rape her, and . . . I will kill her!"

The cobwebs cleared from Ballew's head and the feeling returned to his arms. He saw and heard all, but not until now could he move.

Mustafa pulled and the head came back slowly, then suddenly stopped and began to inch forward. Startled by the sudden response from the Cajun, Mustafa doubled his efforts to break Ballew's neck, but he was unable to pull the head back any farther. Then Mustafa heard a sound like an animal or more like a snarl. The sounds emanated from the lips of Ballew and made Mustafa's blood run cold.

Mustafa hesitated and Ballew's arm moved like lightning. His elbow caught Mustafa full in the ribs, sending him tumbling from Ballew's back and grasping the injured area.

Both men recovered simultaneously and were again on their feet, facing each other. Mustafa yelled at the top of his lungs and also made a headlong charge for Ballew. Just before he made contact, he sprang in the air, aiming his feet forward, planting them firmly in Ballew's chest, knocking him down.

Ballew jumped to his feet as quick as Mustafa. Again both men went at each other. The right foot flew through the air, aimed for Ballew's head, but Ballew moved to the side and planted a left fist in Mustafa's ribs, sending him to the ground.

Ballew moved towards Mustafa but as he bent over Mustafa rolled over and grabbed Ballew by the shoulders. In the same motion he planted both feet in the midsection, sending Ballew in a flip over his body. Instantly both men were on their feet.

They moved in close again. Ballew swung with his right fist, but Mustafa knocked his arm harmlessly away. Mustafa followed this with a clockwise circle in the air, landing his left foot to Ballew's back. In an instant, they were facing each other again. With two motions of his foot, Mustafa kicked Ballew in the stomach, then followed with a blow to the face, sending him wobbling back on his feet. Mustafa moved in for a death blow, bringing his left foot up hard under Ballew's chin in an effort to break his chin or snap his neck.

Ballew had watched the deadly moves of Mustafa's feet. He caught Mustafa unaware, moving quickly to his left and sidestepping the foot. His right hand flashed as it caught the ankle of the left foot, catching it in a vise-like grip, while his left fist came crashing down with tremendous force, backed by all his strength, directly on the left knee cap.

A scream of excruciating pain came from Mustafa's mouth as the leg below the knee bent down at a grotesquely unnatural angle. The sickening sound of breaking cartilage could be heard above the screams of pain.

No sooner did the hand come down on the leg, than Ballew raised his left foot and sent his whole body into Mustafa's right leg just above the knee. The left leg started to bend and then came the same sound of snapping and breaking bone as both men crashed to the ground with Ballew over Mustafa. Ballew pulled himself from the ground, towering over his victim. The right leg was bent at the same awful angle, two bones protruding through the skin behind the knee.

Writhing on the ground, screaming from the pain of both broken legs, Mustafa clasped both hands about his head and cried in torment.

Without as much as a backward glance, Ballew moved to where Kelli lay, propped on one arm. Gently, he raised her to her feet. She wrapped both arms around his neck and clung to him.

After a moment, Ballew pulled the arms from his neck, "I told you not to come back. How come you did dat?"

"Because I was worried about you. You big ass! I did help you, you know!" she said defiantly.

"What say you be right. Maybe you don't need Ballew. Maybe I leave you," he said, turning and walking away.

"Whoa! Wait!" she pleaded, jumping in front of him. Then she threw her nose in the air. "I want to go with you."

Ballew paused, rubbing his chin, "You do as Ballew say?"

"Okay," she said, somewhat subdued. Then she thought of Kaja's other men, "But what of the rest?"

He looked over to where Mustafa lay, "There is only one other. Kaja."

"Only one? Where are the others . . .?"

"Dead. Only Kaja remains," he stated indifferently. Then he put his hand on her shoulder. "Wait."

She did as he said and Ballew moved toward Mustafa and knelt to the ground. He said nothing. He just looked directly into Mustafa's eyes.

"Kill me! Kill me," Mustafa pleaded.

For the longest time, Ballew watched Mustafa, saying

nothing. Still Mustafa asked for death. Finally, Ballew spoke: "Got a big curious. Why dat you came? Never mind why dat. You came dat Atchafalaya . . . now you die Atchafalaya. Should killed you dead, but I let you think. Why you want came here?"

Without another word he turned, took Kelli by the hand and moved out of the clearing. The words grew fainter but even in the distance, they could still hear Mustafa begging to die.

A few minutes later they came to the same spot where Ballew had told Happy Jak to meet him. He stopped and turned to Kelli, "Stay here, I come back before dark."

Ballew was about to disappear into the thick undergrowth when Kelli yelled, "Where are you going?"

In answer, he turned and shrugged his shoulders. "I go to get Kaja." With those few words, he returned to his quest.

Chapter 21

CAJUN TERROR

They came to the Atchafalaya to deal death swiftly. The trained and expert terrorists had not anticipated the likes of Ballew Dragun, the Cajun. These thoughts and others remained at the front of Kaja's fear.

Every move was that of a terrified man. All his thoughts and actions were of escaping from Devil's Island . . . an island from which there was no escape. A fear prevailed that he would find no means of escape and a fear he **would** find the Cajun. Kaja, the master of terror, was afraid and he was lost.

In survival, he had committed the master sin. He drank the water of the swamp and now his body paid dearly for his mistake. Sickness took hold of his body, but fear controlled his mind as he continued nowhere.

Suddenly, Kaja burst from the trail, falling to his knees. Ten feet in front of him stood the silent Cajun, bow slung over his shoulders and arms crossed. He wore the cap in reverse.

With a shriek, Kaja gained his feet, reversed direction, and darted from the area, running as fast as his shaky legs would carry him. Every noise and every movement spurred him on to greater speeds. Once, he came abruptly upon a wild pig roaming the island. Although usually aggressive themselves, the poor animal and Kaja let out equally terrified squeals when Kaja thrust himself within touching distance of the animal. Both exploded in opposite directions at undetermined speeds.

His heart pounding and his legs cramped, he finally slowed down his pace. He had no idea how long he had run, only that he could run no more. His chest heaved with every breath; still, his eyes were open wide in terror, searching for what he knew somehow must be near. The Cajun.

Clinging to a huge cypress, Kaja regained his composure. Slowly, he slid his left hand about the exposed roots of the large tree, pulling himself along as he scouted for evidence of the man who pursued.

For a brief moment, he heard a whistle through the air, followed by a dull thud that sent pain from his hand through his whole body, momentarily making him forget the fever. The new problem was more serious and painful. A long wooden shaft embedded in the cypress pinning his hand to the tree. He had seen it before, an arrow from the quiver of the Cajun.

He screamed more in fear than in pain while reaching for the shaft to free his left hand. Just as he put his hand against the tree trying to push free, another shaft sailed through the air, pinning his right hand to the tree. Again, Kaja shrieked and moans of pain and fear gurgled from his mouth as he hung helplessly pinned to the tree.

Kaja detected a slight noise and twisted his head to look over his shoulders. Directly behind him, watching his predicament, stood the Cajun.

Slowly, he moved near. Kaja jumped up and down like a caged animal and continued to cry out in pain, begging for mercy in his native tongue, but the cries no longer sounded human as sanity began to slowly ebb from his brain.

When Ballew was near enough to touch Kaja, he just looked at him. The lack of action only terrified Kaja more. Ballew's hands flashed like lightning as he grabbed Kaja by the hair, pulling his head back. Slowly, deliberately, while Kaja watched, he moved his face to Kaja's ear and whispered, "Now you get to see how my God's son felt when he died."

Ballew twisted Kaja's hair in his hand, then reached to the shafts protruding from Kaja's hand and bent them back and forth till each shaft broke near to where they entered the hands. Each time he moved the shafts back and forth, Kaja would let out a whimpering moan.

After he disposed of the shafts, he bent Kaja's head back one more time. "Go! Maybe you can escape. If you do, you will be the first," Ballew said, letting go of the hair and stepping back.

Screaming for mercy, Kaja pulled away from the tree, while

trying to free his hands.

"By Allah, don't kill me. Please let me live. I have money, you . . . ," Kaja pleaded.

Finally freeing his hand, he turned to present his offers. The Cajun was gone!

Without a moment's hesitation, Kaja was off and running, with the speed and quickness of a rabbit, in the opposite direction he last saw his adversary. He ran and ran and then ran some more. Once, while running through thick undergrowth, a harmless green tree snake fell about his neck, setting off another chorus of screams and again sending him off blindly in the opposite direction.

Exhaustion again gripped his body and he finally slowed his pace. With every passing minute he failed to see the Cajun, his confidence reached new heights. He tried to cross a fallen tree when he heard the now familiar whistle approach followed by a thud--but no pain. He looked down to see an arrow protruding through his boot between his big toe and smaller toe. The arrow had missed. He pulled frantically to dislodge the shaft from his boot, but without success. With no seeming alternatives, he removed the boot and set about running with one shoeless foot . . . running in any direction that might offer safety.

He ran faster than he had ever run in his life and when he felt he would surely fall from sheer exhaustion, fear pushed him to greater feats of strength, and miraculously, he continued to run and run. Between the safety of dozens of cypress trees, where the water was a foot in depth covered with a green fungus, he crossed a tangle of roots rising above the water. Suddenly the same noise with the same result, only this time the slender wooden shaft embedded in the heel of Kaja's remaining boot.

Trembling in fear, he pulled and tugged at the shoe to break it free. Again, with his strength fading, he managed to pull his foot from the leather boot holding it prisoner. The noises he made sounded like the incoherent gibberish of a monkey gone mad. He cast furtive glances about for a glimpse of the Cajun, so he could run safely in the other direction. Kaja saw nothing, then terror took control.

In an instant he was off and running, crying out in despair as he went. With every noise, he changed direction.

The sudden surprise of an open clearing startled him and made him back against the base of a tall tree for security. Through the whole ordeal, he continually dodged brush and trees. Now, for the first time, an opening where he could see ahead. Kaja, the master of terror, was afraid to cross.

Instinctively, he hid his injured and bleeding hands from the expected cruelty of the Cajun. Both feet bled from being cut by the brush and debris matting the swamp floor. The Cajun was there in the shadows. Every shadow was the Cajun . . . he could sense it.

Suddenly, the sound came at him again, bringing a scream of anguish from his lips. He tried to move, but froze in terror. This time he felt only a slight pain at the base of his neck. The feathered end of the arrow vibrated frighteningly close to his face, the other end stuck deep in the trunk of the tree.

Kaja took a step forward, but was yanked back against the tree. The arrow had cut his neck near the jugular vein and locked his heavy shirt against the tree. He refused to take time to remove the shirt, instead taking the easy way, jerking on the front of the shirt popping the buttons off in all directions. He removed his arms, leaving the shirt hanging from the arrow.

Again, he ran headlong through the swamps. So furious his onslaught he never saw the bullnettle he rushed into. Nor did he notice the water moccasin he kicked harshly to the side with his foot. The reptile made a quick strike, just a glancing blow. Not enough to be deadly, but a strike, nonetheless. Kaja was oblivious to all of this as he rushed madly through the swamps of the Atchafalaya to rid himself of the demon chasing him. Kaja wasted no time looking back, because somewhere out there lurked the Cajun.

Kaja never comprehended he was an unwitting pawn being maneuvered by the Cajun. Maneuvered much like a dog herds sheep. Kaja no longer headed aimlessly about, but instead, now in a set direction--a pre-arranged path set by the Cajun!

Kaja crashed recklessly through the swamps and again he burst into an open clearing. The force of his charge brought him directly into the middle of the clearing before he could slow himself down. He mumbled incoherently, jumping and turning his body completely around to see what approached him from the rear. He twisted, jumped, moved, dodged, and turned, to his left, to his right, then he checked his hindquarter. Kaja's terrified eyes rolled to his right, then his left, but no sign of the predator he knew pursued.

Belle Rose's words returned to haunt him -- "You will die many times. You will die last." Suddenly, unable to control himself anymore, he raised his clenched fists and shook his arms, "Kill me! By Allah, end this torture. Kill me!"

In answer to his demand, another shaft of death sped through the clearing on a path in line with Kaja's heart. The arrow flew true and accurate, hitting Kaja in the chest, staggering him, and knocking him back.

Stunned by the impact, but shocked by the lack of pain, Kaja turned disbelieving eyes to the ground where the arrow lay, the sharp end broken away and wrapped with his own shirt. The shirt he left hanging on another arrow just a short time before.

Kaja cursed obscenities at the Cajun in his own native tongue. "Kill me, you coward! I demand you kill me now! Show yourself!" Kaja demanded brazenly, knowing he could die any time. The edge of fear dulled by an exuberance and hope of relief by death.

"Not yet," came the whisper of the Cajun. He stood only two feet behind Kaja. "I am not finished yet."

The words renewed the fear and terror temporarily forgotten. When Kaja turned to face his death, he screamed deliriously and ran quickly in the opposite direction.

This time, Kaja moved quickly, but with a slight bit of caution. Then he heard a voice, giving him new hope. The voice came from nearby, and he thought he could detect the sound of an airboat in the distance.

Quietly, he came to the edge of where the campsite once had been. Carefully, he separated the reeds, only to find Kelli on the bank of the island, yelling, and waving at the approaching airboat. In the airboat, less than 100 yards from the island, were Richard and Happy Jak.

His courage bolstered when he knew Kelli was alone and she held a gun. A gun, something he understood, something that could help in his escape. Although sick and weak, he had enough strength remaining to wrestle the gun away and commandeer the boat away from the two men in exchange for the woman. A wild plan, but his only hope. He took the time to cast another fearful glance behind for the Cajun, then he charged quickly for the woman.

Kaja had taken less than a dozen steps when he turned his head toward Kelli, suddenly coming to a terrified halt. What he saw between him and Kelli was life and death.

Kelli was no less surprised by Kaja's sudden appearance

than she was that of the person who placed himself so quickly between her and Kaja.
Between them stood Ballew Dragun, the Cajun.
The string of the bow pulled taut, an arrow lay against Ballew's cheek, aimed directly at Kaja's heart.
Both Richard and Happy Jak disembarked from the boat.
Richard yelled, "Kill him before he gets away!"
No answer came from Ballew. Like a statue, he waited, motionless, with his weapon aimed for Kaja's heart.
The first to react was Kaja, who yelled incoherent gibberish, much like a crazy man. Screaming and with both arms waving wildly in the air, he spun about and ran from their view.
Richard hobbled toward Ballew, who lowered the bow and gently eased the arrow from its perch.
"You can't let him go. We must go after him. He needs to be brought to justice and punished," ordered Richard.
Ballew looked at Richard and said nothing. Kelli and Happy Jak gathered near. Kelli put both arms about Ballew's waist as he slipped his arm over her shoulders.
In the distance, they heard a shrill scream, followed shortly by another.
Ballew smiled and caught Richard's eyes, "Here his own mind will kill him. He will die a thousand times. Then he will die. Come, let us leave this place and go home. I have a house to build and you, *Ticrot* . . . you must go home and be a policeman again."
"I don't know if I wanta do this shit anymore," Richard mumbled.
They loaded the boat and, as Ballew turned it in the water to return to Happy Jak's store, he removed the Saints cap from his head and put it in the normal position.
The war was over.
Ballew moved to the front of the boat and pointed in a different direction from where home and safety waited. "Happy Jak, go this direction. There are some things that must be done."
The boat turned as Ballew directed. All were curious and Richard was about to speak when they neared the small island where he had deposited Delacroix and Mamou. They were nearing the spot where Ballew stranded the two men the day before. Before they reached the island, they could discern the short, stumpy figure of Mamou standing alone. This time Ballew directed Happy Jak to stop short of the island.

"Hey, Mamou, how you are?" Ballew asked.

"A little tired, a little hungry . . . but I got a big wanta go home," said Mamou with a little whine.

Ballew stared at Mamou. "Where be Delacroix?"

Mamou shrugged his shoulders, "He leave in the night. I not seen him today. Ballew, are you put big hurt on Mamou and leave him here?"

"Maybe. Should I?" Ballew asked.

For a moment, Mamou thought about the question. "Yes, maybe I have it coming," he mumbled dejectedly.

"You and Delacroix try to kill me. Maybe we leave Mamou, huh, Happy Jak?"

"Yes, we leave him to the snakes and the gators!" snapped Happy Jak, as he started the engine.

Instantly, Mamou dropped to his knees whining, "Oh, please, do not leave me die here, Ballew!"

"Don't leave him," Kelli pleaded, placing her hand on Ballew's arm. Then she saw the smile he and Happy Jak tried to hide.

"Oh, please, Ballew! I help you and Happy Jak and I be with Delacroix no more," Mamou begged.

Ballew shrugged his shoulders. "But Delacroix is dead."

"Oh, please, Ballew, take me," he begged.

With a frown and a shake of his head, Ballew waved his hand, "Okay. Hurry, get in. We leave."

Ballew scarcely finished saying the words before Mamou plodded through the shallow water and toward the boat that would take him to safety. Soon they were on their way again.

"Hey, Ballew, how 'bout we get back, 'ol Happy Jak make you some fritters."

"That sound good," said Ballew in a relaxed tone as though nothing had ever happened. He settled himself in the boat with his arm still snug about Kelli.

Finally Richard understood Ballew's justice. Richard had thought only of the code of justice established by the civilized world, but now, for the first time, he understood the Cajun's justice. He had no idea as to what had happened to Kaja's men and he didn't want to know. What was eerie to him was the look of terror he saw in Kaja's eyes before he turned and ran in fear. Richard was thankful Ballew was his friend.

Chapter 22

Goodbye, Ballew Dragun

A week had passed since Kaja disappeared, and Belle Rose was complaining, ready to vanish back into the swamp. Richard and Happy Jak had developed a unique relationship, with Happy Jak teaching Richard all about his business. Ballew and Kelli would disappear for longer periods and on the two previous nights they had vanished completely, only to return late the following mornings, laughing and singing. They became inseparable.

Ballew collected items to rebuild his house, making a trip to his island once a day. Rocky was recovering, and as Richard had said, "healing up and hairing over" from his burns. On one such trip, Ballew retrieved the painting he had hidden, the one he gave to Kelli.

The week passed so quickly, it was time for Richard and Kelli to return. Richard placed calls to friends in the Bureau, who were able to make arrangements for him and Kelli to be picked up. Everyone gathered for one last time, all save Belle Rose who had disappeared back into the swamps two days before. They sat together in a private room at Happy Jak's store.

After Ballew passed drinks to the other three and pulled a chair near the table, he placed the briefcase on the table with all the money Kaja had brought.

"I give money to Happy Jak for the damage caused by Kaja," Ballew said. "I want you two to split the rest between yourselves."

"We can't do that," Kelli answered.

"I have to turn it over to the FBI," said Richard with a shrug of his shoulders.

"Is it stolen?" Ballew asked.

"Well . . . no," answered Richard.

"In the swamp, if you have it, it be yours. I want you promise me you take it for yourselves . . . or I hide it in the swamp and no one have it."

"What about you?" Kelli asked.

"Yeah, what about you?" asked Richard.

"I need nothing. If **you** don't take it, no one does. You must promise."

Richard smiled sheepishly. "I never thought I'd be reluctant about taking a million dollars. You've got a deal."

Kelli shook her head affirmatively.

The agreement was made.

A few hours later, the two waited patiently for an FBI escort to take them to the airport in Baton Rouge.

"I guess we can trust the FBI this time," Kelli quipped.

"I reckon so," laughed Richard. "There's no bad guys left."

The car arrived and Happy Jak helped them load.

"Where is Ballew?" Kelli asked.

"He waits on the pier 'till you leave," said Happy Jak.

"Wait for me, Richard," said Kelli. She broke into a run for the pier.

"Hurry and tell him goodbye for me!" yelled Richard. He leaned against the car, pulled a cigarette from his pocket, and covering it from the wind, lit up. He took one drag, breathed in deeply, then looked at it while it burned. "Aw, hell! I need to stop this before it kills me."

With those last words, he threw it unceremoniously to the dirt, grinding it in until it burned no longer.

Kelli found Ballew just as Happy Jak had said, standing near his airboat. He smiled as she approached.

"I want to thank you for the painting. I will always cherish it," she said. "Ballew, I want you to come to the city with me."

He shook his head. "Stay with me . . . you be safe."

"I have to return. You understand, don't you?" she asked.

Ballew shook his head side to side, then gently pulled her close, kissing her long and passionately. Suddenly, he stopped, putting her at arm's length and looked into her eyes.

For a moment, she thought she detected tears. "Ballew?"

Somehow, he managed a smile. He released her, then

reached for his head, pulling the Saints cap from its familiar position and shook his long dark locks in the breeze.

Ballew looked at the hat, beat it twice against his left leg as though it were now clean. He looked at Kelli, then extended his hand and the cap toward her. His voice cracked: "For you . . . remember me . . . I will not forget you!"

Ballew turned abruptly, scrambling aboard the boat. The engine quickly jumped to life and in a moment, he turned the boat and slowly pulled away.

Kelli stood there, clutching the old cap to her chest, watching Ballew until he disappeared. A tear rolled down her cheek. "Goodbye, Ballew Dragun."

* * *

For two months Kelli Parsons again controlled her magazine office in New York. The only difference was, she occasionally wore jeans to the office, enticing the women working for her to hang loose and not be so rigid. Her department was no longer regimented as before, with production up 100 percent, due to the relaxed atmosphere.

Kelli touched the button on the intercom and summoned her secretary into the office. When Margaret entered, she carried a notebook and was wiping her eyes with a tissue.

"It's beautiful," she said. "I didn't know you could write fiction. The man is such a hunk. Where did you come up with that swamp idea?"

"That's a long story. You really liked it?"

"Oh, yes," she answered enthusiastically. "Oh, I almost forgot. Some things arrived for you. Did you really order something from Marvel Comics?"

"It's arrived!" said Kelli. She started to bolt from her office when Margaret pulled her to the side.

As Margaret spoke, she kept raising her eyebrows and pointing with her eyes to the top of Kelli's head. "Really, don't you think you should . . . "

"Oh, this," laughed Kelli, reaching up until she felt the black cap with the New Orleans Saints logo. "It's fine, don't worry."

Outside her office, next to Margaret's desk, was a cardboard box. Inside was a note that read, "Thanks for the story. Hope this is what you wanted." Inside were four Spider Man T-shirts, similar to the ones Ballew wore, three extra, extra, large and one medium. Beneath the shirts were Spider Man comic books, 30 in all.

Kelli held the medium against her chest, "How's it look?"

All Margaret could do was shrug her shoulders. "Uh, great. Are you okay? Kelli, is this a trick question?"

"Never mind."

"I almost forgot," Margaret said, reaching for an envelope on her desk, "these are for you."

Inside the envelope were two tickets to a football game--between the New York Giants and the New Orleans Saints . . . a game not be played for two months.

"I think they made a mistake," Margaret noted. "The game is to be played in New Orleans, not here."

"That's right."

"Hey, kid," came a familiar voice from behind.

She spun on her feet and came face to face with Richard. She gave him a quick hug and kiss, "Have you come to rescue me?"

"Of course," he said with a smile. "Got some place we can talk?"

Kelli dismissed Margaret and returned to her office with Richard. He walked to the window of her office and looked out, taking in New York. "Did you do as I told you?"

"I have the airline tickets in my purse. What about your job? They'll fire you when they find out."

Turning his back to the window so he could face her, he stuck his hands in his pocket. "Not really. You see, in the morning, they'll get my resignation. It's on my desk now."

"Do you believe the terrorists will make another attempt?"

"Don't know, but I figure the swamp will be the safest place. God knows, he can take care of you." Richard smiled, "Hey, kid, next time you want to write about those guys, would it be okay if **I** said a few things?"

"Sure."

"You'll print 'em?"

"You bet." Then she asked, "What are **you** going to do?"

"I've got the money--or did you forget? Or should I say, I have **some** of it left."

"What did you do with the money?"

"Well, there was this barmaid I've always had drinks with. Sarah's not too bad, for an older woman. She's my age, forty-four. Anyway, I always said, if I got rich, I'd take her to the Caymans, buy a bar, and settle down."

"Did you?" Kelli asked.

"What, settle down or buy a bar?"

"Richard!"

"She's in the Caymans now," Richard said with a sly smile. "Got a sailboat, and Sarah and I are gonna charter it out. Always wanted to do it. I hope you get to come down some time and meet her."

"I'd like that."

"Oh, yeah . . . I call her--the sailboat that is--the *Ticrot*."

Kelli laughed when she heard the name of the boat. "I almost forgot; did Happy Jak get the lumber?"

"Yeah. He said Ballew refused for a while, but gave in. All the lumber for the new place is there, and the compressor, generator, and those windows you wanted to send him."

"Good."

"Well, guess I'd better get going."

"Me, too," said Kelli with a sigh.

"I'll drop a line to Happy Jak when I get settled. I expect you and Ballew to come see me. The first visit is on me."

"You have a deal," she said, slipping him a wink. She gave him another hug and a kiss.

A sheepish grin covered his face. "Say, you couldn't give me another one of those hugs and kisses?"

"Richard!" she admonished, shaking a finger at him.

As if in surrender, he held his hands high in the air, "Kidding! Just kidding." He started to leave, but stopped in his tracks. "Tell Ballew 'Hi' for me."

Richard slipped through the door and was gone. Kelli called the garage and had her car readied. She called a porter, who took her things and loaded them into the car, including the box of comics and shirts. She had a trip planned and it was time to leave.

* * *

The new lumber was piled high and the bronze-framed windows lay nearby, protected with plastic covers. The new air hammer lay idle, Ballew having returned to the hammer he was accustomed to. He straddled a wooden joist, while trying to brace one of the roof trusses, when he heard an airboat approaching.

Standing on the roof, he shaded his eyes with his hands to cut the glare. The boat had almost reached the island before he recognized the person. Neither the cap with Saints printed on it, nor the long Spider Man T-shirt, could hide the long hair or beautiful figure.

Instantly, he recognized Kelli. With little effort, he swung gracefully from the rafters to the wood floor below. He watched from the unfinished porch as she jumped from the airboat and tied the boat to a log lying nearby. He moved away from the porch, stopped and smiled.

Kelli stood there facing Ballew for a moment, with both hands forming fists resting on her waist. Then she took the old Saints cap from her head, turned it around, and placed it back on top of her head. Much in the same fashion as a baseball catcher, then Kelli started running toward her Cajun.

Look for these exciting novels by author

JOE BARFIELD

Published by Moran Publishing, L.L.C.

☐	1-884797-00-8	**FORMULA 2000 - THE DREAM**	$9.95
☐	1-884797-03-2	Chem Storm	$9.95
☐	1-884797-02-4	Moon Shadow	$9.95
☐	1-884797-04-0	URBAN KILL	$9.95

Look for the above books at your local bookstore

Moran Publishing, L.L.C., P.O.Box 655, Sealy, Texas 77474
Please send me the books I have checked above. I am enclosing $_____
Add $2.00 to cover postage and handling, and $.50 for each additional book.
Send check or money order (no cash or C.O.D.s)
    Mr/Ms_____
    Address_____
    City/State_____ State_____ Zip_____

Please allow four to six weeks for delivery. Prices and availability subject to change without notice.

FORMULA 2000 - THE DREAM

A Novel of a Promise and a Dream

    Grant Kelly's son, Shannon, age 19, has developed into more than just a good racer. Because of a **promise** and a **dream**, Grant sells his house buys an Indy type car called a Formula Continental and with the remaining money the father-son team enter SCCA's tough American Continental Championship series run in the United States and Canada--and begin an odyssey neither dreamed.

    But the competition has money and experience. Two Canadian teams control the series along with a California team, BRM owned by the drivers rich father, Anthony Benson. The driver, TJ Benson, has the best including one of the finest mechanics, Charlie Pepper.

    It is Charlie who sees the potential in Shannon and his inferior car and comes to his aid. Charlie helps Grant unload the old race car for a Swift, a better car Charlie knows is still competitive.

    As the season progresses, Shannon becomes more competitive, begins to assert himself and win.

    In the last race Shannon gets the pole but his car is destroyed in qualifying. Then an unexpected competitor comes to his aid, offering Shannon a VanDiemen and a chance to fulfill his fathers dream. There is only one condition--Shannon must win!

Chem Storm

A Novel of Action and Adventure involving a Chemical Disaster

Jean Alexander a reporter for the Houston Post has made a discovery. She has found that the Houston Ship Channel is a time bomb waiting to go off. Along with the help of an Engineer, Travis Selkirk she makes many terrifying discoveries. There could be a chemical disaster worse than ever imagined from a nuclear disaster. Plants that store chemicals with the explosive force of an atomic bomb but that will unleash chemicals that can kill with delayed effects, some by breathing and others with simple contact to the skin.

But some are not happy with what Travis and Jean find. One owner, afraid of discovery, tries to have them eliminated.

Suddenly an accident occurs that rapidly creates a domino effect, killing nearly 50,000 people. Jean and Travis are caught in the cataclysmic incident. Both must rely on Travis's experience and knowledge to escape the chemical disaster--the Chem Storm!

Chem Storm is terrifying and the details realistic, but the odds of this happening are a million to one. Then again the Texas lottery is 14 million to one and somebody usually gets it every week.

-Howard White
-Houston Engineer

Moon Shadow

A Novel of War, with Love, Friendship, Honor and Treachery

Before the Aurora Project can be completed, the United States has been invaded by the Coalition, a group of Mid-East and South American countries.

The Aurora Project is the combination of a unique space station, Starburst, locked in a geosynchronous orbit above the United States and used as a terminal to explore space, advance science technology, with anti-missile and aircraft lasers of pin point accuracy to within two thousand miles of Americas borders. Access to Starburst is with a half dozen fully developed space planes, including 4 converted SR-71 Blackbirds. All capable of flying directly into space.

The invasion finds Beau Gex, along with ten of Americas best pilots, caught deep behind enemy lines. Only Gex has the ability to lead the small group out of enemy territory and to the remains of Americas retreating forces far to the North. The task becomes more difficult because Gex is thought to be a traitor to America and a murderer by others, while some do not want to follow him.

During the small groups effort to flee, they discover a dozen old World War II aircraft. Gex convinces the others to fight back with the old planes. Mike Marix wants to lead the group, but the others want to follow Gex because of his experience. Both men have fallen in love with Krysti Soccoro, and only Beau's best friend Ruben Alonzo can prevent a fatal conflict.

The group learns the Coalition has found one of the Blackbirds, and intend to destroy the space station, Starburst.

Now it is up to Gex and his men to destroy the Blackbird with their antiquated aircraft. They must fly one last deadly mission.

But some want Gex dead and sabotage his P-51 Mustang. To survive Gex must rely not only on his skill but also an old Indian legend. The legend of Moon Shadow.

The technical aspect of Moon Shadow is well covered making what the P-51 Mustang accomplishes even more believable. A wonderful and thrilling adventure

-Pat Moran-
1st American Pilot to fly the Mig 29 and Sukhoi 27

URBAN KILL

A Detective Novel

Near Hollywood, California two men prepared for the hunt. Every thing was ready, the two hunters wore only jeans and t-shirts as did their driver-guide. Strange for hunters. All they were equipped with, other than two expensive, high powered rifles were an ice chest with food and beer. They also had a police band radio. Strangest of all was when the guide guaranteed a kill by midnight or their money back. At that point one of the hunters handed him an envelope with $50,000.

It wasn't long before they were in place. But all three waited in the van, while the driver listened to the police radio.

Suddenly the guide spotted the quarry, for which they had waited so diligently. The hunters prepared by opening a small slot in the side of the van. Still they remained inside while one slipped his rifle into position. A few minutes later an alarm sounded only a short distance from the van. This was followed by two shots from a pistol. A black man raced from a liquor store directly across the street from the van. In one hand he held the money he had just stolen and in the other he held a pistol.

"This is it," whispered the guide to both hunters.

A single shot from a high powered rifle rang out, piercing the heart of its intended victim--killing the black man instantly!

"Congratulations!" said the guide. "That's your first urban kill!"

About the Author

    Joe Barfield was born in Corpus Christi, Texas, in 1949 and currently resides in Houston, Texas. For 25 years he has worked as an architect. Divorced at age 27 he raised his son and daughter by himself and remains single today.

    Over the last 19 years he has taken an active part with his children and his hobbies. His hobbies enticed him to write *The Cajun*. Today he still continues activities such as flag football, softball, scuba diving and road racing. Road racing got him involved with Cajuns when his racing took him to Louisiana.

    The things that intrigued him most were the unusual Cajun accent, humorous stories and spicy food. From these he developed *The Cajun* into what he likes to think they are--adventurous and romantic. After years of racing in Louisiana the author says you can find no friend more loyal than a Cajun--or no enemy worse. The author said, "The only thing I regret about being Texan is not having been a little Cajun."